Harvard
Square

Harvard
Square

A NOVEL

ANDRÉ ACIMAN

W. W. NORTON & COMPANY

New York • London

Copyright © 2013 by André Aciman

All rights reserved
Printed in the United States of America
First Edition

A portion of this book appeared in different form in *The Paris Review*.

For information about permission to reproduce selections from this book, write to Permissions, W. W. Norton & Company, Inc., 500 Fifth Avenue, New York, NY 10110

For information about special discounts for bulk purchases, please contact W. W. Norton Special Sales at specialsales@wwnorton.com or 800-233-4830

Manufacturing by RR Donnelley, Harrisonburg, VA
Book design by Chris Welch
Production manager: Anna Oler

ISBN 978-0-393-08860-1 (hardcover)

W. W. Norton & Company, Inc.
500 Fifth Avenue, New York, N.Y. 10110
www.wwnorton.com

W. W. Norton & Company Ltd.
Castle House, 75/76 Wells Street, London W1T 3QT

1 2 3 4 5 6 7 8 9 0

for my brother Allan

Harvard
Square

PROLOGUE

"CAN WE JUST LEAVE?"

I'd never heard my son say anything like this in all the weeks we'd been visiting colleges together. We'd seen three universities in the Midwest, then stopped at liberal arts colleges in New England, Pennsylvania, and New York. Now, on the last leg of our summer college tour, in that corner of Massachusetts I had known so well, my son had either reached the limits of his endurance or simply lost his nerve.

"I don't want to be here," he said. I told him that leaving was not an option. "Of course it is," he replied. To avoid being overheard by the families assembled around us in the Office of Admissions, I lowered my voice and told him that leaving before the welcoming speech was totally inappropriate. But he nixed that argument with an equally terse and snappy "Let's just split." The wood-paneled room with the thick carpeting was filling up with more visitors. "Like now," he hissed, almost threatening to raise his voice.

"I don't get it," I whispered. "The best university in the world, and all you want is to leave. Seriously?"

But arguing wasn't going to work. Besides, he must have sensed, just by looking at me, that I wasn't going to put up a fight. Perhaps I too was tired and had had my fill of these guided college tours. He didn't wait for me to yield. He stood up and picked up his large brochure and baseball cap. I was forced to stand up as well, if only to avoid looking awkwardly at odds with him in front of the others. Then, before I knew it, the two of us were discreetly making our way out of the admissions office. Almost immediately, our seats were taken by another father and son.

In the vestibule, where more parents had gathered before entering the hall, we heard a member of the admissions staff announce, with a slight, informal giggle in her voice, probably meant to sound kind and reassuring, that following a few words of introduction, she and her colleagues were going to walk us over to such-and-such a place, then to that other place, then head over to yet another spot where we'd all stop at the so-and-so memorial to get a breathtaking panoramic view of yet another Harvard favorite. I recognized at once the slightly smug lilt with which she delivered an itinerary that couldn't have been more thoroughly planned but that wished to convey we were all in for improvised good fun in an otherwise routine trundle through yet another college campus.

As we walked out, more parents with prospective applicants were still filing in, headed to the staff desk, then directly to the assembly hall.

Outside, on the patio, we inhaled a breath of early morning air. I recognized the incipient pall that heralds a typical muggy summer day in Boston.

I could tell my son felt uneasy. He had run into a familiar face on the patio. The two had tried to avoid each other. When they couldn't, the other hastily grunted what must have passed for a cordial greeting among students from rival schools. At least that young man knows the rules, I thought. There was contention and muted feuding in the air, and for everyone, parents and children alike, the choices couldn't have been clearer: either play the game or fold.

We left the building and were cutting through Radcliffe on our way to the river. I wanted to ask why the sudden change of heart, why the itch to leave. But I thought better than to raise the matter quite yet. The tension underscoring the silence between us was palpable enough and couldn't be dispelled. Then, and almost by way of an explanation that was also trying to pass for an apology, he hesitated a moment and finally said, "I'm so not into this."

I didn't know what *this* meant. Did it mean college tours, college towns, college admission officers, colleges, period? Or was he referring to college visitors who'd been deftly showcasing their children with both awe and muffled pride, each vying not to look too eager or too diffident or too summery to be taken seriously by the admissions staff? Or did he mean Harvard in particular? Or—and this suddenly scared me— was what really irked him most the thought of being asked to like the school because I had?

We had arrived a day earlier and had already visited many corners of Harvard: the Radcliffe Houses, the River Houses, then I'd taken him up the stately stairway of Widener Library where we tiptoed into the main reading room. I stood there for a moment, without moving. It was clear I missed my days as a graduate student here. An almost empty reading room on a beautiful summer day was still one of the wonders of the world, I said as we were about to leave the room. All he could do was to utter a wistful but no less tart "I guess."

I showed him all the places where I had lived: Oxford Street, Ware Street, Lowell House. Didn't Lowell House remind him of a turn-of-the-century grand hotel on the Riviera?

"It's a college dorm."

As I showed him around town, I kept wondering what it must feel like to walk with your father and watch him stop at places that couldn't mean a thing to you. You listen to tidbits about his life as a graduate student long before your parents met and find yourself unable or unwilling to relate to any of it, and probably feeling a touch guilty because you can't even work up the show of interest your father seems to want to stir. Everything he sees is steeped in a stagnant vat of nostalgia, and for all its rosy cheeks, the past always gives off that off-putting, musty scent of old pipes and mildewed rooms that haven't been aired in years. I tried to tell him about Concord Avenue and Prescott Street, where I'd also lived; but it was like asking him to join me in getting a haircut at my favorite barbershop on Dunster Street. He'd be humoring me, that's all. But it would mean nothing. Had I asked, he'd have said: *I don't need a haircut.*

I told him I knew of a place where they made good burgers. "You sure it's still there?"

Once again, the sneer and dash of irony in his voice. He'd already heard me say that much had changed after thirty years, not the layout of the streets or of the stores, but the stores themselves, their awnings and marquees, perhaps even the feel of the place. Harvard Square had gotten smaller, felt cramped, crowded. It also seemed that things had been moved around a bit, new buildings had gone up, and the Harvard Square Theater, like so many movie houses around the world, had been drawn and quartered. Even the immutable Coop— short for the Harvard Cooperative Society, the large department store located right on Harvard Square—was no longer the same; a good part of it had become an insignia and souvenir store for visitors. I still remembered my Coop number. I told him my Coop number. "Yes, I know, I know," I immediately threw in a hasty attempt to preempt yet another quip from him, "it's just a department store."

Like many parents who had been students here, I wanted him to like Harvard but knew better than to insist for fear he'd dismiss the school altogether. Part of me wanted him to walk in my shoes. He'd hate that, of course. Or perhaps I wanted to walk in them myself again, but through him. He'd hate that even more. Walking in daddy's footsteps as daddy's stand-in come to expiate the past! I could just hear him say: *No one's idea of college.*

I wanted to share with him and bring back all of my old postcard moments: the day I crossed the bridge in the snow while friends ran across the frozen Charles and I thought *how reckless*; the first time I entered my beloved Houghton Library and sat waiting for the librarian to hand over my very first rare book written by Mademoiselle de Gournay, Montaigne's adopted stepdaughter; the aging face of my long-gone Robert Fitzgerald who taught me so much in so very few words; my last drink at the Harvest bar; down to the stifling reluctance to head out to class on a cold November afternoon when all I'd rather do was curl up with a book somewhere and let my mind wander. I wanted to walk the cobbled lanes leading up to the river with him and, in a spellbound instant, seize the beauty of this sheltered world that had promised me so much and in the end delivered much more. The buildings, the feel of early fall, the sound of students thronging to class every morning—I couldn't wait for him to heed their call and their promise.

Finally I found the courage to ask if he liked what he'd seen.

"I like it fine."

But then, unpredictably, he turned the table on me and asked the same question. Had I liked it here?

I said I had. Very much.

But I knew I was speaking in retrospect.

"I learned to love Harvard *after*, not *during*."

"Explain."

"Life wasn't easy," I said, "and I don't mean the course work—though there was plenty of that, and the standards were high. What was difficult was living with the life Harvard held out for me and refusing to think it might be a mirage. I had money problems. There were days when the margin between the haves and have-nots stood not like a line drawn in the sand but like a ravine. You could watch, you could even hear the party, but you weren't invited." What was hard, I was trying to say, was remembering I'd already been invited.

I was the outsider, the young man from Alexandria, Egypt, forever baffled and eager to belong in this strange New World.

The rest I didn't want to think about or remember, much less discuss right now. Besides, the *during memories* of my years at Harvard felt tucked away still—not necessarily for-gotten, but as though put on ice for a day in later life when I'd have the strength and leisure to revisit them. But now wasn't the time. For now, it was the magical *after love* I wished to convey. It had stayed with me all those years and yanked me back to days I missed a great deal but knew I would never for a minute wish to relive again. Perhaps the *after love* was what made me embark on this odyssey of college stops with my son, because I longed to set foot in Cambridge again—with him as my shield, my cover, my standby.

How to explain this to a seventeen-year-old without destroy-ing the carousel of images I'd shared with him since his preschool days? Cambridge on quiet Sunday evenings; Cambridge on rainy afternoons with friends, or in a blizzard when things went on as usual and the days seemed shorter and festive and all you wanted to imagine was tethered horses waiting to take you to Ethan Frome places; the Square abuzz on Friday nights; Harvard during reading period in mid-January—coffee, more coffee, and the perpetual patter of typewriters everywhere; or Lowell House on the last days of reading period in the spring, when students lounged about for hours on the grass, speaking softly, their voices muffled by the sounds of early summer.

"I loved it," I finally said. "I still do."

By then we had entered the Coop.

"Don't ask if they still have your Coop number," implored my son, who knew how my mind ticked and didn't want me to embarrass him by growing nostalgic about times past with a salesclerk who couldn't have cared less.

I promised not to say a thing. But when I bought two T-shirts, one for him, and one for me, I couldn't help myself. "346-408-8," I said.

I told the clerk that I still remembered the number because I would always say it out loud when buying a pack of cigarettes at the Coop. And in those years I'd buy a pack a day, twice a day.

The salesclerk checked his computer and said I wasn't in their system.

The way my old phone number here was no longer in my name, I presumed.

The way, unless we do something with our lives, some of

us come to Cambridge, spend a few years here, then leave this place and then the planet without a trace.

Not in the system, it was called. It made me question whether I'd ever really been in the system here.

I belonged here once, but had it ever been my home? Or was it my home, though I could never really claim I'd belonged here? *Not in the system* covered both options.

My son was urging me not to engage in a conversation with the salesclerk. But something in me didn't wish to accept that I was not in the system or had never been. I asked the clerk to check once more and repeated my Coop number.

"Apologies, sir," blurted the young man. "Your number is still under your name, but you will need to reactivate your Coop number."

So I was in the system but inactive, like a mole, or a spy, forever in but on the fringes. That summed it all. I did not wish this for my son.

When we approached Brattle Street, I suddenly realized how much and yet how little the block had changed. The Brattle Theatre hadn't budged; but it had a new entrance underground. Casablanca too hadn't budged, but they'd gutted and truncated it. And finally Café Algiers had moved from downstairs to upstairs, though its green logo hadn't changed. I stood outside the old coffee shop where I'd spent years reading and where, one summer long ago, I'd run into someone who came so close to altering the course of my life that today I might not even be my son's father.

"What do you mean 'not my father'?" asked my son, who'd never heard anything like this before and was more than mildly miffed by what I'd just said.

I didn't want to answer, partly because I wasn't sure I knew the answer, but also because I wanted to spare him the thought that so much of who he was depended on tangents and the whims of fate.

"There were days when I wasn't sure I wanted to stay here any longer—when I too wanted to split." I wanted him to know I was using his word. "And I don't mean just from Harvard, but from the United States."

"And?"

"I wasn't even a citizen in those days and a side of me, just a side of me, craved to move back somewhere on the Mediterranean. This fellow was from the Mediterranean as well and he too longed to go back. We were friends."

I was still staring at the emblem of Café Algiers and, without even trying, could almost heed the loud slap of backgammon chips summoning me from decades back. I used to hang around here to put off heading home, to find light and fellowship in my evenings, because there were days when nothing else promised light or fellowship.

"Why did you want to leave?"

"Many things. I had failed my comprehensive exams. They said I could take my exams a second time, but not a third. I just wanted to leave before they'd throw the book at me if I failed again."

But these were all words. And I wasn't sure I wanted to share any of this with someone who was himself already having a hard time making up his mind about Harvard.

"I passed," I finally said. "Harvard was generous, magnanimous even."

But I couldn't forget my days and evenings at Café Algiers where I'd come because that small underground café at the time was the only place this side of the Atlantic I could almost call home. The smell of Turkish coffee, the French songs they played here, the verbal fireballs of a Tunisian nicknamed Monsieur Kalashnikov and the chatter of the men and women who'd gather around when he presided, down to the clammy, wooden dampness of my tiny square table next to which hung a makeshift poster of a deserted beach in a coastal town called Tipaza, its turquoise sea forever limpid and beckoning, everything in this small coffee shop reminded me of a Middle East I thought I had lost and put behind me and suddenly realized I wasn't ready to let go of. At least not just yet. Not for Harvard, not for America, not for anyone, not even for the children I wished one day to be a father to. I was not like everyone else in Cambridge, I was not one of them, was not in the system, had never been. This wasn't really my home, might never be. These weren't my people, were never going to be. This wasn't my life, wasn't my birthplace, wasn't even me, couldn't be me. This was the summer of 1977.

1

CAMBRIDGE WAS A DESERT. IT WAS ONE OF THE HOT-
test summers I'd ever lived through. By the end of July, you
sought shelter wherever you could during the day; at night you
couldn't sleep. All my friends in graduate school were gone.
Frank, my former roommate, was teaching Italian in Flor-
ence, Claude had gone back to France to work for his father's
consulting firm, and Nora was in Austria for a crash course
in German. Nora wrote to me about Frank, while Frank
wrote about Nora. *He's losing all his hair and he isn't even 25.*
She, he'd write, was a jittery flibbertigibbet who should be
flipping burgers instead. I was trying not to take sides, but
I found myself envying their love and fearing its dissolution,
sometimes more than either of them did. One would quote
Leopardi to me, the other Donna Summer. Both had sprouted
quick romances abroad.

My other friends who had stayed in Cambridge to teach summer classes had also left. Postcards trickled in from Paris, Berlin, Bologna, Sirmione, and Taormina, even Prague and Budapest. One of my fellow grad school friends was doing the Petrarch route, from Arquà to Provence, and wrote that, like Petrarch himself, he was about to ascend Mont Ventoux with fellow medievalists. Next year, he added on his postcard with his stingy, minuscule script, he was planning a climb up Mount Snowdon in Wales; I should come, since I loved Wordsworth. Another friend, a devout Catholic, had set out on a pilgrimage to Santiago de Compostela. Both were to meet in Paris and come back on the same plane before we'd all start teaching this fall. I missed my friends, even those I didn't like very much. But I owed them money and didn't mind their extended grace period.

All the summer school kids were gone, as were the foreign students who flocked to take classes at Harvard every summer. Lowell House was empty and its gate padlocked and strapped with a chain. Sometimes, just the thought of stopping by and standing in its main courtyard, flanked by a row of balusters, was sufficient to stir the illusion of Europe. I could knock at the window and ask Tony, the gatekeeper, to open the gate for me, say I needed to get to my office. But I knew that my visit might take no more than a minute or two, and I'd hate to disturb him.

This was a different Cambridge.

As happened every year once its students and most of its faculty were gone by midsummer, Cambridge began to acquire a different, gentler, working-class character. The pace slackened; the barber would stand outside his shop to smoke a cigarette, salesclerks at the Coop would be chatting it up among themselves, the waitress at Café Anyochka would still not have made up her mind whether to leave the glass door open or if it was time to turn on their rickety air conditioner. Cambridge in early August.

I was staying the whole summer, holding a very part-time summer job in one of the Harvard libraries. The job paid a puny sum per hour. To make ends meet I tutored French. Money went toward rent. Other priorities were: food, cigarettes, a drink whenever possible. When money ran out, which it inevitably did by the end of each month, I'd put on a shirt, a jacket, and a tie and have lunch at the faculty club, where, amidst the established Harvard faculty and visiting dignitaries, I would eat on credit. I had failed my comprehensive exams in January, which left me just one more chance to retake them. I was reading books for my second try, scheduled for early in the new year, always lugging books wherever I went. Inside me I had the sinking feeling that graduate school would wear on and on with no end in sight till, before I knew it, I'd turn thirty, then forty, then die. Either this, or I'd flunk my comprehensives again, and they'd find out what they probably suspected all along: that I was a fraud, that I was never cut out to be a teacher, much less a scholar, that I had been a bad investment from the get-go, that I was the black sheep, the rotten apple, the bad seed, that I'd be known as the impostor who'd hustled his way into Harvard and was let go in the nick of time. All I'd been doing these past four years was hide from the merciless world outside the academy, burying myself in books all the while resenting the very walls that sheltered me and made it possible for me to read more books. I hated almost every member of my department, from the chairman down to the secretary, including my fellow graduate students, hated their mannered pieties, their monastic devotion to their budding profession, their smarmy, patrician airs dressed down to look a touch grungy. I scorned them because I didn't want to be like them, but I didn't want to be like them because I knew that part of me couldn't, while another wanted nothing more than to be cut from the same cloth.

When I was not working at the library, I would go upstairs on the roof terrace of my building to sunbathe—with my folding chair, my bathing suit, my cigarettes, my books, and an endless string of watered-down Tom Collins which I dutifully replenished every two hours or so in my apartment, situated right under the terrace. I had taken the magnum bottle of Beefeater gin at the end of a departmental party in late spring; the bottle had a long way to go yet. I liked to read while listening to music. Often a couple sat next to me, reading and drinking as well. One of them, in a bikini, liked to chat every once in a while. She introduced me to John Fowles. I introduced her to Tom Collins. Sometimes she brought cookies or sliced fruit. On that terrace above the fourth floor overlooking Cambridge, all I had to do was stare at my book, smell the suntan lotion around me, and, in the silence of a weekday morning right there on Concord Avenue, drift away and think I was finally lying by some beach on the Mediterranean, or my long-lost Alexandria which I knew I would never again set eyes on except in sleep.

Sometimes I would offer to fill an iced drink on my next trip downstairs for another neighbor who like me was also reading for her orals. She'd accept, and for a few seconds we would talk. I loved her glistening tan shoulders and slim, bare feet. But before I was able to have a conversation with her, she'd be back to reading. Was my music too loud? No, it was fine. Sure it wasn't bothering her? It didn't. Apartment 42 was clearly not interested. Apartment 21, who also came up to sun-bathe sometimes, was a bit more talkative, but she lived with her twin sister, and there were times when I could hear them go at each other, some of the vilest insults I've ever heard flung between two humans. Better stay away—though the idea of twin sisters in the same bed at the same time never failed to arouse me. Apartment 43, who lived next door to me, already had a boyfriend, which explained why she was so seemingly forthcoming. Like me, they were both in their mid-twenties. In the morning, they would leave the building together, the spitting portrait of the world's healthiest relationship. She'd accompany him to the Square, where he'd catch the train to Boston and she'd turn around with their collie and come back by way of the Cambridge Common. We shared the same ser-vice landing, their kitchen door facing mine. They liked pancakes in the morning. Sometimes, the smell of their breakfast wafted into my kitchen, especially when I opened my service door and they left theirs open for cross-ventilation, which is when I'd catch them in boxers and pajamas. On weekends they cooked French toast and bacon. I loved the smell. It stood for family, hearth, friendship, domestic bliss. People who cooked French toast lived with people, liked people, understood why people needed people. In three years, tops, they'd have children. On Saturdays sometimes he would head off to work. Later she'd come upstairs on the terrace in her bikini, eager to make small talk, carrying a towel, suntan lotion, and always something by a British author. Did she know I could hear her passionate cries at night? I was sure she knew.

When she stepped onto the roof terrace on Sunday mornings carrying her folding chair, she'd beam a smile at whomever was lounging there, amused, sly, and self-conscious. She wanted me to know she knew I knew. But it stopped there. When I would take a break and offer to bring her a Tom Collins, she'd decline with a smile—as always amused, sly, and self-conscious. She knew what I was thinking.

On weekday mornings, I loved to look down from my window and watch them leave. Their life was perfectly rounded. Mine had transcendental homelessness written all over it. They headed out and came back, while I stayed put, getting progressively more tanned, more bored. There was nothing to do but read all day. I was not teaching, barely tutoring; I was not writing; I didn't even own a TV. I would have loved to drive out somewhere. But no one I knew had a car. Cambridge was a fenced-in, isolated strip of parched land.

Upstairs, on the terrace, is where I had decided to reread in the space of six months everything I needed for my comprehensive exams on seventeenth-century literature. Mid-January was far off yet, but in the middle of the night it felt like minutes away. Every time I was done reading a book, I'd discover many more I needed to read or reread. I'd budgeted two books a day. When it came to French prose writers I'd read three a day. The Elizabethan, Jacobean, and Restoration prose writers, definitely two a day. But then came the picaresque writers of Spain, and the prose writers of Italy, one adulterous tale after the other until the whole history of European fiction seemed written by P. G. Wodehouse on steroids. And finally German and Dutch authors. Here the solution was very simple: if I hadn't already read them, they were never written. Ditto with some of the great French gossipmongers of the royal court: if I couldn't remember them, they were not important. Meanwhile, I'd reread *The Letters of a Portuguese Nun* and *Don Carlos* many times and was still awed by their brilliance, which gave me hope. I was slashing my way through a jungle of books, constantly finding clever ways to assuage the pangs of conscience each time I realized I'd omitted an important work. Not exactly scholarship—but under the blazing summer sun and the near-hypnotic scent of suntan lotion around me as I watched so many thighs lounging about on tar beach, no one could ask for more.

My dissertation advisor, Professor Lloyd-Greville the redoubtable seventeenth-century scholar, had admitted me into the department with high hopes. He had always tried to throw a few financial-aid dollars my way, and he had once expected me to pass my comprehensives with cutlass and steed, like the caliph Haroun al-Rashid jumping over impossible human hurdles. He always brought up Haroun in my company, either because Haroun, like me, came from the Middle East, or because, in addition to being a great soldier and statesman, Haroun was also a patron of the arts and sciences, all of which Lloyd-Greville aspired to. But I couldn't begin to know what he thought of me or of Haroun. Born, bred, and blooded at Harvard, Lloyd-Greville was a paragon scholar who also happened to be an authority on Yeats. I could just picture myself knocking at his door after taking my exams a second time and hearing him say, with his courtly smile followed by that unmistakable little cough that cleared his throat before he'd utter one of his lapidary pronouncements, that this time, he was so very sorry to say, I'd definitely missed the boat to Byzantium. "Even third-class passage?" I'd ask. "Even third-class passage," he'd say. "How about the bilge area, there are always ex-convicts and stowaways in bilge class." "Even bilge class," he'd declaim, as he'd put on a strained *much as we regret to announce* smile and screw in the cap of his Montegrappa pen that had just signed my death warrant.

My other advisor, Professor Cherbakoff, was more lenient but would never deign sign off on my exams if Lloyd-Greville demurred. He liked me, I knew, but his paternal concern for me had grown downright oppressive. He too came from a Jewish family that lost everything in France owing to war and politics. His return to France after the war as a student had filled him with such horror that a few years later he was lucky enough to find a position in the United States and put France behind him. His was a sobering reminder that France, the France I dreamed of when there was no other place left to dream of, either had never existed or might never open its doors to me.

Lloyd-Greville, by contrast, worshipped France. He owned a sixteenth-century mansion in Normandy. A legendary leather-framed picture of it, which was always the talk of the department, sat in his office: wife, two daughters, maid, cook, gardener, dog, and two to three de rigueur cows sprawled in the distant fields. "Yes, it is perfect," he once said when I sat in his office and, to soften him up after staring at the picture, said that his house, his life looked perfect. Cherbakoff would never have had the nerve to agree with me, at least not so readily. He knew exactly what I was going through, knew how self-doubt scrapes down the soul, till all that's left is a flimsy sheath as thin as a sliver of onion skin. He wanted me to follow in his footsteps, which is also why I avoided him.

Usually by one o'clock on the rooftop, I had enough energy to read for at most an hour or so in my apartment. I liked when it was dark and cooler inside. After that came the small library where I worked and where I'd read some more. Then

I'd wander about Harvard Square in search of another place, preferably an indoors café, after which there'd be another place, and maybe another, before I turned in.

RIGHT NOW, BETWEEN me and the elements stood a blow fan at Café Algiers, just as between me and my rudderless summer sat the two volumes of Montaigne's *Essays* which I'd been promising Lloyd-Greville to comb through, essay after essay. Pascal I'd promised to reread afterward. As for all the short novels ever penned by Europe's middlebrow hucksters, I'd just have to do what they themselves claimed they did: wing it.

One could spend an entire day at Café Algiers. It was a tiny, cluttered, semi-underground café off Harvard Square that held no more than a dozen tiny, wobbly tables and that looked like a miniature Kasbah about to spill on the floor. How they managed to stuff so many tiny, rickety tables, chairs, and a giant antique espresso maker, plus a whole kitchen area in one-tenth the space needed was beyond me. The owner must have been an engineer by training who doubled as part-time cook, cashier, waiter, and busboy. They served coffee, juices, sandwiches, and cakes. Weather permitting, Algiers boasted a tiny alfresco area on what could have passed for a terrace but was really no more than a narrow passageway between Brattle Street and the bar Casablanca on the way to Mount Auburn Street. People parked their cars in a lot right behind the bar.

I hadn't spoken to a soul all weekend. It was Sunday, everything was closed, and I'd been roaming from one coffeehouse
to the next. It was now late in the afternoon. Another scorch-
ing weekend like this and I'd wilt, no one would miss me, no
one would even know. I found myself thinking of the young
couple in Apartment 43. They were having people over for
dinner, she told me. Gazpacho and lamb chops and God
knows what else—wine, always wine. He liked to cook. She
liked books. After dinner, they'd wash and dry the dishes in
the kitchen, and he'd playfully bump her hips with his, as I
watched him do once downstairs when he stood by her while
she took forever to empty their mailbox. Had he bumped her
ass in jest, or simply to mean *Will you hurry?* They had two
names on their mailbox. Soon they'd have just one.

I was reading Montaigne's *Apologie de Raimond Sebond* that
afternoon, and was sitting in a relatively quiet corner of Café
Algiers drinking an iced coffee that was to last me at least two
and a half hours. Nursing a drink is one thing. But watching your ice cubes melt and turn the watered-down brew into
clear soup and still pretend that your glass is half full was like
trying to preserve the polar icecaps with a paper fan.

Then I heard him. He was sitting at a table not far from
mine, speaking French. Correction: he wasn't speaking. He
didn't speak; instead, he rapid-fired machine-gun style, in
bursts and sputters. *Rat-tat-tat*, he took down civilization,
Western and Eastern, no difference, he hated them both.
Cranky, jittery, crazed, strafing his way from one subject to

the next—it didn't matter which—he'd mow it down. *Rat-tat-tat*, like shattered glass spun in a blender. *Rat-tat-tat*, like a jackhammer, like a chainsaw, like a power drill, every syllable spiked with venom, vengeance, and vitriol.

I had no idea who he was, what exactly he was talking about, or why he kept raising his voice, but in this underground café on a quiet midsummer Sunday afternoon, his was the only voice you heard.

Oui, oui, oui—rat-tat-tat. Bien sûr, bien sûr—rat-tat, rat-tat. Et pourquoi pas?—rat-tat-tat-tat? Long sentences, spoken with spitfire accuracy, while all around him sat cigarettes, napkins, matches, a cheap lighter, home keys, car keys, leftover change from his previous coffee before he'd decided to order a second and then a third—debris strewn helter-skelter about his table like the spat-out bullet shells of his hysterical prattle. *Rat-tat-tat*, down with capitalists, communists, liberals and conservatives, Old World, New World, the League of Nations, the Arab League, the League of Women Voters, the Catholic League, the Great Wall of China, the Berlin Wall, down with them all! Whites, blacks, men, women, Jews, gays, lesbians, rich, poor, cats, dogs—a flint storm of curses as unmistakably North African French as the cicadas on sleepy Mediterranean afternoons when they drown out every other sound with the raspy musketry of their hindquarters.

At that moment he was fulminating against white Americans, *les amerloques*, as he called them. Americans loved all things jumbo and ersatz, he was saying. As long as it was artificial and double the value if you bought five times the size you'd ever need, no white American homemaker could resist. Their continental breakfasts are jumbo-ersatz, their extra-long cigarettes are jumbo-ersatz, their huge steak dinners with whopping all-you-can-eat salads are jumbo-ersatz, their refilled mugs of all-you-can-drink coffee, their faux-mint mouthwash with triple-pack toothpaste and extra toothbrushes thrown in for the value, their cars, their malls, their universities, even their monster television sets and spectacular big-screen epics, all, all of it, jumbo-ersatz. American women with breast implants, nose jobs, and perennially tanned figures— jumbo-ersatz. American women with smaller breasts, contact lenses, mouth spray, hair spray, nose spray, foot spray, scent spray, vaginal spray—no less ersatz than their oversized sisters. American women who were just happy to have found a man to talk to in a crowded café on a midsummer afternoon in Cambridge, Mass. would sooner or later turn out to be jumbo-ersatz all the same. Their lank, freckled toddlers fed on sapless, bland-ersatz, white-ersatz bread and swaddled in ready-to-wear, over-the-counter, prefab, preshrunk, one-size-fits-all, poly-reinforced clothes couldn't be more bland-ersatz than their big, tall, fast-food lumbering football giant daddies with outsized shoes, penis enlargers, and sculpted, washboard, eight-pack abs who personify the essence of all that was ever jumbo-synthetic on God's ill-fated, jittery little planet.

This, I would soon find out, was standard fare whenever he found someone to buttonhole. He'd start with the First World, work his way down to the Second, then to the Third, till he'd wipe out every visible bare-bottomed savage in the rain forest and thrown the hapless survivors to the Huns, where they all belonged anyway, or to the Ottomans, who'd know what to do with them, or worse yet, to the Jesuits who'd sing a prayer before burning them alive and making missionaries of their children.

He couldn't have been older than thirty-four, wore a faded army fatigue jacket with many pockets, and was speaking in a Maghrebi accent to a bearded American college student who was clearly trying to look like Hemingway. The American occasionally dared to interrupt with tepid pieties in decent enough French, while Machine Gun Mouth was catching his breath to take lingering sips from his coffee cup, which he held from the rim, as if its handle were missing. "But you can't generalize about all Americans," said Young Hemingway, "nor can you say all women are this or that. Every human being is unique and different. Besides, I don't agree with what you say about the Middle East, either."

Machine Gun reclined on his seat as he rolled his nth cigarette, licked the glued end of his cigarette paper after filling its midsection with tobacco, and like a cowboy who'd just spun the cylinder of his revolver after carefully reloading its chambers, pointed a stiffened forefinger that almost touched the temple of the startled young American, who had clearly never had a finger, much less a loaded pistol, pointed at his head: "All you know is what you learn from newspapers and your *boolsheet* television. I have my own sources."

"What sources?" asked the bearded American, who was beginning to look like a timid prophet about to bicker with the Lord God Himself.

"Other sources," snapped the North African. And before the young man had a chance to cross-examine him, there it was again, as good as new, oiled, rammed, reassembled, and reloaded, louder and more articulate yet: *rat-tat-tat-tat-tat-tat-tat.*

I knew I'd heard his voice many times before at Café Algiers, but on that late Sunday afternoon, the hammering staccato of his words was impossible to ignore. I could tell he knew people were looking over in his direction. He pretended not to notice, but it was clear he was picking his words and buffing his performance, like someone who while speaking to you is looking over your shoulder at the mirror behind you to make sure his hair is well combed. His speech was growing a touch too studied, as were his gestures and the exaggerated pitch of his explosive, out-of-control laughter. Obviously, he liked people to wonder about him. And I was—there was no doubt—wondering about him. I'd never come across anyone like this before. Primitive, yet completely *civilisé.* He crossed his legs in a very distinguished manner—but the look, the clothes, the hair were a ruffian's.

Suddenly I heard him again. *Rat-tat-tat.*

"American women are like beautiful manor houses with lovely rooms and lavish art, but the lights are switched off. Americans are not born, they are manufactured. Ford-ersatz, Chrysler-ersatz, Buick-ersatz. I always know what Americans will say, because they think alike, speak alike, fuck alike."

Young Hemingway was listening to this tirade, trying to sneak in a few words edgewise to draw some sense from the diatribe; but there was no stopping the string of invectives that came rattling forth like pellets fed on a bullet belt. Rapid-fire Kalashnikov stuff, G.I. Joe ducking in the trenches with bullets whistling overhead and mud-buried mines exploding underfoot, and all about him senseless strafing and detonations. No sooner had he lambasted the female sex than he took a swipe at human greed, at Mormons, at underpaid Mexican waiters who steal food when the owner isn't looking, finally taking on NATO, UNESCO, Nabisco, Ceauşescu, Tabasco, Lambrusco, you name it, all of them big, shameless signs of a world gone completely mad and ersatz. I had never heard such abominable agitprop in my life. The American president he renamed *le Boy Scout*. "The Italians are rotten thieves. The French will always sell their mothers, throw in their wives, then their sisters; but their daughters they'll sell you first. As for Arabs, we were infinitely better off as colonies. The only one who understood history was Nostradamus."

"Who?"

"Nostradamus." No sooner named, than out poured a litany of quatrains predicting one catastrophe after the other. "Nostradamus and the myth of the eternal return."

"You mean Nietzsche."

"Nostradamus, I said."

"How do you know about Nostradamus?"

"How do I know!" he asked rhetorically. "I know, OK?"—

which he pronounced *oké?*—"Must I teach you everything I know?"

I couldn't tell yet whether this was amicable sparring or comic banter about to turn ugly, or if they were engaged in the besotted ramblings of Vladimir and Estragon. But the louder of the two was definitely a cross between Zorba the Greek on steroids and Rameau's nephew on speed.

At some point I could no longer resist. I stood up and headed to his table. "I couldn't help overhearing you. Are you students here?" I asked in French.

No answer. Just a dismissive shake of the head, immediately followed by that sinister gimlet stare of his, which seemed to ask, *And if we are, what business of yours is it, anyway?*

I wanted to say that I hadn't spoken to a single person, much less in French, for two days, and with Apartments 42, 21, and 43 I traded nothing but distant glances, and frankly this sitting on the roof terrace every day was not good for my soul, and eating by myself was no better, to say nothing of the watered-down swill they called coffee here. But the silence between us was hard to take, because it came with a decidedly hostile stare. I was already preparing to apologize and bow out, saying that I hadn't meant to interrupt, thinking to myself that I should have known better than to barge in on perfect strangers and expect to make small talk with a street ruffian and his acolyte.

Before I returned to my table, the words slipped out of my mouth:

"Sorry to disturb. I just felt like speaking to a Frenchman."
Again the stare.

"Me, French? What are you? Blind? Or is it deaf you are? With my Berber skin? Look here." And with this he pinched the skin of his forearm. "This, my dear friend, is not French skin." As though I'd insulted him. He was obviously proud of his Berber skin. "This is the color of wheat and gold."

"Sorry, my mistake."

I was determined to step back to my table and pick up Montaigne where I'd left him face down.

"How about you, are you French?" he asked.

I couldn't resist.

"With my nose?"

He was playing with me. I knew he wasn't French, just as he must have immediately guessed I wasn't either. Each was basically letting the other think he could pass for French. A tacit compliment that hit the mark in both of us.

"How come you speak French if you're not French?"

Anyone born in the colonies would have known right away the answer to that. He was definitely playing.

"For the same reason *you* speak French," I replied. He burst out laughing. We understood each other perfectly.

"Another one of us," he explained to Young Ernest, who was still trying to sort out what possible importance Nostradamus could have in today's complex geopolitical conflicts.

"What do you mean *one of us*?"

"*Il ne comprend rien du tout celui-là*, this guy doesn't understand a thing," he said, with typical mock hostility prickling his voice.

We exchanged names. "You can call me Kalaj," he said, as though yielding to a public nickname he preferred to his own name, but also because there was a vague suggestion in his voice that one could call him Kalaj "for now"—until, that is, he got to know you better.

He'd been here for six months only. Before that Milan. This was home now.

He threw out a word in Arabic at me.

I threw back another.

We laughed. We were not testing each other; more like feeling the ground for how to improvise a tentative pontoon bridge.

"Perfect accent," he commented, "even if it is Egyptian Arabic."

"Yours is difficult to place."

"I seldom speak Arabic," he said, then asked, "Jewish?"

"Moslem?" I replied.

"Just like a Jew: always answers with a question."

"Just like a Moslem: always answers the wrong question."

We were both laughing, while Young Hemingway stared uneasily, thrown off as he was by our chaffing and mock-religious slurs.

"Why did the Arab store owner buy fifty pairs of jeans from the Jew?"

"I don't know."

"Because Isaac promised Abdou to buy them back at a higher price."

Laughter.

"But why did Isaac buy them back in the end?"

I didn't know the answer to this either.

"Because the Arab agreed to sell them at half price."

"Did the Arab ever buy blue jeans from the Jew again?" I asked.

"All the time! You see, the jeans were made in Egypt and cost the Arab a fraction of what the Jew paid for them to begin with." We laughed heartily.

"The Middle East!" he said.

"What do you mean *the Middle East*?" asked bewildered Hemingway.

Kalaj ignored the question.

"Were you waiting for someone?" he asked.

"No, just reading."

"But you've been reading for hours. Why don't you just sit down with us, and we'll talk a bit? Bring your books."

So he had been aware of me all along. He told me about his taxi cab. I told him about my forthcoming comprehensives. We were talking. Talking is what humans like to do when they're together, talking is natural. On Sunday afternoons, people talk, laugh, drink coffee. I had almost forgotten that people did this. Before I knew it, he ordered a round of coffee for the three of us. "Talk is good, but someone needs to order coffee," he said.

He was, with this round of coffee—and it happened so fast

I almost didn't notice—celebrating me. This blustering vol-
cano is probably kind, I thought. But crafty, ill-tempered, and
mad. Stay away.

I was the exact opposite. Interest in other people came
naturally enough; but it came the long way around, with
so many bends, hurdles, doubts, and deferrals that halfway
toward a friendship, discouragement and disappointment
would invariably settle in, and something in me would simply
give up.

Once again, Kalaj ranted against American women. He told
us an obscene joke about an Arab who is arrested and beaten
by the police for jumping a naked blond woman sunning herself on a deserted beach in North Africa. As they shackle him
and pound him with more blows and accuse him of defiling
a dead body—"Can't you see she's dead?" shouts one of the
policemen—all the Arab could do in his defense was to shout
back, "But, officers, I thought she was an American."

Kalaj pointed to the various women sitting in the café.
This one over there wouldn't speak to him again because
he'd refused to use protection. This other one sitting with
her beau had turned him down once by saying "I think I'm
going to take a pass." He had never heard such insipid ersatz-
speak before, and he repeated the words to us as if he were
mouthing a ritual incantation spoken by extraterrestrials: *I
think I'm going to take a pass.* In his rudimentary English the
sentence was suddenly exposed for what it was: bland treacle-
speak that sounded as artificial and no more capable of passion

and arousal than a linoleum tile or a Formica tabletop. He pointed to a tall, slender, model type with a stunning figure. "She thinks I'm about to speak to her, but I've seen her come in and out of the bathroom too many times already. She has bathroom problems. Not for me!"

"What do you mean, *not for you?*" interjected Young Hemingway, who by now was utterly outraged by such unmitigated misogyny.

"I mean I wouldn't *neek* her with your *zeb.*"

He was, as always, aware of every woman in the café. "They're here for one reason only, and that reason is us three." Young Hemingway asked him why he didn't make a move if he was so sure. "Too soon." The only people I'd heard speak this way were fishermen. They look at the sky, gauge the wind, the clouds, have a sixth sense about things, then when you least expect it, they'll say, "Now!" The woman with the slender figure had just cast a look at our table. With absolutely no discretion, Kalaj began to chuckle out loud, "She looked!" We caught a smile ripple on her face.

There are two kinds of men about town in France: *flâneurs* and *dragueurs*. As becomes obvious in no time, *la drague*—cruising—is not a hobby, not a science, not an art, not even a question of odds and probabilities. With him it was the perfect alignment of will with desire. His desire for a woman was so relentless that it would never cross his mind that a woman might not desire him back. He never doubted that a woman wanted him. They all did. As far as he was concerned, all women wanted all men. And vice versa. What stood in the way between a man and a woman at Café Algiers was a few chairs, a table, maybe a door—material distance. All a man needed was the will and above all the patience to wait out a woman's scruples or help her brush them aside. As in a game of penny poker, he explained, all that matters was simply the will to keep raising the pot by a single penny each time; a single penny, not two; a single penny was easy, you wouldn't even feel it; but you had to wait for her to raise you by a penny as well, which is when you'd raise her by another, she by yet another, and so on. Seduction was not pushing people into doing things they did not wish to do. Seduction was just keeping the pennies coming. If you ran out, then, like a magician, you twirled your fingers and pulled one out from behind her left ear and, with this touch of humor, brought laughter into the mix. In the space of fifteen minutes one morning, I saw him offer a woman a *cinquante-quatre*—a fifty-four-cent cup of coffee, tax included—put his arm around her each time he burst out laughing, and be off with her.

"But don't get me wrong. In the end it's always the woman who chooses you, not the other way around—always the woman who takes the first step."

"What about all this bit about raising them with a penny each time?" asked Young Hemingway.

"That was bunk," Kalaj replied.

"And Nostradamus, then?"

"Bunk too."

His friend stood up to go to the bathroom, huffing, "Nostradamus—really!"

No sooner has he left our table than Kalaj said, "I can't stand this guy."

"I thought you were friends."

Dismissive smirk again. "With that face of his? Are you serious?"

Suddenly, Kalaj put on a pouting face, stared intently at his cup, meditated on its shape, and began spinning the cup ever so slowly on its saucer. It took me a moment to realize what he was doing. He was mimicking Young Hemingway's way of pondering every syllable coming out of Kalaj's mouth. I burst out laughing. He laughed as well.

AT CAFÉ ALGIERS, people dubbed him Che Guevara or *el révolutionnaire*, but mainly they called him Kalaj, short for Kalashnikov. "Have you seen Kalaj?" they'd say. Or: "Kalaj is haranguing the brotherhood of man over at Casablanca." It meant he is arguing about politics in Cambridge's most popular bar. Or: "Kalaj shouldn't be long, it's almost *l'heure du thé,* teatime," some of the regulars would say to make fun of how ill-suited he was for anything resembling the ritual civility of five o'clock tea. Sometimes you could even hear him arguing with someone on his way to the café, always loud and contentious. "Our soldier approaches," one of the waitresses would say. Told he shouldn't argue so much, he'd snap back and say "I wasn't arguing."

"Then what would you call it?"

"It's how I talk. I can't change how I talk. It's who I am."

And out sputtered louder protestations yet: he was no hush-hush, privacy-enamored ersatz American. Nor was he the simpering, self-effacing, *you do your thing, I'll do mine, and let's all get along fine* type who thronged the bars and coffeehouses of Harvard Square. *Not who I am*, he'd repeat, emphatically, as if this were the simplified version of a complicated syllogism he'd picked up years ago in a crash course on identity, chatter, and wit in some working-class café on rue Mouffetard in Paris where your nickname is branded on your forehead, your clothes, and your feet. *Everything I am and everything I feel is written on my face. I am a man—you understand?*

He excelled at tawdry existential fluff and superannuated clichés pawned off like darned-up hand-me-downs that had just enough bluster to spirit another generation of deadbeat combatants from who knows what battlefield—anything to impress a woman listening in on his conversation at the moment.

And listen in is what most women did. They were there at Café Algiers that first day I saw him, listening at every corner. But it took me weeks to realize that everything he was, said, and did was intended to accomplish one thing only: to rouse a woman's interest—any woman's. Everything was show, everyone knew it, and everyone fell in with it. Identity as performance, courtesy Café Mouffetard. Sometimes a costume was all the identity you needed. Anger itself, like passion, like laughter, like his most ineradicable beliefs, was, when all was said and done, for show.

Sometimes.

Sometimes, after a near squabble had been averted between him and Moumou, an Algerian regular at Café Algiers, I'd draw my chair closer to his and try to tidy things over by saying something as hackneyed as "He didn't mean a thing by it." "He meant every last word of it," he would say, raising his voice as though about to start an argument with me now. One had to be patient with him, yield a bit, reason a bit, give him the breathing space he needed to let off steam, because steam, vapors, fumes he had plenty to let off. Zeinab, the waitress who was also Tunisian and who had a temper of her own, especially with customers when they didn't tip well or asked for too many refills or more variations on the café's bare-bones menu than she wished to remember, would become sweetness itself when she saw him flare up with one or another regular there. "*Oui, mon trésor, oui, mon ange,* yes, my treasure, yes, my angel," she would whisper, and whisper again, as if smoothing down the ruffled hair on a cat that had just seen a mean dog. You didn't argue with him when he got that way; you simply said something sweet and soothing. "I know exactly how you feel, I know, I know," I'd say, until it was time to speak reason, "but how do you know he meant what he said?" I'd whisper. "I just know, *oké*?" *Oké* here meant, *End of argument. Go no further. Get it?* I didn't always know how to tame his temper. *Oké* was his way of nipping what could easily erupt into a squabble between us as well. "Why be so sure?" I'd whisper, all the while trying to press the point and show there was no risk of our ever getting into an argument but also to make him see things from what the rest of the world calls *another perspective*—a totally foreign concept to him. In his world, there was not and was never going to be another perspective. When we couldn't arrive at a consensus, he'd look away from me and say, "Leave it alone, I said." Silence. And he'd right away order a fifth cup of coffee. "Leave. It. Alone," he'd repeat.

To emphasize the silence that had dropped like a dead-weight between us, he'd quietly pick up the emptied cup before him, remove the spoon, which he'd always leave inside when drinking coffee, and place it neatly and deliberately on the cup's saucer, as if trying to straighten things up and bring order in his life. It was his way of saying *See, you've upset me, I'm trying to compose myself. You shouldn't have said what you just said.* A moment later, he'd be all laughter and jokes again. A woman had walked into the café.

Kalaj's place at Café Algiers was always the same. Center table—not just to be seen, but to know exactly who was coming in or stepping out. He liked to sit inside, never outside, and, like almost everyone born and raised on the Mediterranean, preferred the shade to sunlight. "This is where Kalashnikov takes position, aims, and fires," said Moumou, who, like Kalaj, was also a cabdriver and loved to tease him, the way an Algerian and a Tunisian like to chafe at each other before their taunts degenerate into a full-fledged tussle of words—which invariably happened when one or the other or both lost their tempers. "Either he sits there with his Kalashnikov between his knees waiting for you to make a false move or he'll smoke you out, pin you down, and then, when you least expect it, bellyache you to death about his women, his visa, his teeth, his asthma, his monk's cell on Arlington Street where his landlady won't allow him to bring women upstairs because he makes them scream—did I leave anything out? A Kalashnikov with perfect night vision. You name it, he shoots it down." Their arguments and taunts were legendary, epic, operatic. Kalaj would say, "I've got the eyes of a lynx, the memory of an elephant, the instincts of a wolf . . ." ". . . and the brain of a tapir," would interrupt his nemesis, the Algerian. "You, on the other hand," Kalaj would retort, "have the looks and sneaky bite of a scorpion, but you're a scorpion without a tail, a tail without venom, a quiver without arrows, a fiddle without strings—shall I go on, or do you get my drift?" he'd say, alleging the Algerian's notorious failure to achieve an erection. "At least this scorpion here will take anyone to the top of the mountain—ask around!—whereas with you, they'll barely scale a tiny molehill, give out a courteous little yelp to torment the old lady's sleep, and seldom come back. I can go on if you wish . . ." would come the Algerian's not so oblique reference to Kalaj's marriage that scarcely lasted a fortnight. "Yes, but during those few moments up that tiny molehill I've done things you can't even remember doing since you were twelve years old, despite all the horse pills I hear you take four times a day that will do more for your bunions than for the little pinkie the good Lord gave you and which you wouldn't know what to do with except put it in your ear." "Shush, everyone," the Algerian would interrupt when the place was more or less empty in the early morning and their jibes were not likely to disturb customers, "Monsieur Kalashnikov is going to impugn my manhood—speak to him if you dare, but wear a bulletproof vest." "Oh, it's our Arab comedian coming out of his magic lamp, fart end first," Kalaj would retaliate, putting down yesterday's *Le Monde*, which he picked up every day for free from the international newspaper stand on Harvard Square because it was already twenty-four hours old and no one else wanted it.

Sometimes, to quell the rising storm between the two, the owner of the place, a Palestinian, would put on an album of Arabic songs, usually Om Kalsoum. Within seconds, the battle of wits came to a complete standstill, and the plangent voice of the Egyptian diva would fill the hushed four corners of Café Algiers. "Play it louder, play it louder, for the love of God," Kalaj would say. It was always the same song. *"Enta omri,"* you are my life. If Kalaj was having breakfast with a woman in the morning, he'd interrupt whatever they were saying and translate the lyrics word for word in his broken English—"your eyes brought me back to our long-gone days"—pointing to his eyes, then to her eyes. "And taught me to regret the past and its wounds"—and with the palm of his hand draw a gesture signifying the sweeping, painful passage of time.

If we were together having coffee and a croissant, he'd translate the words for me as well, word for word, though I remembered enough Arabic from my childhood in Egypt not to miss the general tenor of the song. If he was sitting by himself and the song was being played, he'd hold his cup by its rim in midair and, caught in a spell, murmur the diva's words aloud and then translate them back to himself in French.

It was not always easy to step out of Café Algiers after such an interlude in our imaginary Mediterranean café by the beach and walk over to Harvard, which was right across the street. But, on those torrid mornings with the blinding sun in our eyes, it seemed constellations and light-years away.

I still remember the morning smell of bleach and lye with which Zeinab would mop up the floor of Café Algiers while the chairs sat upturned on the café's minuscule tables. The place was closed to customers, but they'd let a few of us in—regulars who spoke Arabic and French—and allowed us to wait for the coffee to brew. One look at the poster of Tipaza and your body ached for sea water and beach rituals you didn't even know you'd stopped remembering. All of Café Algiers took me back to Alexandria, the way it took Kalaj back to Tunis, and the Algerian to Oran. Perhaps each one of us would stop by Café Algiers every day to pick up the person we'd left behind in North Africa, each working things back to that point where life must have taken a wrong turn, each as though trying to put time on splints until the fracture and the cracks and the dislocations were healed and the bone finally fused. Sheltered from the morning sun and wrapped in the strong scent of coffee and of cleaning fluids, each found his way back to his mother.

Mornings, however, exerted a second-tier magic all their own because they reminded the three of us of Paris, our half-way home, and of French cafés we'd known at dawn, when waiters are busy setting up the place and exchange pleasant-ries with the street sweeper, the newspaper vendor, the deliv-ery boys, the baker next door, everyone dropping in for a quick coffee before heading out to work. Kalaj had gotten into the habit of a very early coffee in the cafés of rue Mouffetard. Drop in, greet the regulars, speak, snipe, gripe, and take up this morning where you left off late last night.

At Café Algiers he was almost always the first to arrive in the morning. Like Che Guevara, he'd appear wearing his beret, his pointed beard with the drooping mustache, and the cocksure swagger of someone who has just planted dynamite all over Cambridge and couldn't wait to trigger the fuse, but not before coffee and a croissant. He didn't like to speak in the morning. Café Algiers was his first stop, a transitional place where he'd step into the world as he'd known it all of his life and from which, after coffee, he'd emerge and learn all over again how to take in this strange New World he'd managed to get himself shipped to. Sometimes, before even removing his jacket, he'd head behind the tiny counter, pick up a saucer, and help himself to one of the fresh croissants that had just been delivered that morning. He'd look up at Zeinab, brandish the croissant on a saucer, and give her a nod, signifying, *I'm paying for it, so don't even think of not putting it on my check.* She would nod back, meaning, *I saw, I understood, I would have loved to, but the boss is here anyway, so no favors today.* A few sharp shakes of his head meant, *I never asked for favors, not now, not ever, so don't pretend otherwise, I know your boss is here.* She would shrug: *I couldn't care less what you think.* One more questioning nod from Kalaj: *When is coffee ready?* Another shrug meant: *I've only got two hands, you know.* A return glance from him was clearly meant to mollify her: *I know you work hard; I work hard too.* Shrug. *Bad morning? Very bad morning.* Between them, and in good Middle Eastern fashion, no day was good.

Later in the afternoon, when he'd return to Café Algiers, he was a different man. He was back in his element, all pumped up and ready to fire—this was home base, and the night was young.

I would eventually find that Kalaj was gifted with 360-degree eyesight. He always knew when someone was watching, or eavesdropping, or, like me that first time, simply wondering. He'd sit in his center position—what his Algerian nemesis called Kalaj's *état major*, his headquarters—and would instantly recognize people by their footsteps. If he hadn't turned to say hello when he heard your footsteps, it was because he wanted to avoid showing he was aware of you. Or because he was too busy talking to someone else. Or because he never wished to see your face again. He'd scope a situation in a millisecond. He'd walk into a crowded bar and moments later say: "Let's leave." "Why?" I'd ask. "There are no women here." "How about those two over there?" I'd say, pointing out two beautiful women he'd obviously overlooked. "The one in black is crazy." "How can you tell?" "I know, that's how I can tell," he'd repeat, impatience, sarcasm, exasperation bristling in his voice, "I can always tell—*oké*? Let's. Just. Go."

Or with his back still turned to the door, he'd say, "Don't look now, but there's someone making his way toward us." When had he seen him walk in? How had he noticed? And where does one pick up such skills? "He'll buy me coffee, then a pastry, and then he'll want to tag along." Of course, no sooner had he told me not to look than I'd already turned my head to see who it was. "Didn't you hear me say *don't look now*?" "Yes, I heard you say *don't look now*." "Then why did you look?" All I could do was apologize, say I'd always been slow on the uptake. "But this slow?"

Sometimes there'd be a woman he was trying to avoid. Big embrace if he couldn't duck in time, big introductions, kiss-kiss, and kiss-kiss again, then immediately turning to me, "Is he here?" "Is who here?" I'd ask ingenuously. "The immigration lawyer we're supposed to meet?" he'd hiss, brandishing his stiletto grin, ready to hack at me for lacking the remotest sense of man-to-man complicity. It would take me a moment to understand. "No," I'd reply, "he said he'd be waiting at the café across the street." "*Waiting at the café across the street, wait-*

ing at the café across the street," he mumbled under his breath as we'd rush out of Café Algiers. "How long must it take you to come up with something as stupid as *waiting at the café across the street?*" "Why was it stupid?" I'd protest, knowing that it was completely stupid. "Because she could have easily asked to join us!" Never had I felt so useless and callow in ordinary day-to-day affairs. I was a flea tagging after a titan.

One day, as I walked into Café Algiers, I noticed a girl reading a book at what was my usual corner table. The table next to hers was unoccupied. So I walked over to the free table, put my book down, and sat down. She was reading Melville. I was rereading Spenser. When eventually she lifted her head, I caught her gaze and asked where she was in *Moby-Dick*. She told me. I made a face. She smiled. She looked over at my book and said she'd studied Spenser the previous year. The two of us were reading impossible English, I ventured. "It just takes getting used to," she said sweetly. We continued to talk. About the teachers, about our books, about other books. She liked many authors. I wasn't so sure I liked so many. Then, with the conversation drying up, I let her go back to her reading, and I picked up mine. Not long afterward, she stood up, left some change on the table, and was about to leave the café. "Maybe you should reread Melville," she said before walking out.

"Maybe," I said.

I felt I had made an enemy.

"Couldn't you tell she wanted to keep talking?" Kalaj said

when he walked up to my table. I hadn't noticed he'd been watching me all this time. He asked what we'd spoken about.

"So you spoke about books. Then what?"

I didn't know that there was a *then what*.

"You could have said something about her, or at least said something about yourself. Or the people around us. Or tea leaves, for the love of God. Anything! You could have asked questions. Helped her answer them. Suggested things. Made her laugh. Instead you told her you hated things. You're a champion—seriously."

"It's where the conversation went."

"Because you let it go there."

"Because I let it go there."

"Exactly."

"What will you do the next time you speak to a woman in a café?"

My silence said it all.

"Do you not understand women or are you just inept?"

I looked at him in dismay.

"I suppose both," I finally said.

The two of us burst out laughing.

He knew the whereabouts of everyone, understood why and how things worked, trusted no one, and at all times expected the worst from each and every one. He foresaw what people might do or say, figured things out even when he couldn't understand the first thing about them, and sniffed out deceit and shortcuts most mortals were simply unaware even existed. In this, as in so many other things, he belonged to another order of beings. Gods, heroes, and monsters hadn't been invented when he burst in on the fifth day of creation all wired up and set to go. Mankind would arrive much, much later.

Kalaj also remembered faces. While walking with him one day I ran into a Syrian fellow I knew and said, "He's a good guy." "He's a sick fuck," Kalaj replied, and right away related how, a few weeks earlier, he'd seen this exact same man argue with his girlfriend and slap her across the face outside a nightclub in downtown Boston. "Actually, of all the people I know here, he is the only one I fear. He could stab you in cold blood, bugger you afterward, then run you over with his car. I'll bet you anything he's a spy."

I didn't believe Kalaj at the time, but years later, I heard that this same man, after disappearing in the Massachusetts penitentiary system for assault, rape, and battery, resurfaced as a book dealer in the West.

Kalaj had another gift. He not only remembered faces, he saw through them as well. *Your friend So-and-so, I don't trust him. Your other friend Such-and-such, he hates you.* The list was endless. So-and-so always sits sideways so as never to look you in the eye. Such-and-such seems kind, but only because she's scared to tell you she dislikes anyone. As for this guy over there, he is not intelligent, just crafty. She is not happy, just laughs a lot. She is not passionate, just restless. He is not wise, just bitter. Hysterical laughter means nothing—like bar chatter, like telephone intimacies, like saying I love you instead of a plain goodbye. He hated people who said I love you before hanging up. It meant they didn't. He mistrusted people who cried easily at the cinema. It meant they felt nothing in real life. So-and-so always affects to be giddy, but it's only to avoid telling you the truth. So-and-so says he has a great sense of humor. But he never laughs. It's like saying one's aroused without getting hard.

So-and-so this, So-and-so that. *Rat-tat-tat-tat, rat-tat-tat-tat.*

Did I want to know why Young Hemingway has a beard? he once asked.

Why?

To hide he has no chin.

Did I know why So-and-so covers her mouth when she laughs?

Why?

To hide her big gums.

Did I know why people say So-and-so is smart?

Because everyone else says it.

Did I want to know why So-and-so complains that things are so expensive?

Because his father is wealthy and he doesn't want you to think he's a daddy's boy.

Did I know why he claims he should stop buying expensive clothes?

Because he wants you to know he was born with a taste for them.

On and on and on.

He measured everyone on a Richter scale of either passion or authenticity, usually both, because one invariably implied the other. No one passed. His universe thronged with people who were never who they claimed to be. Where had he learned to think this way? Was any of it real? Or was it all arrant nonsense spewed out of a private Aladdin's lamp fanned by nightmares and demented demons? Or was this just one very unlucky man's way of staying afloat in a New World he couldn't begin to fathom except by thinking he was onto all of its mean and cozy little tricks, that he could read the face behind the mask, that he knew which way the world turned because it had turned on him so many times?

In the end, all he was left with was guesswork and rapid-fire Third-World bluster and paranoia—the perfect cross between desert seer and street hustler.

"Did you notice how you always cross the street on the slant?" he asked me one day.

"Because it's the shortest distance," I replied, thinking hypotenuse.

"Yes, but that's not why you do it."

I had never considered this before and tried to give it no thought. But I knew he'd seen right through me: I did things on the sly, I was born oblique—read: disloyal.

I pretended not to hear.

He probably saw through this as well.

I was shifty, he was up-front. I never raised my voice; he was the loudest man on Harvard Square. I was cramped, cautious, diffident; he was reckless and brutal, a tinder box. He spoke his mind. Mine was a vault. He was in-your-face; I waited till your back was turned. He stood for nothing, took no prisoners, lambasted everyone. I tolerated everybody without loving a single one. He wore love on his sleeve; mine was buried layers deep, and even then . . . He was new to the States but had managed to speak to almost everyone in Cambridge; I'd been a graduate student for four years at Harvard but went entire days that summer without a soul to turn to. When he was upset or bored, he bristled, fidgeted, then he exploded; I was the picture of composure. He was absolute in all things; compromise was my name. Once he started there was no stopping him, whereas the slightest blush would stop me in my tracks. He could dump you and never think twice of it; I'd make up in no time, then spite you forever after. He could be cruel. I was seldom kind. Neither of us had any money, but there were days when I was far, far poorer than he. For him there was no shame in poverty; he had come from it. For me, shame had deep pockets, deeper even than identity itself, because it could take your life, your soul and bore its way in and turn you inside out like an old sock and expose you for who you'd finally turned into till you had nothing to show for yourself and couldn't stand a thing about yourself and made up for it by scorning everyone else. He was proud to know me, while, outside of our tiny café society, I never wanted to be seen with him. He was a cabdriver, I was Ivy League. He was an

Arab, I was a Jew. Otherwise we could have swapped roles in a second.

For all his wrath and dislodged, nomadic life, he was of this planet, while I was never sure I belonged to it. He loved earth and understood people. Jostle him all you wanted, he would find his bearings soon enough, whereas I, without moving, was always out of place, forever withdrawn. If I seemed grounded, it was only because I didn't budge. He was temporarily unhinged yet forever on the prowl; I was permanently motionless. If I moved at all, I did so like a straddler standing clueless on a wobbly raft in the rapids; the raft moved, the water moved, but I did not.

I envied him. I wanted to learn from him. He was a man. I wasn't sure what I was. He was the voice, the missing link to my past, the person I might have grown up to be had life taken a different turn. He was savage; I'd been tamed, curbed. But if you took me and dunked me in a powerful solvent so that every habit I'd acquired in school and every concession made to America were stripped off my skin, then you might have found him, not me, and the blue Mediterranean would have burst on your beach the way he burst on the scene each day at Café Algiers.

In another country, another town, other times, I would never have turned to him, or he given me the time of day. I was not in the habit of approaching a complete stranger, would never have done so had I not seen something of me in him, something muted and forgotten in me that I recognized right away when it flared in his speech. His rants, for all their distorted, senseless dyspepsia, spoke to me, took me back to my past, the way Café Algiers took me back to something distant, unnamed, and overlooked in myself.

He, I would soon find out, was the only other human being in Cambridge who not only had not seen *Star Wars* but who refused to, who deplored it, who scorned the cult that had suddenly sprouted around it that summer. Obi-Wan Kenobi and Darth Vader and Luke Skywalker were on everyone's lips as though they were familiar characters in a Shakespeare play, with R2-D2 and C-3PO trailing like minor fools and obsequious courtiers. But for Kalaj, it stood for all that was jumbo-ersatz.

ONE OF THE things that drew me to Kalaj at first had nothing to do with his mischievous sixth sense, or his survivor's instincts, or his cantankerous outbursts that had strange ways of wrapping their arms around you till they choked you before they turned into laughter. Nor was it the mock-abrasive intimacy which put so many off but was precisely what felt so familiar to me, because it brought to mind those instant friendships of my childhood, when one insult about your mother followed by another about mine could bind two ten-year-olds for a lifetime.

Perhaps he was a stand-in for who I was, a primitive version of the me I'd lost track of and sloughed off living in America. My shadow self, my picture of Dorian Gray, my mad brother in the attic, my Mr. Hyde, my very, very rough draft. Me unmasked, unchained, unleashed, unfinished: me untrammeled, me in rags, me enraged. Me without books, without finish, without a green card. Me with a Kalashnikov.

If I liked listening to him, it was not because I believed or even respected the stuff he mouthed off every day at Café Algiers, but because there was something in the timbre and inflection of his words that seemed to rummage through a clutter of ancestral fragments to remind me of the person I may have been born to be but had not become. If I didn't take his daily rants against America seriously, it was because it was never really America he was inveighing against, nor was his the voice of a bewildered Middle East trying to fend off a decaying and implacable West. What I heard instead was the raspy, wheezing, threatened voice of an older order of mankind, older ways of being human, raging, raging against the tide of something new that had the semblance and behavior of humanity but really wasn't. It was not a clash of civilizations or of values or of cultures; it was a question of which organ, which chamber of the heart, which one of its dear five senses would humanity cut off to join modernity.

Which is why he said he hated nectarines. *Brugnons*, in French. People were being *nectarized*, sweet without kindness, all the right feelings but none of the heart, engineered, stitched, C-sectioned, but never once really born—the head part plum, the ass part peach, and balls the size of Raisinets.

The nectarine didn't have a single living relative in the king-
dom of fruit. It was all graft.

"Grafted like us, you mean?" I said to him one day at Café
Algiers after I'd heard him go on and on about President
Carter's *nectarined* face, to say nothing of his smile. The face, I
agreed, was pure nectarine. But were we any better? We were
no more authentic than anyone else, and we, having lived on
three continents, were pure graft.

"Yes, I suppose like you and me," he conceded. But a
moment later: "No, not like you and me. The nectarine thinks
it is a fruit. It doesn't know it's not natural and won't believe
it however hard you argue. And to prove it, it can even have
children, the way robots too will have children of their own
one day."

He suddenly looked pensive, almost sad.

"You don't know you're human until you have children."

Where did he come up with such notions?

"Do you have children?" I asked.

"I don't have children."

"Then?" I was teasing him

"I have my skin. That's all." And again, as he had done the
first day I met him, he pinched the skin on his forearm. "This.
This is my proof. The color of the ground in my country, the
color of wheat. But," he added as though on second thought—
because there was always a second thought to everything he
said—"I would have liked a child."

All this was spoken out loud in French the better to intrigue a woman sitting next to our table who was probably wondering whether she was a nectarine herself, hoping that she wasn't, all the while trying to guess what kind of a lover this strange rogue-preacher was in bed.

Which was exactly the purpose of the whole diatribe.

And yet, what finally cemented our friendship from the very start was our love of France and of the French language, or, better yet, of the idea of France—because real France we no longer had much use for, nor it for us. We nursed this love like a guilty secret, because we couldn't undo it, didn't trust it, didn't even want to dignify it with the name of love. But it hovered over our lives like a fraught and tired heirloom that dated back to our respective childhoods in colonial North Africa. Perhaps it wasn't even France, or the romance of France we loved; perhaps France was the nickname we gave our desperate reach for something firm in our lives—and for both of us the past was the firmest thing we had to hold on to, and the past in both cases was written in French.

Every night, in the bars and coffeehouses of Cambridge, we'd seek each other out, sit together, and for an hour or so speak in French of the France we'd both loved and lost. He was in Cambridge because he was running away from debt, from alimony, from who knows what ill-fated scrapes and illicit ventures he'd gotten himself mixed up in in France. I was in Cambridge because I still hadn't found the courage to pack up and try to make France my home. We were, when we eventually ran into each other every night, the closest the other would ever get to France. Even the skittish intensity of his tidbit notions plucked from working-class cafés on rue Mouffetard and transposed to the dim-lit bar Casablanca kept the illusion afloat. Until last call. Last call made things more urgent, more desperate, for when they turned on the lights and we finally walked out of the bar to face a deserted Brattle Street, we already presaged the sobering realization yet again that night, as always at night, that this was not France, was never going to be, that this was all wrong, would always be, that France itself was just as wrong, because we were wrong everywhere, here, as in France, as in our respective birthplace that no longer was our homeland. We blamed Cambridge for not being Paris, the way over the years I've blamed many places for not being Cambridge, which is like blaming someone for not being someone else or for not living up to who they never claimed they were.

All that echoed in our minds as each said goodbye and finally made his way back to a place neither could in good conscience call a home was the evening's attempts at French wit in a language we spoke with joy and bitterness in our hearts, because we spoke it with the wrong accent, because it was our mother tongue, but not our native tongue. Our native tongue—we didn't even know what that was.

A Berber by birth, Kalaj had grown up to love France in Tunis, while I, since childhood, had worshipped Paris in Alexandria. Tunis had no more use for him when he jumped a navy ship in Marseilles at the age of seventeen than Egypt had for me when it expelled me for being Jewish when I was fourteen. We were, as he liked to boast when we'd run into women at a bar, each other in reverse.

He had as little patience for Islam as I for Judaism. Our indifference to religion, to our people, to the never-ending conflict in the Middle East, to so many issues that could easily have driven a wedge between us, our contempt for patriotism, for flags, for causes, or for any of the feel-good ideologies that had swept through Europe since the late sixties, left us with little else than a warped sense of loyalty—what he called *complicité*, complicity—for anyone who thought like us, who was like us. There was, however, no one else like us. I'm not even sure we knew what "being like us" meant, since we were so different. We adhered to nothing, nothing clung to us, nothing ever "took." Our capital was an imagined Paris. Our country the two of us. The rest was bunk. *De la merde.* Passports were bunk. Newspapers were bunk. Cambridge was bunk. My exams were bunk. The books I was reading were bunk. The massive Checker cab he drove every day, which his nemesis called *le Titanique*, was bunk, his women, his green card application that never seemed to be headed anywhere, his lawyer, Casablanca, his impacted wisdom teeth, his first wife, his second wife, his marriage to the second wife before he'd divorced the first and whom he'd grown to hate no less than the first, because both, in the end, had kicked him out of their lives, because everyone was always kicking him out of their life, all, all was bunk. Even the personals, which he loved to read on the day they were published in the *Boston Phoenix*, were bunk, just as his replies, which I had to write for him in English, were pure bunk. He contradicted everyone and everything because in contradiction he heard his own voice, but no sooner had he heard it than he'd turn around and contradict himself and say he was as full of bunk as the next fellow. In the end, even France, when we'd talked long and hard enough about it, was bunk. The only exception, he said, was family and blood. His youngest brother, his mother, even his sister who ran away with an Algerian in Paris and whom he refused to have anything to do with though he kept sending her occasional care packages from America. And perhaps, in the end, he included me as well in his tiny clan. For us he'd have laid down his life. He must have known, as I'd always known, that for him I probably lacked both the courage and commitment to risk a thing.

If I did help him, as I did when I spent hours coaching him for his interview with Immigration Services, it was probably either without thinking or because I couldn't come up with a good enough excuse not to. Or maybe I did it to take my mind off my own work, to feel that I was doing something worthwhile besides reading all these books I knew I'd probably never reread. He thanked me profusely and said that help came so seldom in his life that he knew how to value those who had any to give. I dismissed the whole thing and said it was nothing. He insisted I was wrong, that a sure sign of being a good friend was the inability to see how good a friend one was. I knew better than to start arguing the point. My gesture had come too easily, carried no risk, no obligation, no scruple, no hesitation or difficulty to overcome. I knew the difference between a good deed and instant charity tossed like a cheap coin on a salver. "Let's just say it made you happy to help me," he added to cut short our discussion as we left Café Algiers one day after consuming five cups of coffee. His profuse thanks was probably meant to veil what he'd always suspected: that for me he was no more than a buddy in transit, while I was the long-lost sibling he never knew he had until we'd crossed paths in Café Algiers. "One day you'll have to tell me why you've allowed me to be your friend," he'd say, "and then I'll tell you why as well. But you'll have to speak first." When he said things like this, I'd always throw him a vacant *Come again? What are you talking about?* stare. "One day," he'd repeat after sizing up my intentionally blank gaze that hadn't fooled him.

If we read each other so well it was also because the other thing that bound us was our very peculiar scorn for everything and everyone. Our scorn expressed itself differently, but it must have flowed from the same wellspring of self-hatred. Mine was a festering boil filled with bile and muted resentments; his erupted with rage. No one starts as a self-hater. But rack up all of your mistakes and take a large enough number of wrong turns in life and soon you stop trying to forgive yourself. Everywhere you look you find shame or failure staring back.

He had that. I had it too. Blunders everywhere, each damn-
ing in its small, insidious way. Blunders and bunk. Bunk was
our protest, our way of talking back. He shouted *bunk* and
boolsheet the way you pour alcohol over a wound you hoped
wouldn't grow worse. You said *bunk* to deal the first blow. To
have the last word. To show there was more where that came
from. To check out so you wouldn't have to fold in front of the
others. We shouted *bunk* at ourselves as well. *Bunk* was the last
thing you said to shore up your pride, the last stop on a shaky
landfill called dignity. After that, you wept.

I saw him weep twice. The first time was when he learned
that his father in Tunis had been rushed to the hospital with
peritonitis. After that, no letters, no phone calls, complete
silence from Tunis. Meanwhile, here he was, holed up in far-
flung Cambridge. He was, like a character in *Casablanca*, a
stranded soul waiting for letters of transit that never came,
striking up all manner of friendships in dubious establish-
ments. Why was he in Casablanca? Well—as Bogart says in
the film—he'd been misinformed. He should never have come
here. But here he was, like a lone gunrunner in a world that
had grown tired of galled, self-hating anti-heroes, because
anti-heroes themselves had long become bunk and passé.

He was not crying for his father only. He was crying for
himself, because he couldn't take the first flight out to Tunis,
because he couldn't go back poorer than when he'd left seventeen years earlier, because leaving now meant he'd never be
allowed back to the U.S., because he was ashamed of who he'd

become. He was trapped. I had never seen someone pound his head with both fists before. But pound it he did, until I clenched his fists and told him, "Stop, stop, for the love of God stop hitting yourself."

Neither of us believed in God. I put my arm around him. I had never done this before. He continued to sob against my shoulder, I could feel his chest heaving, and heaving again, then he burst out laughing. Twenty minutes later he was telling everyone in the café that he had sobbed in my arms like a woman, just like a woman, he repeated.

I knew what he was doing.

Behind his rage, his volcanic eruptions, and hyperbolic indictments of mankind whole, he had never grown up. He thought or pretended he had. The worst you could do to him was to spot the boy of seventeen. This is where his life had stopped. All the rest was error and bunk.

The second time I saw him weep came much later.

"I'M HUNGRY. HAVE you eaten?" Kalaj asked at Café Algiers, that day we first met.

"No."

"Well, let's get a bite for free."

He looked so grubby and unkempt when he stood up, that I imagined he must have meant something by way of a soup kitchen. There was clearly a first time for everything, and, given my cash flow, I'd been sacrificing food for too many cigarettes. I was ready to admit defeat and head out for a free bowl of chicken broth or whatever was the pauper's fare on the menu that Sunday.

"They're serving *'appy hower* at Césarion's." He pronounced happy hour as the French do: *'appy hower*, by eliding *h*'s where they belong and inserting them where they don't.

I had no idea what happy hour was. He looked totally baffled. "It's when you buy a cheap glass of pale red wine for a dollar twenty-two and have as many *petits sandwiches* as you can eat," he explained. Why hadn't I known about this?

We walked out of Café Algiers, then made our way through the narrow corridor leading to the tiny makeshift parking lot that stood in front of the Harvest. This was where he liked to park his cab.

He entered Césarion's with all the poise and self-assurance of someone who's been a longtime friend of the owner, the manager, the headwaiter. "Frankly, I'm sick and tired of Buffalo wings," he said as soon as he spotted a large ceramic bowl filled with the greasiest fried wings that had ever been mired in bogs of sauce. We ordered two glasses of red wine. You took a little plate *comme ça*, like that, he explained, and you filled it with *petits sandwiches* or *brochettes* or wings, *comme ceci*, like this.

Soon, some of the same faces I'd observed at Café Algiers began to straggle downstairs into Césarion's. I had always thought it was an expensive establishment. Yet, here, half of Cambridge's riffraff was busy stuffing itself on larded wings and *petits sandwiches*. I'd been living in this town for four years, and yet someone who had landed at Logan Airport six months ago already knew all the ins and outs of every Sunday freebie around town. How and where did one pick up such a skill?

"See this guy?" Kalaj pointed to a bearded man wearing a large leather-brimmed hat. "He was here yesterday too. And the day before. He comes in here like me: to eat for free." Kalaj wedged himself to where the cheeses were. I followed. He pointed to a woman holding a glass of wine. "She was at Café Algiers too this afternoon." I gave him a blank stare. "You don't remember? She was sitting right next to you for two hours."

"She was?"

"*Franchement*, frankly . . ." Exasperation speaking. "Now watch this guy."

I watched *this guy*. Unlike Young Hemingway, he had a studiously stubbly unshaven beard. There is nothing to watch, I finally said. Of course there was, snapped Kalaj. "Learn to see, can't you!" He took a breath. "He's just spotted the woman at the corner and is going to try to pick her up. He never succeeds."

Sure enough, the studiously unshaven young man sidled up to a woman in a paisley summer dress, and without looking at her, muttered something. She smiled but didn't say anything. He muttered something else. Her smile was more guarded, almost forced. Anyone could tell she was not interested just by the way she leaned against a pillar. "He never learns." But I admired the man's courage, his persistence, I said. "Courage he has lots of; persistence also, and certainly no shame.

Desire too he's got. But it's all in his head—not *here*. Which is why he's never convincing, because he isn't very convinced himself. He'll wake up one day at the age of fifty and find he's never liked women."

"How do you know all this?"

"How do I know! Easy. He's going through the motions, but you can tell he's hoping she'll ask him to stop. Either this, or he's decided it's a loss but keeps at it to prove that at least he tried. And besides, there's another reason." Here, with his back leaning against the wall, he finally lit the cigarette he'd been dangling from his lips ever since rolling it at Café Algiers. "The fact is he's ugly, and he knows it. All that stubble on his face is intended to make him look cool, but it doesn't work."

I was beginning to wonder what he thought of me. Had he already figured me out? I was not sure I wanted to know.

One of the waiters came and asked if we wanted another glass of wine. "In a moment," said Kalaj, almost offended that management was trying to push drinks now. "Can't he see I'm still drinking?"

Meanwhile another waitress had removed the empty bowl of chicken wings only to return moments later and put down another bowl brimming with more of the same. "A few more bites won't hurt us," he said.

Soon, the friend he had left behind at Café Algiers also stepped in. "There he is again. Let's leave."

I was just starting to like Césarion's. I had grown to like the *petits sandwiches*, and the chicken wings weren't so bad either.

"There's nothing happening here tonight."

"What do you mean?"

"The women are taken."

"What about the one leaning on the pillar," I pointed out, if only to persuade him to stay a while longer.

"She works here."

I didn't have to leave or follow him, and yet I walked out with him. As we stepped out into the early evening light, he muttered, "*Je déteste 'appy hower.*"

It was nearing sunset. I never liked sunsets around Harvard Square, never liked Mount Auburn Street, especially late on Sunday afternoons when its tired, declining light and its shuttered, old New-England-town look suggested a mix of lingering wealth, incipient decrepitude, and the stealthy patter of movements in quiet nursing homes where early supper is being served as soon as Sunday's visitors have left. Mount Auburn had always stood for the grungy backside of Cambridge, and now that the students were gone, its deserted sidewalks and ugly post office looked as gray and wretched as an aging dowager sans makeup.

I was growing restless and needed to get back to my reading. Besides, Kalaj was beginning to buttonhole me, and I didn't like it.

Suddenly, as we were still on the stairway leading up to the street, he gave me his hand and shook mine. "Time went by faster than I thought. I must drive my cab."

He must have read what was going through my mind. It

would be just like him to end a conversation abruptly. It made saying goodbye easy. "Maybe we'll see each other another time. *Bonne soirée*." Snap!

Before going home, on impulse, I headed back downstairs to Césarion's. I had always been a light eater and what I'd seen during happy hour there could easily pass for tonight's fare if I managed to wolf down more wings. Yet after only a few moments downstairs by myself I couldn't have felt more out of place. Not my crowd, not my scene. Without Kalaj and the unreal France he projected on everything around us that afternoon, I felt awkward, exposed; everyone seemed to be an habitué here, whereas I needed to be seen talking to someone, someone who knew his way around this strange ritual called happy hour and who had lived long enough on the fringe of things not to feel uncomfortable or even louche when caught slumming for more than five minutes. I couldn't even find the gumption to pick up another chicken wing. So, before daring to touch the food, I hesitated, then finally managed to order another glass of wine. By the time the bartender served me a glass of red, the big bowl of chicken wings had disappeared. Perhaps they would replenish it soon. But the large bowl of *petits sandwiches* had also been taken away. It took me a while to realize that happy hour was over and that the price of wine, when I finally asked how much I owed the bartender, had doubled.

Crestfallen, I walked back to the Square and headed toward Lowell House. The locked gate made me feel more lonely and homesick. But if Kalaj were sitting in his cab near the Square and happened to spot me on my way to Lowell House, I wanted him to know that the world I was headed back to right now was the furthest thing from the greasy-fingered warren of shabby happy-hour scavengers who'd champ down whatever was dished out with a cheap glass of pale red wine for a dollar twenty-two. I was angry. I wanted him to envy me, perhaps because I needed another's gaze to help me look more kindly on my life and not see that, like so many left over in Cambridge this summer, I too was reduced to slumming. Perhaps I wanted to prove to him, and to myself through him, that I hadn't sunk so low, that however privileged my life had once been in Alexandria, I had found ways to put both the Middle East and Europe behind me now and discovered, if not a new home, at least a new place in the world that could, to anyone who didn't know better, pass for a baronial estate. I could never allow myself to think this was a home, because I knew that the precarious smidgen of privilege that Harvard doled out to people like me could, at a moment's notice and with little more than a few scratches from Lloyd-Greville's vintage Montegrappa pen, be readily taken away and put me back on the street by mid-January.

As I walked on the quiet cobbled sidewalk that led up to the locked gateway of Lowell House, I knew I was momentarily allowing myself to slip into the comforting childhood memory of erstwhile summers back in Egypt where you showered just before dinnertime, put on clean clothes after spending the day at the beach, and awaited whatever life might throw your way that evening. I peered through the locked gate entrance and spied the entirely deserted grassy courtyard where, months earlier that year, I'd sat and taught my class after students had begged me to hold the class outside. Now students and teachers were summering at places that weren't necessarily far from Cambridge but whose whereabouts along the eastern seaboard I knew nothing of. I envied them their beaches, their summers.

Maybe Kalaj and I were not so different after all. Everything about us was transient and provisional, as if history wasn't done experimenting on us and couldn't decide what to do next.

But there was a difference: he was the control in the experiment; I the experimented-on. He was given the placebo, I the real medicine. I had witnessed the effects of the new drug, while he couldn't understand why it wasn't working. Neither of us belonged, but he was still the nomad, I had a ground to stand on. I had a green card, he a driver's license. He saw the precipice every day of his life, I never had to look down that deep. There was always a fence or a hedge to block the view; he had run out of all partitions. But there was another difference between us: he knew how to wiggle his way around the precipice; I, however, put him right between the precipice and me. He was my screen, my mentor, my voice. Perhaps his was the life I was desperate to try out.

2

A WEEK LATER, ON SUNDAY, I CAME ONCE AGAIN TO Café Algiers, hoping that Kalaj wouldn't show up, yet sensing all along that he might. This was another hot, stifling late summer day, and there was nowhere to go for cool air except the movies, but I didn't want to spend the money. I looked at where he'd been sitting last week. A couple with a baby was occupying that table, so I found a table elsewhere in the café, sat down, and took out a copy of La Rochefoucauld's *Mémoires*. Suddenly, I heard his voice. He was seated not far from me and was arguing with his backgammon opponent.

"You've done it again; don't do it. This is a warning."

I couldn't tell whether this was the common verbal squabbling between backgammon players or an earnest warning.

Just then Kalaj slapped a black ivory chip very loudly on the backgammon bar, almost in a rage.

"*Nique ta mère, neek* your mother!"

Another dice throw, and his opponent, Moumou the Algerian, yelped, "*Nique la tienne, neek* yours!"

"With what?" bandied Kalaj.

"Just play!" said Moumou.

Kalaj rolled the dice again, a double something, I couldn't tell what, but I knew it was a double because I immediately heard *slap, slap, slap, slap,* four times. This was the endgame and he was going to win. But then he exploded.

"Not again! I refuse to play with you!"

"Why?" the Algerian asked.

"I will never, never, never play with you again."

"Did I cheat?"

"Did I say you cheated?"

"Then what are you objecting to, what are you saying?"

"I am saying that you cannot keep rolling threes and ones every single time."

"Why?"

"*Parce que c'est mathématiquement impossible.*"

Kalaj insisted on having him throw the dice again, because he was persuaded there was something fishy in his manner of holding the dice that kept rolling a three and a one. The Algerian was glad to oblige but said that the three and one he originally played still counted. He threw a five and a six.

"No," objected Kalaj, "hold the dice the way you did before, in that underhanded way you have of slamming the dice against the corner of the box. Everything about you is underhanded. Like your people."

"Like this you mean?" asked the Algerian, holding the dice in the way Kalaj had described.

"Exactly."

"But that's how I always throw my dice."

"Just play!"

The man threw his dice and rolled a three and one.

"What did I tell you? Every time you throw the dice that way it's a three and one."

"But you're absolutely mad, no wonder you have the brains of a tapir."

"I am not mad."

"You try then."

Kalaj grabbed the dice and rolled a four and a two.

"Well, it's because I don't know how to do it your way. I'm never playing with you again. *Bonne journée.*"

He stood up, looked around, saw me, and walked over to my table. I knew I'd have to give up reading my book. He pulled up a chair and sat at my table, gave me a big handshake, tousled my hair, scanned the place from where he was now sitting in case he'd missed something during backgammon, and ordered coffee. "It's way too hot," he said. After ten or so minutes, he stood up, gulped down the remaining coffee, and said he knew of a place where it might be cooler—"Let's go!"

Together we walked out to a small French patisserie on Holyoke Street. This was where the younger members of the faculty sometimes had coffee with graduate students when they wished to seem less formal. This was where you griped and groused and poured your heart out to teachers who meant well but couldn't really change the system or do anything to help. This is also where they met you when they didn't get tenure and grumbled on and on only to remind you that you were no less ineffectual as a friend than they were when you yourself were in the doghouse. Yet this, I told Kalaj, was where I had tutored French to Heather twice a week during the previous spring term.

"*Hezer*, who?" he asked. Heather an undergraduate rower. I could just imagine the jokes he'd make at the expense of a woman whose voice was far lower than mine. I told him how at one point Heather had looked up at me during one of our tutorials and, on a whim it seemed, asked if I was interested in becoming a tutor at Lowell House. Of course I was interested. But how would she be able to help? Her answer couldn't have been more lapidary. "No problem, then!" I didn't understand what *no problem* meant. "No problem, as in *pas de problème*," she joked in the French she knew she'd never learn to speak. Gruff, husky, a touch butch. Seeing I wasn't persuaded, she added, "I mean gladly!" "You're sure?" "Sure I'm sure." But noticing I continued to nurse lingering doubts about her offer, she finally blurted, "Look, I have pull." Abrupt, no-nonsense, to the point. This, it took me a long while to realize, was how

Park Avenue WASPs spoke their candor and how they went out of their way to make things happen when they wished to make them happen. I didn't believe she had pull, or anything like it. But a month later I was asked to apply to become a non-resident house tutor.

She liked rowing every morning, she liked George Eliot, and she worshipped *Parsifal*. Go figure.

Kalaj was not surprised. He asked if I had to sleep with her after that. "No," I said. "This was not about sex."

"Of course it's about sex," he shot back. "You're the type who never sees that it's *always* about sex. Always, always." Maybe he was right, I said, thinking back to Heather and suddenly realizing that perhaps she'd been trying to tell me something I had failed to hear. "Was she ugly?" he asked. "No. Despite the voice, quite sexy." He made me imitate her voice, her manner of speaking, her gestures, finally bursting out laughing when I consented to imitate her French accent.

"They're put together differently, these women," he finally said, and right away launched into his sermon on nectarines.

Two minutes.

Anyochka's was totally empty that night, its large glass door wide open. The AC was broken. We ordered two *croque monsieurs*, a luxury in my budget, but it was summer vacation, and I felt like spoiling myself. Amid the dimmed lights and the whir of an old ceiling fan, he told me all about his childhood in Tunisia and about his studies in France. His specialty: *informatique*. He explained what precisely a byte was, 1's and o's. I couldn't understand a thing. He explained again. Still couldn't understand. He tried a third time. Then he let the matter drop. "You're simply *incapable*, hopeless." Seeing no immediate future in *informatique*, he became a self-employed caterer. He married his sous-chef, though it became obvious enough by the rest of the tale that it was her money that had set him up in business. "She betrayed me. She destroyed me. And she ruined me." He was now married to an American.

"Where is your wife?" I asked.

"No idea."

"Does she travel a lot?"

"I told you I have no idea. Don't you understand when I speak?"

Rat-tat-tat, but aimed at me this time. What was I even doing having dinner with this creep? I was about to explain my question.

"No need to apologize. I don't give a damn. Well," he changed his mind, "let me explain."

Five minutes.

They met in an underground station in Boston. He had just missed the train to Park Square and, without thinking, had muttered a curse in French. You seem upset, the woman on the platform had said. I *am* upset. She thought he was speaking to her. No, he wasn't. He was just cursing out loud. But one thing led to another. Things invariably did with him. Within days they were married. Soon after their wedding he filed his application for a green card.

What had made him come to the States?

"Let me explain."

Four minutes.

And how did he come to be interested in computers?

"Well, you see—"

Four more minutes.

The tales were gnarled together and could take forever to sort out, but I listened because they had all the makings of a latter-day picaresque novel. After his French wife had abandoned him—she had kicked him out, actually—he befriended an Italian businesswoman who was staying in Paris and who had hired him as her personal chef. From cook he became her driver, then her social secretary, till he graduated to a more meaningful occupation and was invited to live with her in Milan while her husband was away. The husband returned, heard all he needed to hear, and threatened to come after Kalaj. That is when Kalaj believed it was time to flee, and through her contacts, ended up in, of all places, Harvard Square, to stay with her best friend, who was an Italian graduate student at Harvard and whom, it happened, I knew quite well and I liked. "Like her all you want," was his reply. After about two weeks, the graduate student and her live-in boyfriend took Kalaj aside and informed him that perhaps he should start thinking of moving elsewhere.

Perhaps you should start thinking of moving elsewhere, he mimicked, making fun of their couched language. He moved out that same afternoon. Better a park bench. Better the grimy floor in a soup kitchen. Better a public bathroom. They needed *space*! *Space* was a concept that was totally foreign to him— as though humans had suddenly become galactic mutants in need of huge magnetic shields. "Me, impose on people?—God forbid." In fact, he had just been kicked out from his newer digs when he missed that underground train to Park Square. This time last year, he finally said, he had never even heard of Cambridge, much less of Harvard Square. Now he knew more than he'd ever wished. He and his *amerloque* wife had split up. Actually, she too had kicked him out. She was a lay analyst. Shelley. Very rich parents. Jewish.

"Probably didn't like having an Arab taxi driver for a husband," I threw in.

"No, that wasn't it."

"She didn't know French and you didn't know English well enough?"

"No, not that either."

"What, then?"

Out poured yet another screed against American women. Did I know the one about the Arab necrophiliac? Yes, I did. He had told me the joke last week. Well, she was the dead woman in his bed. Even his left hand was more sensual. After sex, it was like leaving a motel room: you slammed the door shut, slipped your keys under the doormat, and headed for your car. You didn't even bother switching the TV off.

Now she was divorcing him.

"At some point," he went on, "I couldn't do it with her any longer. I became numb. Like my friend the Algerian, whose ship doesn't sail, and whose arrows won't fly—you understand, right?—poor fellow. I didn't want to ask him for his pills, but a friend told me that peanut butter helped a lot. So I downed so much peanut butter that the color of my skin began to change. But no waking my *Monsieur Zeb*. I was so worried. Because without him, you know, I am nothing, I have nothing. Because he's all the gold I carry. But then I met someone else . . . and *bam!* I'm a Sputnik, a Kalashnikov, a Trans-Siberian locomotive with triple the horsepower of the mounted cavalry at the battle of Friedland, stiffer than oak and harder than marble and bigger than Zeinab's broomstick." He laughed. "Still, I do miss her sometimes. She was my wife, you know."

"Here," he said, producing a tiny pocket notebook. He removed the rubber band around the notebook and slipped it around his wrist. I had never seen his handwriting before. It was everything he wasn't: neat, tentative, timid, the product of a frightened child in harsh, French, colonial schools where they taught you self-hatred for being who you were (if you were half French), for not being French (if you were an Arab), and for wishing to be French (if you were never going to be). The handwriting of someone who had never grown up, who'd had calligraphy beaten into him. It surprised me. "Read," he said.

Dresser.

Turntable.

Television.

Striped ironing board.

A standing lamp to the left.

A night table to the right.

A tiny reading light clasped to the headboard.

She sleeps naked at night.

Cat snuggles on her bed.

The stench from the litter box.

Bathroom door never locks.

Toilet flushes twice.

Impossible to repair. Shower drips too.

I see the Charles. And the Longfellow Bridge.

Sometimes nothing because of the fog.

And I hear nothing. Sometimes an airplane.

No one sleeps in the adjacent room;

It used to be her mother's once,

She died in her sleep.

They never emptied her closet,

The dresser and the turntable were hers too.

No one plays music in the house.

After all his put-downs and vile words about his current wife, he had written a poem for her in the style of Jacques Prévert. Was he trying to tell me he'd grown fond of her?

"It's all true," he finally said, taking back the notebook,

slipping the rubber band around it, and putting the notebook back in his vest pocket.

I was tempted to say it felt very true to me as well. "Have you ever shown it to her?"

"Are you out of your mind?"

I must have looked totally baffled.

"I just wrote this because I didn't want to forget what her apartment looked like."

Because I didn't want to forget was the heart and soul of poetry. Had any poet been more candid about his craft?

I was speechless with admiration. This cabdriver was a minimalist poet. He not only trained a pair of fresh yet jaundiced eyes on the world around him, but he saw into the very heart of things simply by describing stray objects. The whole thing capped with the magic of two verses: *No one sleeps in the adjacent room* paralleled by *No one plays music in the house*. Leave it to a man born in North Africa to capture the hapless, gritty lives of local Cantabrigians.

"She claims I married her for a green card—"

"Well, did you?" I asked, expecting an outraged, heartwarming denial.

"Of course I did. You don't think I married her for her good looks."

"Then why did you write her a poem?"

"What poem?"

"This thing about the dresser, turntable, ironing board."

His turn to look entirely nonplussed.

"What are you, stupid?" Baffled looks on both our faces. "Poem? Me? My lawyer gave me a list of questions they ask you at Immigration Services. They're cunning people and they want to make sure you actually live together as husband and wife and that your marriage isn't just a ploy to get a green card to stay in this country. So they ask you to describe the bedroom, the kind of pajamas she wears, where she keeps her diaphragm, if you fuck in the kitchen . . ."

Rat-tat-tat.

"Me, write a poem . . . for her? You should see her face first."

Right away, he mimicked her mouth by pulling his nether lip all the way down to expose the roots of his gums. "When she laughs with these gums of hers your penis runs for cover. When I kiss her all I can think of are dentists. As for oral sex—!" He shakes his shoulders and feigns a shiver. Once again he emits his loud, thunderous laugh.

"And yet she took away the only roof I had in this country. The only thing I own now is my cab. And my *zeb*. That's it. I sew my own buttons like a woman and mend my own shirts like a fisherman, and I hate fish, and in my world, a man who darns his own socks is not a man."

He was reaching for the trigger. Any moment now and a string of invectives would come shooting out of his mouth.

But soon a woman walked into Anyochka's. She was svelte, beautiful, with lovely skin. "French," he said. "French and Jewish."

"How do you know," I whispered.

"I know. Trust me!"

I told him to hush. "She's looking at us."

"All the better. She's looking at us because she wants to speak to us."

But he went on with his rant about his wife, her teeth, his teeth—"Your teeth aren't so hot either," he said, referring to my own. He heaved a sigh. "Pretty soon," he threw in, "we'll have to go back to listen to Sabatini, the guitarist who's playing tonight at Café Algiers, because I love guitar music."

There was something strained, staged, and velvety in the way he pronounced *Sabatini*. Declamation rippled in every syllable as his voice rose an octave. This, it suddenly occurred to me, was being said for the benefit of the woman who had just walked in. He was setting the scene. He didn't look at her, but his thoughts and speech seemed aimed at no one else.

At some point, he could no longer stand the silence between our tables.

"You're looking at us because I can tell you understand."

"Yes, I do," she said in French. She was blushing.

"We didn't happen to say anything offensive, did we?"

"No."

"We are staying here for dinner. It's way too hot everywhere else." She smiled back. "I think it's *croque monsieurs* or cold soup today."

"Cold soup sounds like a good idea," she said, not even looking at the crinkled menu. The waitress came and took the order. There were no other customers except for us this evening. He looked at her, she looked back, then looked away.

"Unless you're thinking of eating all by yourself or have other plans, would you like to join us?"

It turned out that she had no plans for dinner and was happy to join us.

He immediately shifted to the end of his side of the table. The next thing we knew we were sitting all three together. No one had told her Boston could grow this hot in the summer. She missed home. Toulouse, she answered. He missed home too, but it was much hotter there than here, though the sea helped. Obviously he was waiting for her to ask *where?* She did. Reluctantly, he named a tiny town in Tunisia, Sidi Bou Saïd, adding, the most beautiful whitewashed town on the Mediterranean, south of Pantelleria. Ever heard of it? No, never. There was a reason why most people had never heard of it. Why was that? she asked. The Tunisian Tourism Office was even more incompetent than the Massachusetts Tourism Office. She laughed. Why? Why? He asked rhetorically—because everyone told you about Paul Revere, John Hancock, and Walden Pond. But he still couldn't understand who Walden Pond was or what role he played in the American Revolution. I noticed for the first time that her laughter was not simply convivial; she was laughing heartily, and Kalaj couldn't have been happier.

The ice was broken. He told her his name, then told her mine. But she could call him Kalaj. How long had she been here? Six months. Same exact thing with me, he exclaimed, as though the coincidence was a prescient sign of something far too meaningful to be neglected. Everything she said meant a great deal in the Book of Fate. And was she happier here than in Toulouse? A long story, she replied. You? she asked. My story is surely far longer than yours; it has good people and some not very good people. Does yours have good people? he asked, obviously a leading question. I don't know, she replied, maybe there are fewer good people than I thought. "Others can be cruel, and we too can be cruel. Life makes us behave unfairly, doesn't it?" he said, to show that some people are big enough to take the blame and learn from their mistakes. She shrugged her shoulders, meaning she didn't know, hadn't decided, didn't care to discuss. "But let me tell you one thing?" he said, and waited a few seconds before continuing with his sentence. She turned her face to him, waiting to hear what he had to say. "Amazing things still happen."

"Oh?"

"Take tonight for example. I ran into my friend here but had no idea I was going to. We came here because it was boiling hot at Café Algiers. And yet, after dinner we're headed back to Algiers to listen to Sabatini play the guitar. And in between this, that, and what else, we run into you." Meaning: *Isn't life full of miracles?* Kalaj ordered three glasses of wine. A silent look from him asked me if it was all right to order more wine, meaning he and I were splitting the bill. I nodded. But then I remembered and panicked. I immediately signaled as discreetly as possible: *Could you lend me ten dollars?* He read me loud and clear. *Pas de problème* came his immediate message. From under the table he handed me a crisp twenty-dollar bill. I signaled *tomorrow, I promise.* He signaled an exasperated *Please!!!* Meaning, *Not to worry.* We were all happy. The wine came, he took up the joke about Walden Pond and the Tunisian Tourism Office and Sidi Bou Saïd, then skipped back to Sabatini. "Let's face it," he added, "the man is no concert master with the guitar. But it's Sunday, and this is only Cambridge, Cambridge is dead tonight, and I always like to make the best of things and end a week with friends and good cheer. Don't you?"

"Yes, I do," she said.

Santé!

And with this both he and I put our worries aside. He forgot all about his green card, I about my exams, my Ph.D., everything. I liked forgetting my cares. Thanks to wine, you didn't forget them, they just stopped scaring you for a while.

IN NO TIME we reinvented France with the very little we had that evening. Bread, butter, three wedges of Brie, *croque monsieur*, a bowl of vichyssoise for her, a green salad to share, still more wine, dimmed café lights, laughter, French music in the background. Cambridge was just a detail.

Her name was Léonie Léonard. Kalaj couldn't resist. But it's a pleonasm. Yes, it was, she said shyly. *Pléonie Pléonasme.* Laughter, laughter. I told them that this wasn't a pleonasm, that he was confusing a pleonasm with a tautology or, more plainly, with a redundancy. He looked at me with startled eyes and said, "Are you crazy, Professor?" We burst out laughing again.

Within minutes, we had her entire life story. He listened, posed leading questions, listened, joked, and on occasion, especially when he was laughing, reached out to touch her elbow, her wrist. He had picked up shrink talk from the women he'd met in Cambridge and understood that once a woman bares her soul there's little else she won't bare, the way he'd say that once a woman tells you she's dreamed of you, you know what else she wants from you. It was just a matter of how you let her get there. He asked, she answered, he asked again, she answered, then asked, each essentially leading the other on, provided none went too fast and none folded. You were not allowed to pass. That was his rule. You had to remain in the game, at the table until everyone showed their cards. Getting bored, he once told me, was unthinkable. I interrupted their back-and-forth once or twice, and both times would have ruffled their seamless Mozart duet had either paid any attention. I had never seen someone turn *la drague* into a way of life. He desired women no more than anyone else, nor was he better-looking than other men. But without women he was nothing. He said so himself but never quite understood it. The important thing is that women did. He wanted women all the time. As soon as he saw a woman, a light flared in his eyes. He became excited, alert, grateful, sweet; he needed to touch, caress, kiss, bite. Women picked this up immediately. Just the way he stared at their skin, their knees, their feet screamed *If I don't touch, I am as good as dead, I don't exist.* He would stare at them straight in the eyes, brazenly, and then, eventually, let a quiver on his lips suggest a smile. He felt passion first, love much later, but interest always. Being so visibly and so boldly desired made women desire him back, which stirred his desire even further. In this as in other things, there was no ambiguity, no hesitation, no shame, no running for cover. The moral couldn't have been simpler: if you desired someone badly enough, and desired them in the pit of your stomach, chances were they desired you no less. What you wore, who you were, what you looked like were altogether insignificant.

He was available to all women, yet he always ended up with the same type. They were between twenty-five and thirty-five, sometimes in their early forties. They had either been married or just gotten out of terrible relationships and were clearly ready to hurtle into one that promised no better. All were handicraft artists of one stripe or another, which, in his eyes, meant they came from money and were all in therapy. They were also nurses, paralegals, florists, musicians, hygienists, decorators, hairdressers, babysitters—one was even a closet organizer/consultant, another a dog walker. It did not matter what they did, what they said, who they were. He was after passion, because he had so much of it to give; after hope, because he had so little left; after sex, because it evened the playing field between him and everyone else, because sex was his shortcut, his conduit, his way of finding humanity in an otherwise cold and lusterless world, a vagrant's last trump card to get back into the family of man. But if you asked him what he wanted most in life, he'd have said, without hesitating, "Green card." It defined who he was at the time, how he lived, and ultimately what everything, including getting laid, was intended to procure him: *la green carte*. I had a *green carte*. Zeinab, the girl behind the counter at Café Algiers, had a *green carte*, so did her brother, another cabdriver. Kalaj simply looked on, like a Titan staring at the goings-on of lesser divinities from across the crags of exclusion. As for the women who'd have done anything for a man who spoke Kalashnikov when he was hot and could reach out and touch their wrist and outshrink the sharpest therapist on Harvard Square, they had probably never even seen a *green carte* in their lives. They were bona fide through and through. He, on the other hand, was Monsieur Pariah, an unharnessed thoroughbred with a touch of France, a few tricks from the East, and enough gumption in his fist to remind the parents of every freethinking, ill-behaved suburban daughter that she could have brought home someone far, far worse had she really meant to scare the neighbors.

After Anyochka's, the three of us ambled back toward Café Algiers. She walked between us, leisurely and friendly. We'd stop for no reason, chat, pick up our pace, then stop again. At one point she even lingered before crossing the street as I went over some of the oddest aspects of English grammar.

They laughed. I was laughing as well. I looked forward to iced coffee, the music, and the three of us talking about anything that came our way. But suddenly, Léonie said she had to leave. *"Bonne soirée,"* Kalaj said, as abruptly as she announced her departure. *Bonne soirée* was his version of a gallant, almost rakish send-off. It suggested that the evening was far from over yet and held out wonderful and unexpected prospects for you.

"She must have felt the heat," I said, trying to show I too knew a few things about women.

"Maybe. My guess is that she is a live-in babysitter and that it's time for her to relieve the parents. There'll be another time."

He ordered two *cinquante-quatres* for us.

"I give her at the most two to three days. She'll show up."

"How do you know?"

"I know."

"Did she give you a *sign*?" I said, emphasizing the word in an attempt to be humorous and show how unfounded was his assumption.

"No sign at all. I just know." He looked at me. "With all your Harvard education, you don't understand women, do you?"

"Oh?" I said stressing yet more irony in my voice to suggest that I did understand them, and how.

"No you don't. You're too flustered, so you're either too quiet or, my bet is, you rush things. In all things, and not just women, it's how you manage time—how you sit and wait and let things happen." Knowing how to distend the moment and linger—*savoir traîner*, he called it—dragging one's feet and letting the things you want come to you. Luck behaved no differently.

I said nothing, felt chastened. Was I so easy to read?

Did he see into the future as well?

Sabatini, as it turned out, played a few Spanish songs on his guitar. He played too slowly. But people clapped, and some cheered. A typical Sunday crowd. Fringe people. I was fringe people too. Then a young teenager, Sabatini's pupil, borrowed his master's guitar and played a short piece. The applause couldn't have been more enthusiastic, and before the clapping died down, the boy immediately launched into a dreamy rendition of Chopin's *Andante spianato*. It was a moving, extended tribute to his teacher, and after the applause, Kalaj immediately walked up to the boy's father and said, "You watch, one day, one day soon . . ." He couldn't come up with the right words or finish his sentence, but the father accepted graciously.

Kalaj, I could tell, was shaken. Maybe it was the boy's youth, or the son he never had, or never knew he had, or wished he had. Maybe it was just Chopin.

"Let's hope he plays something else," I said, trying to ease the tension on Kalaj's face and allow him to stay without having to ask whether I minded.

"No. Enough classical music for one night."

I knew what he was thinking: there were no women at Café Algiers that evening.

That night we ended at the Harvest, which was across the narrow passage connecting Brattle Street to Mount Auburn Street. Just some wine, we agreed. Poor man's fare. It cost a bit more than a dollar twenty-two, but not much more. Kalaj rolled his cigarettes, which saved him a lot of money, because he was constantly smoking. From time to time, I'd glimpse a woman staring as he rolled a cigarette. He would keep rolling and rolling, seemingly unaware of everyone around him, and then suddenly, once it was rolled and he seemed happy with it, he'd whip out his finished cigarette, turn around, and hand it to the woman who'd been staring all along. It was a conversation piece. Everything was or became a conversation piece. You started with almost nothing, it didn't matter what—Walden Pond, the weather, vichyssoise, anything—provided you started. If the other was interested, and there was no reason why she shouldn't be, she'd raise you. Then, all you did was raise her again, always by a penny, never more. Never rush, never hesitate, never stop staring, and never fold. And be cheerful. Things, as he also liked to say, always led somewhere, most likely to a bedroom, but as long as you kept the pennies coming, they always took you by surprise, even when you knew where they were headed all along. One day in a very small café in Paris he had kept them coming. She was a rich magazine editor from Italy. They spoke about food, she loved food, she needed a cook, he knew how to cook . . . The rest, well, he'd already told everyone in Cambridge.

In this case, the woman to whom he offered a cigarette was the model with bathroom problems we had seen the week before at Café Algiers. Even before I'd noticed anything, he had already scanned the room, spotted her seat, and then zeroed in on the table next to hers with the instant accuracy of a sharpshooter. The conversation started. Over a nothing.

"Do you like the cigarette?"

"Very much," she replied.

He nodded at her answer, then paused before speaking, as though appraising the deeper meaning of her answer.

"You know, though, that Dutch tobacco is better than regular Virginia."

She nodded.

"But the tobacco I like best is Turkish."

"Well, Turkish, yes, of course," she immediately said. She too, it seemed, was an expert in matters tobacco. I wanted to laugh. The glint in his eye when he caught my attempt to stifle a laugh told me that he too had caught her attempt to put on a show of knowing a thing or two about tobacco.

"I started smoking Turkish tobacco in my native city."

"Where is it?"

"Sidi Bou Saïd, the most beautiful whitewashed town on the Mediterranean, south of Pantelleria. In the summertime, the pumice stones roll to the shores and the children gather them up in large wicker baskets and sell them to the tourists for nothing."

She looked totally spellbound by his description. "Where is Pantelleria?"

"Where is Pantelleria?" he asked, as though everyone was supposed to know. "It's an amazing island in the Straits of Sicily. Ever been to Sicily?"

"Never. Have you?" she asked.

His thoughtful, drawn-out nod was meant to suggest that Pantelleria was not just a place but an experience to which words could do no justice.

I knew where this was going and excused myself to go to the bathroom.

On my way there, I peeked into the main dining room, and bumped into Professor Lloyd-Greville. He was the last person I wanted to be seen by in a bar, given my standing in the department. I'd been avoiding him since failing my comprehensives. He was having dinner with his wife and an academic couple from Paris in the more fashionable and far more expensive French part of the establishment. Would I mind coming and saying hello? Of course not. I knew his wife from departmental parties. She and I always ended up making small talk in what she called "our intimate little corner" in their large living room overlooking the Charles. Departmental parties are usually the bane of academic wives, but she had turned her husband's position into a thriving source of clients for her real estate business, which she operated non-stop, even when they were away during their long summer stay in Normandy. She was originally from Germany but had lived and studied in France and enjoyed playing the role of the deracinated soul cast ashore in New England who was forever sympathizing with equally deracinated sister souls, especially if they were younger, callow graduate students. "And how is the thesis coming along?" she asked. I affected a horrified gasp as though to say: *Lady, would you please, it's still summer.* She put on an amused if mildly mischievous pout to mean: *So what naughty things have you been up to this summer that are keeping you away from your work?* It was not flirting, just verbal ping-pong. I was dying to slam the ball but too polite to stop the back-and-forth.

I told her about my comprehensives. She was sad, thought a while, then almost winked, meaning, *I'll look into this,* as she gave her husband a reprobatory gaze to suggest he had been a bad boy and should have known better than to flunk a young man like me. It meant: *I'll see what I can work at my end.* But it could just as easily have meant nothing at all.

She had spotted me once having lunch by myself at the Faculty Club and never forgot it. *Playing the impoverished grad student, are you? Well, you're not fooling anyone, my dear.* Trying to disabuse her would have required making too many admissions, and she'd still think me a liar, which would have made things worse. So I let her think I was not starving. To keep up appearances, I'd always manage to send her a new book that we happened to discuss in our "intimate little corner" during the monthly evening get-togethers in her living room. A new hardcover book was out of the question in my budget, but calling the publisher in New York and claiming I was eager to review a specific title was easy, and they usually fell for it when I alleged to have an assignment from some obscure journal. I called it reading on credit, since I'd always make a point of looking over the volume before wrapping it with gift paper and dropping it with Mary-Lou, our departmental secretary, who'd make sure to let Mrs. Lloyd-Greville know there was a *petite surprise* waiting for her. A few days later a small, thick, square envelope, lined in pearl gray paper bearing her embossed name on the outside, would arrive in my mailbox with a friendly thank-you message written in royal blue ink. You were not meant to spot—but of course were definitely meant to notice—the crested, semi-faded watermark bearing the expensive jeweler's name.

At the dinner table at the Harvest, the professor and his friend made perfunctory pleasantries on the subject of comprehensive exams and dissertations and recalled how dreadful and humiliating these public spectacles used to be in their day when the two were students in Paris.

"Remember So-and-so, and then such-and-such?"

"Say no more," replied his guest, "but let me tell you"—turning to me—"you guys have it easy."

"Oh, I don't know," said Mrs. Lloyd-Greville, twitching her features in a coded expression that mimed a look of subtle solidarity with yet another *wink-wink.* "Are you still going to write on *La Princesse de Clèves* one day?" she asked with a peevish little grin implying, *See, I haven't forgotten.* I nodded.

"Oh, *La Princesse de Clèves*, it's been ages," said Lloyd-Greville's guest.

"I've just reread it," added Lloyd-Greville's wife. Trying to earn points, was she? A moment of silence passed over all five of us.

"Would you like a glass of wine?" asked the professor, almost standing up to make room for an extra chair in case I was going to be gauche enough to accept. I hesitated, and was practically tempted to give the matter a second thought, when I caught Mrs. Lloyd-Greville slicing a corner off her artichoke heart, as though she had totally failed to notice her husband's gesture and was already assuming I would turn down the offer and let the four of them return to their meal without further intrusion from this graduate student who had shown up at the wrong time and wasn't going away fast enough. I apologized before declining—I was with friends in the small bar. "Ah, youth!" they said in a chorus. Then, with one or two nodding motions meant to signify something I wasn't quick enough to catch, they returned to their oversized appetizers. A moment of silence passed. Then it hit me: I was being *congédié*, dismissed. Very cordially, the little clan had bolted its door in my face.

I had never even wished to join them but I suddenly understood why people burst with road rage, brandished Kalashnikovs, and mowed down real or imagined foes, it didn't matter which, because no one was your friend here, and bunk was forever closing in on you, no matter where you turned. Bunk, their foodie palates; bunk, *La Princesse de Clèves*; bunk, their venomous little white canines darting from behind their puckered smiles as they nodded goodbye and savored their fried *Carciofi alla giudía* that would turn cold if they didn't gobble them up right away while I stood there trying to negotiate a gracious exit. Why was I being reminded that I was a hopeless, feckless, unkempt, unwelcome, and thoroughly unfit waif on this niggardly strip of earth called Cambridge, Mass.?

I would never forgive them, never forgive myself. Why ask me to their table, why overstay my welcome, why couldn't I read the signs? Kalaj would surely have known how to read the signs.

I was, it occurred to me, no different from Kalaj. Among Arabs he was a Berber, among Frenchmen an Arab, among his own a nothing, as I'd been a Jew among Arabs, an Egyptian among strangers, and now an alien among WASPs, the clueless janitor trying out for the polo team.

I hated everything this side of the Atlantic.

Come to think of it, I hated everything that side of it as well.

I hated America, I hated Europe, I hated North Africa, and right now I hated France, because the France everyone else worshipped in Cambridge wasn't the imagined *douce* France I'd grown up loving in Egypt, a France of Babar and Tin-

tin and illustrated old history books that always started with Caesar's ruthless siege of Alessia and ended with the heroic battle of Bir Hakim between French legionnaires in North Africa and the German Reich—a France even the French no longer cared for, much less remembered. France had become jumbo-ersatz as well, a gourmet haven for puckered lips and highborn gluttons.

A decade ago, I began thinking, none of them were good enough to step into my parents' service entrance; now they were snubbing me with a ghetto dish my grandmother wouldn't be caught dead serving to her guests. *Artichokes à la Jewish!*

The thought might have brought a smirk to my face, but it couldn't soothe me. I might as well have been barking jumbo-ersatz at the poor artichokes themselves and their distant cousins the nectarines, before grabbing each choke on their plates and forcibly stuffing them into Mrs. Lloyd-Greville's leering kisser and down her dewlapped bill.

I knew I was beginning to sound like Kalaj. I liked sounding like him, I wanted to sound like him. I liked how it felt. He was the voice of my anger, my rage, a reminder that I hadn't imagined the insult tonight, even when I knew no insult was intended. I was bruised all over and yet no one had cut or meant to injure me. Still, I liked mimicking his rage, liked wearing it. As senseless as it was, it made me feel stronger, made things simpler, gave me courage, and filled my chest. It reminded me of who I was here. I had for so long stopped knowing who I was that I needed a total outcast to remind me that I was no nectarine, that not being able to graft oneself onto this society came with a price but was not a failure.

I wanted to shout out the words. *Nectarines ersatz, nectarines ersatz!*

I went to the bathroom and as soon as I had shut the door read the prophetic inscription over the urinal: *I'm OK, you suck.*

Everyone sucked. Everything sucked. The world sucked. Kalaj sucked. I sucked.

WHEN I RETURNED to our table, Kalaj had already managed to invite the woman sitting next to us to our table—or, rather, he had asked her to move over to his spot on the cushioned bench and come closer to him. "You'll have to forgive me," he whispered when he pointed to my books, which now stood in a neat pile on the far corner of his table, "but I think it's time we separated."

I was obviously cramping his style. Perhaps I was a touch stung, but I liked the honesty. It confirmed our camaraderie. He was a survivor. Tonight he wasn't sleeping alone. He reminded me of hunters, who wake up at dawn and are determined to forage for food and won't come back till they've dragged a fresh carcass to feed their clan on. I was a gatherer: I waited for things to grow, to come my way, to fall into my hands. He went out and grabbed; I stayed put. We were different. Like Esau and Jacob.

In this I was still wrong: I didn't even know how to wait. There was haste, not hope, in my waiting. Kalaj had seen through this as well. He called it *savoir traîner.*

And yet it dawned on me that evening as I headed home through Berkeley Street, where guests at a garden party were still lingering long past party hours, that I was finally glad to be rid of this guy who could waylay you for hours and, just because I didn't know how to brush him off, assumed that I had nothing better to do than trail after him and watch him troll every woman. A sleaze and a freak, I thought. That's what he was. I decided to avoid Café Algiers for the next few days.

What a contrast he was to these quiet, contented academics on Berkeley Street who seemed perfectly capable of extending their weekend hours by gathering a few friends and sitting about on their wide porch drinking gin and tonics, and whose only worry that Sunday evening as they sat together in the dark, was how to avoid attracting bugs. I always envied my neighbors on Berkeley Street.

Thank God I hadn't run into anyone from Harvard in his company. The last thing I wanted was to have Kalaj show up next to me somewhere and, by virtue of just a grimace, a grunt, a word, let alone his bearing and his clothes, give away the sleazy underworld that had brought us together. I could just picture Professor Lloyd-Greville giving Kalaj the once-over before turning to his wife and saying, "He's hanging out with drifters now."

Then I remembered their artichokes, their foodie snouts doused in claret and scholarship. Nectarines at the pumping station of art. The world was filled with nectarophiliacs plying away at their hollow, nectarosclerotic little professions where people shuffled about their nectaroleptic lives.

If only I had the courage to get out now.

WHEN I ARRIVED at my building, I saw the girl from Apartment 42 sitting on the stoop, a book in one hand, a cigarette in the other. She was wearing a white tank top, her bare, tan shoulders glistening smoothly under the light from the lobby.

"The heat got to you?" I said, trying the blandest greeting in the world dabbed with a touch of irony. I suspected something else was bothering her, but weather was better than silence.

"Yes. Dreadful. No fan, no AC, no TV, no draft, *nada*. I figured better here than indoors."

"What about the roof terrace?" I asked.

She shook her head. "Nah, too spooky this time of night."

So this was going to be it, I thought. There was nothing more to say. There were, of course, plenty of silly things to say, but I couldn't think of one with which to raise her by one tiny chip. Still, I lingered on our stoop.

"Actually, it's quite spectacular up there at night, have you ever been?" I asked. "Cambridge as you've never seen it. There's always a breeze upstairs. It's all dark, with tiny lights speckling all around you that remind me of small towns on the Mediterranean."

Before she could ask which towns, at which point I'd have to come up with the name of one real fast, I don't know what took hold of me but I told her I'd been planning to grab something to drink and sit up there. "It's stunning, you'll see."

It took me a moment to realize that I myself had never been up there after sundown, let alone at night. *You'll see* was the verbal equivalent of touching her elbow, her wrist.

"I don't feel like dragging a chair up."

"I'll bring one up for you too," I said. "And they're director's chairs," as though that would persuade her, which made us both laugh.

She followed me up the stairs. Ours was the top floor, and it had become a source of good neighborly relations whenever you met someone going up or coming down the stairs to joke about the wide stairwell in a building that could easily have housed an elevator. *It explains our low rent*, was the thing to say. *Yes*, the expected reply. We were both slightly uneasy, and neither wished to say anything about the stairs, or about the rent or the heat, perhaps for fear of showing that what was taking our breath away was not the climb. When we reached my apartment, I opened the door trying to look very relaxed and left it wide open, a gesture meant to show I was just going to look for the chairs, mix the drinks, and head upstairs to the terrace with her. *This is going to take just a sec*, I was signaling, not sure yet whether all this body language suggesting haste was meant to put her or myself at ease. She dawdled in the foyer, crossed her arms, and watched me head to the kitchen, then slowly she followed in, her way of showing she was waiting for the drinks, her arms still crossed, her shoulders as always glistening, her whole posture saying *Just don't take forever.* She looked around. Her one-bedroom apartment was exactly like mine, she said, but strangely everything, down to the door handle, was right-side left here. Mine faced west, hers east. As she was talking, I took out a can of frozen lime juice, ran some hot water on it, and emptied an ice tray into a large bowl.

"What's that?" she said, pointing to a rubber mallet I had taken out and placed on the kitchen counter.

"You'll see." I took out a roll of paper towels, tore out two sheets, and placed a few ice cubes between them. Then, with the rubber mallet, I pounded the cubes on the kitchen counter and emptied the cracked ice into a glass jar.

"Is this how it's done?" she asked.

Breathless, I could do no more than repeat her words, "That's how it's done." Did she want to try? I handed her the mallet. To steady her hand, I held the hammer with her and then let her pound it once. She liked cracking the ice. She pounded again, then one more time after that. We emptied the cracked pieces into the bowl. Then, just as I was opening the bottle of gin which I'd removed from the freezer, something suddenly seized me and, before I could think twice, I turned toward her and kissed her on the shoulder and then on her neck. It must have startled her but she did not seem to mind, perhaps wasn't even surprised, and let me kiss her again on the very spot on which for days now I'd been yearning to bring my lips. Then, facing me, she met my lips and kissed me on the mouth, as though I'd been taking forever to make up my mind to kiss her there. We never made it to the terrace that evening.

Around four in the morning, though, when the heat in my apartment had become unbearable, we did go upstairs for a short spell and, standing naked on the dark terrace within sight of the neighboring buildings all around us, we watched Cambridge gleam in the misty summer night just before sunrise. It was her idea to go upstairs naked. I loved it. We came back downstairs and made love again.

SHE WAS ALREADY gone by the time I woke up the next morning. I put on some clothes and knocked at her door. No one answered. She must have already gone to the library.

The smell of her body was still on my sheets, on my skin. I didn't want it to go away. I would shower later, but not now. Without a bite or a cup of coffee, I headed straight for Café Algiers.

Along the way down Brattle Street, I kept wondering why I was rushing. Was I gloating? Had I already forgotten her and was I thinking only of telling Kalaj about her? Why had she left so quietly? I had no answers.

Before I could begin to fathom the joy I was feeling, I was

struck by an unsettling pang of horror. Had we made love because I had come with anger in my heart, because sex feeds on anger, the way it feeds on beauty, love, luck, laughter, spite, sorrow, desire, courage, and despair, because sex evens the playing field, because sex is how we reach out to the world when we have nothing else to offer the world? Is this what had happened—because of the Lloyd-Grevilles' dismissal, because Kalaj had suddenly put distance between us when I was just about ready to embrace him as a fellow drifter? Or had I borrowed his lust, caught his lust as one catches a fever?

I had no answers there either.

At the café, Kalaj was already sitting at his old table with a *cinquante-quatre*, his usual objects strewn around his table, his hair still wet. He was rolling up a cigarette, telling Zeinab, who was standing next to him, that asparagus was indeed a renal cleanser—a diuretic and a detoxifier. It increased urination, which helped flush out toxins from your kidneys.

They always spoke in French.

"And I who thought the smell was the result of an internal infection," she said, holding her wooden tray with one hand.

"No, the smell is evidence that the body is cleaning itself. As the body breaks down asparagus, it releases an amino acid called asparagine which is easily detected in the urine of people who've eaten asparagus."

She was filled with admiration. "Do you know everything, Kalaj?"

"I'm an encyclopedia of bunk."

She smiled when she heard him put himself down, perhaps her way of sympathizing with him for thinking so poorly of himself but also of showing she was not taken in by any of it. She probably saw it as an intimate admission of personal foibles he wasn't likely to disclose to anyone else. "I don't like it when you speak about yourself this way. Compared to you, I am so ignorant."

"Yes, Zeinab, you are." He sat motionless as he began to inhale. "But you're like my sister, and I'll kill the first man who lays a finger on you."

"I'm not your sister and I don't need you to kill anyone for me, Kalaj, I can take care of myself."

"You're a child."

"I'm no child, and I can prove it to you in a second, and you know exactly what I mean, even if you're pretending not to."

"Don't speak like that."

He was, to my complete surprise, blushing.

"It's as you want, Kalaj. I know how to wait," she said, heedless of my presence as I stood there on my feet transfixed between them. "All I need is a sign, and I am yours for as long as you want me. When you're tired, you'll let me know. *Sans obligations.*"

"Speak to him, not to me," Kalaj pointed at me, which was his way of greeting me that day.

"Him? He doesn't even look at me. At least you do. As I said: for as long as you want and not a minute more."

With that she was gone behind the counter.

"Another one," said Kalaj when she was out of earshot. Using his right hand, he pulled up a chair with the effortless grace of a defense attorney preparing a chair for a prisoner who's just walked into the visitation room.

"So tell me."

"You tell me first."

We exchanged stories.

He had been right about the woman with bathroom problems. "She has bathroom problems . . . during orgasm." He laughed. Even Zeinab, who was arranging small pastries on a large platter behind the counter, snickered on hearing the story. "You men are swine," she said. "Nothing is sacred to you, Kalaj. And you want to treat me like your little sister?"

He ignored her and asked about my evening. I told him about the woman in Apartment 42, and how we'd stood naked on the terrace facing all of Cambridge in the dark. He immediately dubbed her *la quarante-deux*, Miss 42.

"Her name is Linda," I said.

He preferred *la quarante-deux*.

"We were probably overheard by our neighbors—especially by the woman next door to mine."

"All the better."

He asked if we'd done it on the terrace. I didn't know how to answer without giving everything away. "Let's say we started there," I said.

"You too are a pig," came Zeinab's comment.

"Who told you to listen? This is man talk."

"The things I could teach you men . . ." she echoed from the kitchen.

Kalaj did not like to skimp details, so I heard all about his night. She lived in Watertown, but liked to come to Cambridge in the evening. Big smirk, meaning: *We know why.* She worked in the art section of a university library, had beautiful art in her house, lived alone, not even a pet. Very uninhibited in bed, wild sex. Then, on second thought, mechanical sex. Passion with eyes shut tight. Which was why he wasn't going to see her again. One night was enough. What was wrong with her? I asked. Not for me, came his answer. He'd have given her at most four nights, then she'd start asking for this, and then that, then she'd pout, and why wasn't he doing this, sulk some more, and why not that . . . ? He knew the litany well enough. It was called domesticity. These women are always depressed, then they depress you, and when they've got you well and soundly depressed, they hold it against you, lose interest, and look for someone new to depress. As always, his biggest fear was that getting too close to such people would eventually unseat and kill his artisanal, homespun self and replace it, in the dark of night, with his mass-produced, ersatz double. It scared him—because his other fear was that he might grow to like being ersatz, or, worse yet, forget he had once been otherwise. Even his *Monsieur Zeb* would become ersatz, and then where would he be?

But there was another reason why he knew better than to

seek her out. "I burn through things too fast," he told me, and there was no longevity in the things he touched.

After sex she had wanted to sketch him. Absolutely not, he'd said. Why not? I asked. "Take a look at this." And, like Harpo Marx producing a steaming cup of coffee from under his raincoat, he pulled out a sheet of blue construction paper that had been folded in four. He unfolded it, slapped it on the table, and, to hold it down, placed his damp saucer right on top of one of its corners. "This is me?" he asked, outrage sizzling in his voice, "Is this me?"

With Cray-Pas, she had sketched his face and bare shoulders.

"Yes, it is you," I said. It was quite masterfully done. "Stunning and expressive work."

"This is shit. Her parents had spent a fortune on her education, and all she can do at the age of thirty is *neek* the first Arab she meets in some underground café and then ask him to sit still when he is dying to sleep so she can produce this? *This?*"

He yanked out the sheet from under the saucer, asked Zeinab to come over here right away, and held it out for her to see. *This?*

Zeinab stepped out of the kitchen and was already drying her hands on her apron as she rushed toward our table. "What?"

"This," he said.

"Let's see." She held the picture in front of her, made an amused click in her throat, and then, without batting an eyelash, kissed the portrait. *"Tu es beau,"* she rhapsodized, *"tu es vraiment beau,* you are really handsome!"

"Then you keep it. You've already lost your mind as it is."

"I'll keep it and how. Do me a favor."

"What?"

"Write today's date on it. My hands are wet."

Out of one of the many pockets in his jacket, he pulled out a pencil with a rubber band wrapped so tightly around its head that it had formed a ball on the eraser.

"Why do you have a rubber band on your pencil?" she asked.

"Because when I need a rubber band I'll know where to find one. What else do you want to know?"

He held his pencil as would a ten-year-old boy, with his fingers almost touching the lead. Its stubby point showed it has been sharpened not in a regular pencil sharpener but with a blade. I recognized the uneven marks around the edge of the pencil where it was shaved. It took me right back to my childhood, when I couldn't find my pencil sharpener in class and didn't want my teacher to know I had lost it. You took out a penknife—all of us had penknives—and in total silence under your desk shaved the edge of the pencil until, like a new tooth pushing its way out of the hollow of your gum, the new point began to emerge. Using a knife made you feel brawny, like a sailor with a dagger whittling away at a piece of driftwood because this is how he whiled away his hours when there was

nothing better to do, because real men always found something useful to do with their hands.

"And write neatly," she said.

Again, like a conscientious and dutiful young pupil, he
leaned forward, his face so close to the table you'd think he
had eye trouble, and penciled the date.

Voilà.

"Now you two can go back to your slop," said Zeinab.

"Exactly," he said, and turning to me: "So tell me about *la
quarante-deux*."

I told him the whole story again.

Kalaj said that if she had come upstairs with me that night
it was because I had done one thing right: I had lingered, just
lingered, because when I was standing in front of her as she sat
smoking in silence on the stoop, I had not moved, had kept very
quiet, had made it very obvious that I was aching and longing
for her, that all I could think of at that hour of the night was
her shoulders, and that I would make her laugh and be happy,
that I would take care of everything, including the two chairs.

But, as always, Kalaj immediately corrected himself. She'd
probably made up her mind about me the moment she'd seen
me walking toward her, or maybe even on the rooftop weeks
earlier.

"Now tell me about being naked on the terrace."

"Again?"

"Again."

"You mean how she suddenly sat on my lap naked and I felt

the hair of her vagina on my *zeb* and couldn't believe I could go at it again so soon?"

"*Oké*, stop!"

WE HAD HAD such a warm moment together that morning, that in the days and weeks afterward, I made a point of showing up at Café Algiers just as it was about to open. The place smelled of bleach and Mr. Clean, the chairs were still upturned as the floor was drying, and Zeinab was still mopping the kitchen area, all the while making sure the coffee was already brewing and Arab songs playing. When she was in good spirits, she'd put on George Brassens or, as I later found out, her favorite, Barbara, and she'd sing along to *Il n'y a pas d'amour heureux* and, in mock-cabaret-singer, sidle up to the man who happened to be sitting nearest to the kitchen and sing to him, and to him alone, her favorite verses of the song by Aragon.

In the back of Café Algiers, as always, that picture of Tipaza—in case any of us early birds forgot why we were there. This was more like home than anywhere else, and more home now than home itself, since no one really had one to go back to.

Kalaj was always in a rush. He'd stand up before finishing his coffee, busily start collecting all of his stray items on the table, and after taking one last gulp, he'd light up the cigarette he had been rolling while eating his croissant, and dash out through the front door, which took him through the tiny back lot where he normally parked his cab.

Once he was gone, I'd open my books and sink deep into the seventeenth century. I'd sit there till I needed to shake my legs and move to another locale. If too many customers started coming in, I'd leave to avoid the noise. Then I'd head to the library where I read for a good part of the morning.

I liked this ritual. I liked rituals. Rituals were like home.

Sometimes, after Algiers, I'd avoid the Square altogether and, because it was still warm, would head back to my apartment, change, and be back to my usual spot on the roof terrace—bathing suit, sunglasses, suntan lotion, books, everything I needed, including my small radio. There I continued reading until exhaustion set in and the subject matter of my books began to blend with the surrounding scene. The list of Jesuit abuses are now forever inscribed not only in a cheap pocket edition of Pascal's *Provinciales*, but in the scent of Coppertone, the tint of my Ray-Bans, and in the sound of warbling pigeons who sometimes alighted on the roof terrace, where they gathered, before flying elsewhere under the torrid summer sun. Invariably I'd think of Linda.

How easily had things happened with her. Maybe this is what kept stirring me, not just the beauty but the sheer ease of it. Part of me still wanted to understand how it had sprung, or why. Was it because she'd laughed when I'd offered to bring two folding chairs? Because of how I'd mixed the drinks, or left my door wide open? Or was it simply because I had said something instead of saying nothing.

No, it was because I had lingered, Kalaj had said.

I couldn't wait to ask him what exactly had he meant by lingering. What was it about lingering? The refusal to duck after you'd been given the silent treatment? The will to wait things out until the other spoke, until things eventually turned your way? Or was it the laying bare of one's desire, because one could not believe it wasn't being reciprocated? Or was lingering nothing more than the sheer belief in one's body, in one's beauty?

No, lingering was knowing how to stretch things out, sometimes beyond their breaking point. Not everyone had the balls for this. You sat and waited. And waited and waited. Mind you, though, this was not passivity. What was one man's strategic genius was another man's way of sweet-talking fate. Moumou, who had listened in on that conversation, had no patience with Kalaj's philosophic disquisitions. Sometimes all it took was luck, he said. You got lucky. We all get lucky. Sometimes. "Well, with all the vitamins you take . . ." started Kalaj.

"Well, what about my vitamins? The vitamins help—and how."

ONE EVENING, WHEN I was busy reading at Café Algiers, Kalaj walked in looking dazed. He spotted me right away, came over, dropped his bag right next to the empty chair facing my table, and said he wanted to talk about something serious.

I was about to talk to him about *la quarante-deux.* But he cut me short.

"I don't want to talk about women, not last night's, not tonight's, not yours, not mine."

"What is it then?"

"Actually, maybe I don't want to talk at all."

"I see," I said, trying not to show I'd been wrong-footed by the sudden turn from his usual locker-room mirth to his downright hostile tone. "I'll leave you alone then."

I picked up my book and began to read, determined to ignore him.

"Don't be ridiculous," he finally said. "Are you really going to sulk now? Every woman I know ends up sulking—now you?" I didn't reply. "There. He's pouting. Come on, talk to me. I am in a terrible mood, that's all."

"Why are you in a terrible mood?"

Was he sick? Did he get a fine, did he have an accident, was he robbed?

The sudden hand gesture with the flat of his palm waved once in the air meant *Don't ask.*

"*L'enfer.*" he said. "Hell, that's what it is."

In a few days, he announced, he would have to be interviewed by Immigration Services. His wife had originally promised she'd accompany him, but her lawyer had just informed Kalaj that she had changed her mind. Would I go with him instead? Yes, I said. Good. The problem was that he had to rehearse what he needed to say. Would I help coach him before the interview if he gave me a list of questions and answers that his lawyer said they normally asked at Immigration?

"Again?" I asked.

"Yes, again," he replied, as if to remind me this was serious business and not a time for joking. Once again, as he'd done before, he whipped out his notebook from one of his many pockets and tore out four to five sheets on which were scribbled all the questions they were likely to ask. "I need to memorize the answers and don't know how to study them alone, and you're a teacher, so I thought better with you than anyone else, right?"

"When should we meet?"

"In a few days. Or now."

"Where?"

"Right here."

I told him he was welcome to come visit me, where we might focus better without all the brouhaha of Café Algiers. Besides, my door was always unlocked, I said, so he could come in whenever he pleased. "I like the noise," he said. I felt sorry for him. What demonic monsters must crawl around him the moment he is alone, I thought. He preferred bad company to no company, an argument to silence, a twisted life that coiled like barbed wire around him when he sparred with anyone to the protracted beep of a dead patient's heart monitor.

I held the few sheets he handed over to me and went over them in front of him. OK, I could do this. It was like studying the multiplication table; you needed to be blitzed by unexpected questions: four times eight, nine times six, seven times six, on and on. To bring back some mirth in his life, I decided to bombard him with fatuous questions. Where did you fuck last, how many times, who comes first . . . Explosive laughter.

But why wasn't his wife going with him to Immigration?

"Because that's how she is," he said. "Because she is selfish. Because of her gums."

I looked at him with a puzzled look.

He pulled down his nether lip and exposed his gums. "Because I hate my wife! Because she wants a divorce. My God, you are really thick sometimes."

His lawyer had just informed him that, given their probable divorce, Immigration Services was still not sure they would go ahead with the interview but that he should prepare for it nonetheless.

He started rolling a cigarette. It was his way to avoid staring me in the face. Then looking up, "I need to find a new lawyer," he said. Did I know of a lawyer? No, I did not. "With all your Harvard contacts you don't know a lawyer? This school manufactures the best lawyers in the world and you want me to believe you can't come up with a single one?"

"Not one," I replied.

"You're definitely the wrong kind of Jew. And I'm definitely the wrong kind of Arab."

I laughed. He laughed.

"So," I added, taking out the pieces of paper he had given me, "let's go over some of the questions again." He ordered coffee, sat back, and began smoking.

"Have you ever had anal sex with your wife?" I started.

He was such a good-natured soul that this alone brought a smile to his face. "That's the kind of thing they might ask," I said.

"Are you sure?"

"How should I know?"

Then I asked again: "Well, have you had anal sex with your wife?"

"I don't think we have."

"Yes or no?" I said sternly, mimicking an official of the federal government.

"Yes."

And together that evening we went back and forth with questions and answers. I learned more about his life on that day than anything I'd heard him say out loud when he wished others to overhear. He started life as a deserter. Why? Because two sailors had attacked him on the navy ship. He had just turned seventeen, not a speck of hair on his face, and was too shy to fight them off or tell anyone what they had done. From then on, the mere sight of blood, his own or anyone else's, filled him with dread and shame, and then rage. In Marseilles he had met a very kind doctor who was also a Tunisian and who had helped him find a job in a bakery, then in a restaurant. When one of the chefs slit his own finger by accident, Kalaj had yelled at him for being careless and was summarily fired. Even now when he shaves, he hates to see blood. Where does he shave? In front of the mirror, where else? Does his wife shave her legs? No idea what she does with her legs. Her underarms? Her pussy? What does she keep in her medicine cabinet? Never looked. "You need to know," I said. He tried to remember. Aspirin. What else. She jogged and used a muscle pain relieving cream that stinks of camphor and burns your skin so much when you touch her that your *zeb* is ready to wilt. In Marseilles, he went on, he enrolled in a school to obtain his baccalaureate, but he needed to work and eventually stopped going to school. He never got his *bac*. Then he moved to Paris where he worked in another bakery, always bakeries, and then a restaurant, then another, and another, until he got tired of working for others. He befriended Tunisian Jews in Paris who needed someone to cook Tunisian meals for them . . . but kosher. How did he know about kosher meals? He knew. Yes, but how? He just knew, *oké*? Suddenly he burst out laughing. Why was he laughing now? "Because you asked if my wife and I had anal sex."

Was I sure I didn't know any lawyers?

I nodded apologetically.

"What kind of a Jew!"

He was right to be nonplussed. I'd been at Harvard for four years and didn't know a soul in the professional world. I didn't even have a doctor outside of the one I saw at the Harvard infirmary each time I thought I was dying of gonorrhea and needed to be told that I wasn't. As for a dentist, not one either. Psychiatrists, not a clue.

"Psychiatrists I can find with my eyes closed." Every woman he'd known in Cambridge was seeing one at least once a week.

"You're of no help," he said. Then, changing topics, he asked: "And how is your work?"

"My work?" I looked at him, smiled, and said, "Better not ask. Let's just say that by next year I will probably not even be here." I already caught myself missing Café Algiers.

"*L'enfer* for you as well, then."

"*L'enfer.*"

This was the first time that I finally understood how terrible my parents' lives must have been in their final year in Egypt. Waiting to be expelled, hoping they might not be. Waiting for their assets to be seized, waiting for someone to ring their door with terrible news, waiting to be arrested on some trumped-up charge, waiting, waiting.

A FEW DAYS later I arrived a bit late in the evening at Café Algiers after attending a lecture and a dinner. I had had a bit to drink and was in no shape to study. I wanted company. He was there, looking more glum than ever, sitting by himself, smoking, not even reading yesterday's paper. Peeking at the bill under his saucer, I could see that he had already drunk four *cinquante-quatres*. He was fidgety, fussy, ill-tempered, a gathering storm desperately searching for a lightning rod or else it might unleash its fury on the ten to fifteen earthlings minding their own business at Café Algiers. Tonight, he explained, he was driving on the night shift again.

I'd hate to be a driver on the same road, I thought.

Then he started sulking.

We drank our respective coffees in silence. Everyone, it occurred to me, was meant to notice he was brooding. Zeinab was the first. On his way out, even Moumou came and put a hand on his shoulder and asked, *"Ça ne va pas?"* The answer was curt: *"Non, ça ne va pas."* Zeinab brought him a soup. On the house, she said. It was a Tunisian recipe he'd surely recognize. He wasn't hungry. "I brought it and you'll say no?"

He took a spoonful, slurped it, said he liked it very much. It was a good soup—really. But he wasn't hungry.

When she went back to the kitchen, he looked at me, put on a wry smile, and said: "What Tunisian specialty? It's an ordinary chicken soup."

A second later he put his jacket on. "Come, I'll drive you home."

"Let's go then."

We walked out in total silence. When we reached Ash Street, there it was, his glinting off-yellow Titan among cars. He might as well have been introducing me to the love of his life.

"Everything I own I've put into this monster. Life savings that started the day I snuck into Marseilles to the moment I arrived in Paris, then to every menial job I held in Paris and Milan. Here, knock on this hood," he said, clearly proud of the car. "Don't pat it, knock with your knuckles—real steel, can you hear it? *Dong, dong, dong.* Like cathedral bells. Now knock on this car," he said, as he walked over to the first car parked right next to his. Seeing I hesitated to play along, he grabbed my hand and forced me to pound my knuckles on the hood of a green Toyota. "Hear the ersatz dead thud? Hear the hollow rustle of crumpled aluminum foil? Hear?" Yes, I heard, I said. "Well, I'm like my car. I'll outlive every one of these spit-glue men and women whose imagination is as limp as a used condom."

We got into the car. It was my first time. The car was spotless and I liked its smell, the smell of old leather and old steel. When, two minutes later, we reached my building, I began to feel sorry for him but didn't know what to say or how to help. I was too shy to ask him to open up and tell me about this cloud that had cast such a gloomy shadow over him. Instead I suggested something so flatfooted that I'm surprised it did not irritate him even more than he was already. I told him to head home and sleep the whole thing off, as if sleep could free a castaway from his island. No, he needed to work, he replied. Besides, he was looking forward to driving at night. He loved cruising Boston by night. He loved jazz, old jazz, Gene Ammons—especially played *en sourdine*, with the volume really low—as the tenor sax invariably blocked all bad feelings and made him think of romance and of sultry summer nights where a woman dances cheek to cheek with you to the saxophone's prolonged lyrical strains that made you want love even after you'd stopped trusting love exists on this planet. He loved the music on Memorial Drive and on Storrow Drive as he cruised those large damp thoroughfares watching the tiny lights flicker off Beacon Hill and Back Bay and all along the Esplanade. "I feel American when I drive at night, as in those films noirs where all they do is smoke and drive with their Stetson brim tilted down to eye level." Once, when a fare asked him to change the music, Kalaj ignored him. When the man repeated his request, Kalaj slammed on the brakes right in the middle of Roxbury and told the pure white gentleman to get out of his cab.

At another time when a black man told him to turn off the Om Kalsoum tape he'd been playing *en sourdine*, Kalaj once again screeched on the brakes, and when the man refused to step out of the car and indeed threatened to fight it out, Kalaj simply turned around and shouted, "My ancestors sold yours into slavery—now get out before I do the same to you."

Kalaj, who never once said anything against Jews, had told a Jewish passenger, who'd heard him listening to Arabic music and refused to tip him because he was an Arab, that it was a great pity they hadn't shipped his grandmother and his baby father straight into the gas chambers, because, given the chance, he would have loved to light the ovens himself.

He knew where to hurt.

He must have known exactly where I'd hurt. He never touched that spot.

I MET KALAJ over coffee almost every evening after that, sometimes by pure chance, sometimes because we both happened to be at Café Algiers at the same time, sometimes because neither of us knew what to do when the Indian summer evenings wore on long after we'd worked ourselves to exhaustion. I would read all day, pretend I was elsewhere, and find all manner of ways to avoid worrying that the new academic year was just round the corner. I didn't want to think of the academic year with all of its attendant duties and obligations: teaching, tutorials, committee of this and that, responsibilities at Lowell House, students to meet and interview, departmental parties and get-togethers—to say nothing of my second attempt at passing comprehensives in mid-January and, if I succeeded, my orals following immediately after. Lloyd-Greville had told all first-year graduate students to read every book in the English Literature library. Was he serious, I had asked a fourth-year graduate student. He never jokes, he replied. The joke was on me. I knew I was allowing Kalaj to distract me from my work; I knew there'd be a price to pay soon enough; perhaps I even wanted to pay that price. But the thought of losing Harvard would wake me up at night and stir up a massive state of panic. There was no sleeping after that. One night, I woke up with such an overwhelming feeling of dread that all I wished to do was write a poem to a woman I had loved years earlier and had completely lost track of. On another night I started writing what I was sure was going to bring me a substantial income: a pornographic tale about two rogue nuns in a convent. Usually, though, all I did was warm up some milk and try to imagine that someone close by had warmed it for me before heading back to bed. I'd eventually fall asleep on my couch. Sometimes watching dawn from my bedroom window overlooking so many rooftops made me think of the beach, and thinking of the beach brought peace in my heart. If you refused to look out to check the window, the illusion of a resort town lingered, and that was good.

Lloyd-Greville had had Mary-Lou call me to make an appointment. He wanted to discuss Chaucer with me. "Which tale?" I asked her. "All Chaucer," she replied, as though I'd yet once more forgotten what kind of institution Harvard was. The appointment was set for mid-September, following Lloyd-Greville's return from Russia. He taught Russian literature to Russians. He was—I should have known—fluent in Russian as well.

I knew that spending time at Café Algiers was not helping my reading regimen, but Café Algiers helped stave off the many phantoms that seemed to haunt me even during my waking hours. It also occurred to me that, despite having a few friends in Cambridge, I had never been so close or on such intimate terms with anyone else in my life as I was with Kalaj, and I didn't want to lose this. We had a little world all our own here, a house-of-cards world with its house-of-cards cafés and house-of-cards rituals held together by our house-of-cards France. We called Café Algiers *Chez Nous*, because it was so obviously made for the likes of us—part North African, part faux-French, part dreamplace for the displaced, and always part-something-from-somewhere-else for those who were neither quite here nor altogether elsewhere. At Café Algiers we always ordered a *cinquante-quatre* and later a glass of wine with chili at Anyochka's, which he liked to call *la soupe populaire*, the soup kitchen. Wine, all wines, he nicknamed *un dollar vingt-deux*: his girlfriend, when she soon became his girlfriend, *mon pléonasme*; and Linda from my building, whose name he refused to remember, *la quarante-deux*. His other recent conquest never got a name: she remained *Miss Bathroom Problems*. Césarion's, we both agreed, was *le petit trou*, the little hole, and the Harvest, pronounced *Arvèst*, with the accent on the last syllable, became *Maxim's*, or sometimes, *le grand trou*. Casablanca, for some reason, never got baptized and remained Casablanca. Our daily walks usually took us from *Maxim's* to *la soupe populaire*, with an occasional stop back *Chez Nous*. *Chez Nous* was where we read, played backgammon, made friends, and on certain evenings would sit around and listen to Sabatini. From time to time, the guitarist would bring his star pupil along who'd know to play the *Andante spianato*, because Kalaj always begged to hear it. On Sundays evenings, once the school year got under way, we'd always manage to catch an art film at the Harvard Epworth Church, for a dollar each. He called it *going to Mass*.

He renamed everything around him to snub the world and show there were other ways of seeing and calling things and that everything had to go through baptismal fire to be cleansed of all cant and pieties before he'd let them into his world. It was his way of reinventing the world in his own image, or in the image of what he wanted the world to be— his way of taking this cold, inhospitable, ersatz, shallow town and bringing it down a few notches to see it turn into a kinder, more intimate, more complicit, sunnier place that would open up a secret passageway for him and ultimately yield to him with a smile—if only, like Ali Baba, he could find the right nickname for it in this French language of his own invention. He defaced the world by applying improvised monikers, leaving his fingerprint on everything he touched in the hope that the world might one day seek the hand that had left such deep scuff marks at its door and pull him in saying, "You've knocked long enough. Come in, you belong here."

In that huddled, provisional world of his he crammed and made room for everyone at Café Algiers, but to one person he gave the best and the airiest room. And that person was me. He needed an accomplice who was also a blood brother.

What he did not see is that the more he opened other worlds and kept challenging and pushing Cambridge further away from me to show there were other ways of living and doing things, the more desperately I clung to the small privileges and to the tentative promises Harvard held out for me.

3

EARLY ONE AFTERNOON, WHEN I WALKED INTO CAFÉ Algiers with my books and was not expecting to run into him so early, I saw Kalaj sitting with two women. "How wonderful to see you," he shouted, and right away embraced me. We'd never embraced before. "I've been waiting forever." There was something too garrulous and flamboyant in his greeting. He was up to something. "This is the friend from Harvard I told you about." I suddenly had a suspicion that he was drawing on my Harvard credentials to boost his own standing and show he had contacts outside of his immediate circle of Maghrebine cabbies and waiters. If he'd only known how thoroughly threadbare my connection to Harvard felt at the time, especially with the threat of catastrophe in mid-January hanging on my mornings like the rancid aftertaste of an undigested meal gulped down with cheap wine the night before.

But this wasn't what was going on at all. He was using me as a conversation piece. I didn't mind. Or, perhaps, I wasn't a conversation piece at all. He was basically asking me to help. And help under those circumstances could mean one thing only: relieving him of one of the two women. The question was which of the two.

As the girls were speaking to one another, he gestured exactly what I suspected: *Get them away from each other!* But he added something else: *Which of the two do you want?* Since I was doing him a favor, it didn't matter—I wasn't interested in either. Besides, going along with the ploy by pretending to make advances to one of the girls to help his cause with the other seemed a touch too underhanded for my taste. My apparent reluctance to fall in with his plan baffled him. His eyes jumped at me with incomprehension. *Not do anything?* What an insult to *them*. And frankly, to him as well. I had to choose. Even they expected it.

I picked the one sitting next to me.

She was a Persian girl who had read all of Dante in Italian, then in Spanish, then in Farsi. The other was a curly-haired blonde called Sheila who was, I should have guessed, a physical therapist.

It turned out that Sheila didn't interest him. Ironically, *Miss Bathroom Problems* did. She had disappeared following their first night and it was she, not he, who was being difficult now. I should have seen this coming. He wasn't very worried, though. Cambridge was smaller than Paris. They were bound to bump into each other again. Hadn't he taken her phone number? He'd lost it. Didn't he know where she lived? No. Too dark, too drunk that night, hadn't paid attention. As for *Pléonasme* from *la soupe populaire*—who did indeed turn up on the third day and proved to be, as he'd guessed, French from a Jewish-Moroccan family—he had ended up sleeping with her in his room when his landlady, dubbed *Mrs. Arlington* of Arlington Street, was already asleep. In no time—three days!—he'd fallen in love with Austin, the boy she took care of as a live-in babysitter. He'd break his day in two to drive her to his school to pick him up at 2:00 p.m., and together they'd drive to Faneuil Hall, park the car, and buy three ice creams. It was all a big secret, as the boy was not supposed to tell his parents that his babysitter's boyfriend was a cabdriver who would pick them up every day and roam around Faneuil Hall until he found a parking space. He continued to pick up the boy, on his own sometimes, long after discovering that his babysitter was two-timing him with the boy's father behind the wife's back.

"I don't care if she sleeps with someone else. I too sleep with others. But at least show some dignity—cheating on the man who worships the son of the very man she cheats on me with—that no! *C'est de la perversité!* Absolutely not." *Rat-tat-tat-tat-tat.*

"I think he wanted to be alone with Sheila," said the Persian girl once we were alone together that afternoon. We spoke in French, which for the second time that summer kept open a door I'd thought had been shut to me. I liked speaking to a woman in French. I had come home. There were things to say to a woman in French. Not things that couldn't be translated or said in English, but things that would never have occurred to anyone in English and which therefore couldn't exist in an English-speaking mind. And it wasn't just the things themselves or even the words for them that I had warmed up to, but their emotional inflection, their underlayers, their voice, my voice, the voice of so many who had spoken French to me in childhood and whose wings now hovered over every word I spoke, listening in and barging into my speech in not unwelcome ways. Kalaj had met the two women there, at Café Algiers: the cigarette trick, the forlorn expat trying to make a comeback, the exotic whitewashed town on the Mediterranean, south of Pantelleria. She had never met Sheila before; she'd been sitting at one table, Sheila at another, and in between had sat Kalaj. All he'd done was to *rapprocher* the two.

Not knowing where else to go, I took her downstairs to Césarion's for happy hour. She preferred herbal tea to cheap wine. She didn't touch Buffalo wings—assembly-line food for the indigent, she called it.

"Rich girl from Iran?" I hazarded.

She laughed. "Very rich girl from Iran."

There was silence for a while.

"Do you have many friends in Cambridge?" she asked, clearly meaning to change the drift of our conversation.

"No, mostly graduate students," I replied.

She too was a graduate student, she said, though she could easily have passed for a young professor. She had arrived from Iran in July, far too early before the start of classes.

"First time in America?" I asked, hoping to prove useful in helping her navigate her first steps in Cambridge.

"No, been here many, many times," she answered, as if she couldn't help but underscore what had initially seemed a flippant, self-mocking *very rich girl from Iran.*

Her last name was Ansari.

I quoted a few lines from the Persian poet by the same name.

"Yes, yes, everyone quotes the very same verses," she said, as though asking me to come up with a better one.

Like a croupier she had, with a quick sleight of her roulette-table rake, managed to clean up all my chips. I stared at her blankly. Her frank and dauntless gaze seemed to say: *No more chips, huh?*

"Might as well have dinner together," she said, as we loitered outside of Césarion. "I don't expect we'll be seeing more of Sheila or Kalaj this evening."

I suggested we have a quick bite at Anyochka's. Quick bite was my lingo for cheap eats. With Kalaj it couldn't possibly have meant anything else. With her, *quick bite* bordered on churlish haste. "What's the rush?" she asked. I explained: Cervantes, four hours; Scarron, one; Sorel, another one; Bandello, God knows. I told her about my exams.

"When are you planning to take them?" she asked.

"Mid-January."

"But that's in just a few months." Meaning: *Better get cracking.*

No kidding, I wanted to reply.

I admired women with the ready wit to say things as they are. I told her so. Her answer was no less amazing. "*Cher ami,* I live in the *hic et nunc*, the here and now," she said. I wanted to tell her that I, on the other hand, inhabited the *iam non* and the *nondum*, the no more and the not yet, but then I thought it better to leave this for some other time. Not the right time for Saint Augustine. I asked if she had any other ideas about where to eat. She didn't. Maybe it would have to be a quick bite, then, she jibed. All I remember her saying during our short dinner together was "Let me warn you about one thing, though," which she had said while removing the very thin slices of Havarti cheese from her sandwich with her thumb and index finger. She didn't like superfluous cheese in her sandwich, she said, as she tried to separate the cheese from the lettuce, all the while trying to push back the one or two slices of Virginia ham she had unintentionally pulled out in her effort to remove the cheese. Sandwiches were not her thing either. "Let me say it now." I could tell that this might be an awkward admission, not so much for her, as for me. "Tell me," I said. She seemed to ponder it a while longer. "*Je suis plus grande que toi*, I am older than you are." I reassured her as best I could. But her total candor caught me off guard. I thought I'd been maneuvering the situation deftly enough—but this was too fast, too upfront, too *hic et nunc.* More disconcerting yet was the tone with which she seemed to be taking back an offer I hadn't even realized was on the table. Had she spoken an undisclosed yes before I'd even asked? Had things progressed so fast between us without my even noticing? Then I realized what it was. Kalaj had simply put the two women in the mood. He had done all the spadework. How he'd done it was beyond me. Now that she was in the mood, I was as good a man as any. I kept wondering what balloon had he floated to stir her this way. Perhaps she was after him, and I was just a screen. Or perhaps she assumed I was like him and had one thing and one thing only in mind.

We parted twenty minutes after sharing a pecan pie on a bench off Holyoke Street. I could tell she wasn't used to slumming. At least this was a here-and-now moment between us, I said. She appreciated the jest. I already knew Kalaj would nickname her *Hic et nunc.*

There was still some light left for an hour's reading on the roof terrace, I thought. But I kept thinking of Linda. By now she was surely back from the library. I knocked at her door. No one answered. I tried to turn the doorknob, in case she'd left it open. I would walk in and regardless of what she was busy doing, we'd undress in a second. But the knob would not turn. I rang again. No answer.

That evening I managed to turn all the pages of Cervantes. At around eleven o'clock that night, the buzzer rang downstairs. It was Kalaj. "Are you alone?" Of course I was alone. He rushed up four flights. "I thought you'd be with the Persian."

"I'm reading."

"You mean you actually said 'no' to her? Are you out of your mind?"

"I am reading."

"For what, for your doctorate in paperwork?" He could not understand. "Well, I'll leave you to your papers, my friend." Then, on second thought, "Did you like the Persian girl?"

"She's not bad."

"I asked for a yes-or-no, not a more-or-less."

"Fine, yes."

"So why is she not here?"

"Because she is not here," I said.

"What you did was wrong." He thought for a while. "Actually, it was cruel."

"Actually, I was going to knock at *la quarante-deux*'s door when I was done with my reading. She's the fallback," I added, trying to stir the spirit of male solidarity which I knew he'd appreciate.

"Great, you're a fallback, she's a fallback, your whole life is one big fallback. I don't pretend to know more than you do, but the only real thing in your life is your paperwork, and who knows, maybe your paperwork could just as easily be a more devious fallback than the others. I don't understand, and to be very frank I don't want to. *Bonne soirée.*"

Rat-tat-tat.

And with that he was gone.

I couldn't figure why he was so upset with me. Perhaps, without quite knowing it himself, he had come close to realizing that, in my world, he too had acquired the provisional status of a fallback. Fallback fellowship in a fallback city filled with fallback lives.

I found out a few days later that the reason why he had rung my buzzer and raced upstairs was to ask me and the Persian girl to join him and Sheila for a long car ride to the North End to have coffee and pastries in a small Italian café. "We would have been all four of us together, and we would have had a wonderful time—you, me, the women, the Drive and Gene Ammons' saxophone."

I MET NILOUFAR a few times after that. I loved her name. It meant water lilies and made me think of Money's nenuphars and of MoMA on clear September mornings when the quiet rooms are almost empty and the painter's blues are all yours. She told me about her family, her brother, her ex-husband, her son, her mother, some in Iran, others in Europe and South America. We became friends. Dante, Islam, the Provençal poets, and the Sicilian connection—she was going to write about all these someday. Then one afternoon, as we were both sitting waiting for Kalaj at Café Algiers, we ran out of things to say. There were no more words to fill the silence with, nor anything else to put off the unspoken admission that hovered between us. She stared at me, I stared back. This was beyond I'll-raise-you-by-one-chip-if-you-raise-me-with-another.

Is this what I think it is? I asked myself as I tried to parse the silence between us and get a sense of what was happening. Her stare wouldn't subside. *Yes, this is what I think it is.* I stare, you stare, one human with another human—the rest and everything we've learnt so far in life can wait outside Café Algiers. I was twenty-six years old, yet this was the first true, intimate moment I'd known with another woman besides my mother. I wondered if Kalaj and she had spoken about me. Or had they slept together? Suddenly I saw tears in her eyes. "You're crying," I finally said, unable to pretend I hadn't noticed.

"No I'm not," she said, and looked down at the table, and with the heels of both palms covered her eyes, as if she were massaging them after too much reading. Then, with more tears: "You wouldn't understand. Give me a handkerchief." I pulled one out of my left pocket. I didn't ask what made her cry, but all of a sudden I felt a sense of uncertainty and confusion, like a terrible pressure in my chest for which there were no words, no outs. Part of me was praying for Kalaj not to show up and interrupt this interlude between us, while another couldn't wait for him to help us snap out of it. I stared into her eyes, she stared back, meaning *You see now? Now do you understand?* Suddenly I realized that my cheeks were feeling moist, and, without knowing it, that I too had begun to shed tears.

"I don't know what's the matter with us. Do you?" she asked. I shook my head.

"Just hold my hand," I said, as she pushed a hand toward mine over the table.

I suggested we have something light to eat. But neither of us was hungry. "Walk me home?"

"Of course," I said.

"Do you have all the books you need with you?"

"Most of them," I replied. "Why?"

"Because tonight you're sleeping with me."

Outside, on the narrow alleyway between Brattle and Mount Auburn, we kissed.

She lived off Putnam Avenue close to the river. Over a dish of rice and spiced meats plus wine, we sat cross-legged on a rug and spoke about what had happened to us at Café Algiers.

"Do you think I was too forward?"

"Not at all," I replied.

"Too fast?"

"I love how you did it." Then I kissed her again.

I had never in my life spoken to a woman so frankly about courtship as the courtship itself was progressing. We spoke of Fellini, Renoir, and Visconti. She refused to own a television, she said. A few days later I made her buy one anyway. We had tea every evening. Then drinks. Then her spiced meats with rice and minced vegetables. We spoke of my favorite director, Rohmer, and of my favorite singer, Callas. We spoke of the great poets. And of the lesser poets. I was happy to have drifted away from Kalaj. There was talk of living together, and as the days wore on, we spoke of an enduring bond. We could live in Paris part of the year, she said, and after my exams, what better place than Paris to start writing my thesis on *La Princesse de Clèves*, while she'd take courses at the Institute of the Arab World. But first we had to see the Kurosawa retrospective, which started in one week. When I hesitated about the retrospective, alleging the books I had to read between now and the middle of January and my approaching meeting with Lloyd-Greville to discuss the complete works of Chaucer, she said we'd just have to make the time in the here and now. I loved this about her. Our problem, she said, was not Chaucer but how to smoke during those long, uninterrupted films. Simple. We'd each take turns stepping outside while the other filled you in when you came back. Terrible idea. We'd step outside together, have a quick smoke, and rush back in. Voilà! What could one possibly miss during a two-minute break in a two-hour-plus movie? What if we quit smoking altogether, I said. Excellent idea. When? Not tonight. Tomorrow. "Make me quit, oh Lord, but not yet." We both laughed over our play on Saint Augustine's *Make me chaste, my God, but not quite yet.* This was heaven. In an access of tenderness one night, she turned to me and said, "I'd give you my eyes if you asked." She'd said it in French, but she'd spoken in the archaic tongue of bygone worlds. This too was heaven.

"Is this what you want?" Kalaj asked me one day when I

found I needed to speak with him and only him, because I knew he'd understand. "Do you really want to get married?"

I said I didn't know.

"People are always nervous before getting married, but at some point they know."

"Well, I don't know. So there." Why, had he known before getting married how-many-times-now?

"I wasn't in love," he replied, ignoring my little dart. "Are you in love?"

I didn't know that either.

"She wants me to go to Spain during Christmas to meet her family."

He pondered the matter.

"Can you afford the plane ticket?'

"No."

"Then who will pay?"

I didn't know.

I had never thought that marriage could be determined on so paltry a basis as the price of a round-trip ticket to Barajas Airport.

But there it was, my answer.

We decided to put off the trip till early the following summer. Meanwhile we listened to all of Beethoven's Late Quartets during an entire Saturday afternoon. Then, on the following day, to three versions of *The Art of the Fugue*, after which we sat and watched *60 Minutes*. Next came dinner, the usual rice and spiced meats with a glass of wine for each, followed by lovemaking, and more lovemaking—there was a reason for those spiced meats, she joked. I wanted her all the time. I had never lived like this or been so happy with someone before. In the middle of the night sometimes we'd both wake up and stand by the large glass window in her living room and stare at the magical lights on Memorial Drive. Don't take this away, don't take this away . . .

After about three weeks and after classes had started, I felt something coming. She complained once that I didn't cook. "Doesn't even want to learn," I heard her mutter to herself, as though speaking to the kitchen sink, to her rack of spices from Iran hanging in an open cabinet over the sink, to her prized Chantal teakettle, and her tins of teas shipped directly from Mariage Frères in France. At least I should offer to wash the dishes, she said, when she stepped out of the kitchen after we'd had dinner one evening. Maybe also help with laundry. And put some of your things away. Plus, awkward as this was for her, perhaps it was time to discuss sharing expenses here. That *here* cut me to the quick, for it brimmed over with muffled resentment. Who knows how long she'd been stewing over this before coming out with it. Finally, she said, my love-making wasn't what it was in the beginning. I used to speak while making love to her. Now I was as quiet as a mouse. And I didn't wait for her—a man should always wait for a woman.

My heart wasn't in it, and she had spotted it right away, even before I did.

Then, a week or so later, it finally happened. On Sunday

at 2:00 a.m., just one night before my meeting with Lloyd-Greville, I woke up with the usual paralyzing anxiety about what he would ask. I knew he'd prod and prod to see how shallow my knowledge of Chaucer was. But then, with one thought leading to the next, I finally realized that it wasn't just Harvard or Lloyd-Greville's office I was dying to run away from, but from her as well. Suddenly, I had to get out of her bed. Actually, and it took me a few more minutes to realize this, I had to get out of her house—just get out and run away. I decided to put off leaving until we'd discussed the matter later in the morning like two adults. Perhaps I'd cool down by then and know that my exams were the cause of my anxiety. But I knew that just getting out of bed and sitting in the living room for a few minutes might trigger alarm signals for her. One word about considering slowing things down a bit, especially before my meeting with Lloyd-Greville, or of possibly taking a break for a few days—a couple of weeks, no more, I promise—and there were bound to be tears, recriminations, at which point I'd have to tell her what everyone says under these circumstances: that it was me, not her, my exams, not us, the way my life was run, and not the gifts she'd brought to it—she was perfect, I didn't deserve her. Where would I be without her now? The *now* was meant to convey the extent of my loss and despair. It was *just* that I had to go. Please don't fight it, I'd say, I was learning not to fight it myself. The rhetoric, I failed to realize, was lifted from *A Beginner's Guide to Breakups.*

But by 3:00 a.m. I was ready to explode. Every time I'd fall asleep a nightmare would insidiously work its way into my sleep, hover over my shoulders, then quietly work its way through my left ear and wake me up, even when I knew it was a dream, to remind me I was living a lie, that this should not go on, that I no longer wanted to touch her, didn't even want her foot to rub against mine under the sheets. By 3:30 a.m. I got up, put on my socks, my trousers, kept the T-shirt I was sleeping in, picked up a few of my books, and removed her keys from my key ring and silently placed them on the kitchen counter. When I was out of her building and felt the first cool draft of autumn fan my face, I knew that this sudden freedom was the closest thing to ecstasy I'd known since moving in with her.

From an old telephone booth, I called Kalaj. After a few bland apologies for waking him at this time of the night, I asked: "Can you pick me up?"

"*J'arrive.*"

No questions. No explanations. From the sound of my voice he'd already guessed why I was calling. I wasn't the first, or the last man who wanted out—desperately. Clearly he'd done the same thing himself many times before.

I waited in the late September weather, but I didn't have time to feel the chill, for soon, I spotted his yellow Checker cab nosing its way ever so stealthily in between two rows of parked cars. Less than ten minutes had elapsed since I'd woken up and put on my socks.

After more apologies, I got into the cab. It was warm and smelled of cigarettes. All he said was, "You're as white as aspirin."

He laughed, I laughed. He'd learned the expression from a Greek sailor.

"Still, it was cowardly," he finally said.

"Yes, it was cowardly."

Looking straight ahead of him, he added, "You'll do the same to me some day."

I let it pass. Something told me not to argue.

To dispel the awkward moment between us, I asked if he'd known it could come to this.

Yes, he'd known all along, he said.

Why hadn't he said anything then?

"Would it have made any difference?" he asked.

"No."

"That's why I never said anything."

But I knew he had guessed the real why.

As we drove on Memorial Drive, I kept thinking of her, of what she'd feel when she woke up, how she'd look for me everywhere before spotting the keys on the kitchen counter. How long before she'd finally put two and two together and realize that I'd left for good? *He's left me.* I could just hear her mutter those words to herself as she started rinsing last night's wineglasses that we'd left on the tea table before turning in. *He's left*, the irked, embittered rise in her voice betraying how much she wished she had me there if only to unleash her fury, while a plangent strain in her voice would nail the coffin on our brief love.

Tears began to well in my eyes, especially as I saw her sitting on her sofa that had become our sofa, or worse yet, by the very spot where we'd eaten our rice and spiced meats, realizing that her life had just spun out of orbit—Paris, the Arab Institute, my dissertation, our stay in Spain, everything thrashing about her like wild birds fluttering scared before an approaching beast. I was the beast. How could I do this to someone? And the way I'd done it was worse than the offense itself.

I wanted to go back now and tiptoe my way into her apartment, climb into bed with her, and hold her tight to me, and, as we'd hug, begin to make love, for she too loved sex that sprung in mid-sleep, rough, blind, beastly sex that grew ever so tender the more we awoke to what our bodies had started.

But I didn't have a key to get back in, and I was too embarrassed to ask Kalaj to drive me back.

"Why did I do it?" I finally asked him.

"Because you couldn't stand it, because you were choking, that's why. Perfectly understandable."

No, it was not understandable. *Choking* was just a word, a metaphor, a nothing. I myself had found the word crawling under my pillow that very same night. It was not an answer, not an explanation, yet it seemed the only one at hand, and the only word that said everything despite my mistrust of words. Why had I left her? Because I was living someone else's life, not mine. Because I wanted my life back, even if I didn't know

what *my life* was or what I even wanted it to be. Because I
wanted to be alone, or not with her, or with someone else,
or, better yet, with no one at all. Because I wanted to find
something of me in others only to realize that others were
never going to be like me and ultimately had to be unclasped,
thrown out, exploded, because estrangement is branded on
the soul, because love itself was foreign to me, and in its place
sat resentment and bile. Why had I even started with her? To
be with someone instead of no one? To be like him? Or was I
already, had always been like him, but in so different a guise
that it was just as easy to think us poles apart? The Arab and
the Jew, the ill-tempered and the mild-mannered, the iras-
cible and the forbearing, the this and the that! And yet, we
came from the same mold, choked in the same way, and in the
same way, lashed back, then ran away.

He listened to my musings as though I were reciting a
delirious poem. Then he shook his head and came back to his
favorite word. "It just never took. The gluten never stuck."
The onetime baker in him had spoken.

In the quiet car with its twenty-four-hour music playing
en sourdine, I thought about his four words. I liked them. As
if love affairs were puddings and soufflés; sometimes things
took, sometimes they didn't, and sometimes they just curdled,
and there was no one to blame and nothing you could do.

A second later, I realized that the same could be said about
everything else in my life, and his as well. Nothing seemed to
take. Even our friendship . . .

"Do you really like being alone?" he asked.

"No."

He understood this too. No need for words. He dropped me in front of my building.

I offered to make coffee if he wanted, but he said he might as well keep driving his cab until sunup today. He hadn't yet gone to bed when I'd called. He seldom slept. Besides, it was early on a Sunday morning, and people were still coming out of clubs and after-hours bars. Plenty of money to be made on a Sunday morning.

As he drove away, I began to think that what kept us together was perhaps not even our romance with an imaginary France. That was just a veneer, an illusion. Rather, it was our desperate inability to lead ordinary lives with ordinary people *anywhere*—ordinary loves, ordinary homes, ordinary careers, watching ordinary television, eating ordinary meals, with ordinary friends—even ordinary friends we didn't have, or couldn't keep.

We were not outcasts. We were untouchables. No one knew it except us. Harvard helped me hide it so well that entire weeks, sometimes months went by without my getting a whiff of it even once, let alone allowing someone else to glimpse it. Kalaj hid it in plain sight: by shouting it to everyone he ran into.

When I opened the door to my apartment, I realized that I had scarcely seen my home at night in a very long time. It felt unfamiliar. I was more at home with Niloufar off Putnam

Avenue than here. And yet neither place felt right. No wonder Kalaj preferred to drive about all day and hang out in a Cambridge dive than face his own bedroom. I fell asleep with my clothes on and the smell of Niloufar's bed mingling with my own.

THAT SUNDAY WAS probably the worst day of my life. I had no food in the house. I was exhausted, and I had twenty-four hours to master Chaucer before my appointment with Lloyd-Greville. The thought of taking even twenty minutes to go out to find something to eat was out of the question.

Later in the morning the phone began to ring. I knew who it was and decided not to pick up. I could hear my phone ringing all the way up on the roof terrace, where I planned to spend a few hours before hunkering down to type up my notes on Chaucer. I was to meet Lloyd-Greville the next day at 10:00 a.m. By staying upstairs, though, I knew I was also hiding. Cruel, heartless, cowardly. Linda, who happened to be upstairs on this clear, warm, lovely Indian summer day and whom I hadn't seen since I'd been more or less living elsewhere except for an occasional stop to pick up or bring back books and a few items of clothing, could tell it was my phone ringing. "Why aren't you answering?" she finally asked. Then she guessed why. "Will she ever stop calling?" By noon, while we were mixing our second Tom Collins in my kitchen, she asked, "Want me to pick up?" I couldn't do that to a woman who had been my soul mate. Finally Linda grabbed my phone and placed it in the bathroom, shutting the door tight behind it, like a misbehaving pet that was being punished. I wanted her to remove her light blue tank top and the bottom of her bikini and without waiting proceed to my bedroom. I loved her body, loved the untrammeled sex, savage, selfish, and without meaning. I wanted her to erase the other woman in my life; I wanted to kiss her face, her mouth, and with that face bury the other as one might bury a Tanagra statuette that had become unbearable and stirred not a drop of guilt, pity, love, or even ordinary anger, but just this thing that scared me more, because it impugned me, not her: indifference. Or worse yet than indifference: numbness, first of the heart, then of the body. Hating, by contrast was far, far kinder—and perhaps there was a touch of hatred already in me as well, for hatred helps us forget and covers up the wounds we leave on others as fast as it helps heal those they've inflicted on us. "You don't want to hurt her," Linda said. "It's because you're kind." No, it's because I'm a coward, I wanted to say. But I didn't say anything.

KALAJ DROPPED BY to visit me that afternoon. He had frequently gotten into the habit of coming by, knowing the door was never locked.

"The one thing no man should ever do is feel sorry for a woman. You always live to regret it," he said. "It destroys her, and it destroys you."

I could barely think of Niloufar at all. It was the last day for going over Chaucer, and I was hopelessly behind. "Can I do anything to help?" Kalaj finally asked.

"No, you can't help." And then it hit me: "Or maybe you can."

The idea seemed a stroke of genius.

"I need two editions of Chaucer's complete works," I said.

"And how will I find them?"

I wrote down the approximate call number of the books and gave him my library card to borrow the books with. I told him where exactly to look for them inside the Widener Library stacks and suggested he take out any other books about Chaucer sitting on the stacks.

He had never been inside Widener, didn't know where or what Widener was.

"Past the gate on Mass Ave between Plympton and Linden Streets," I explained in cab lingo.

"That's it?"

I nodded.

With that he sped down the stairs.

I was hungry, ravenous. I could knock at Linda's, but she had probably already gone to the library. Strange thing: I felt more comfortable asking Kalaj to run an errand at a place he'd never even been to than Linda, who was right now in the very stacks where I was sending Kalaj.

An hour and a half later he was back. He was carrying a brown paper bag which he rushed into the kitchen because it was about to leak and emptied it in a salad bowl. More than a dozen chicken wings. Heavenly. From one of his other pockets he produced a small bottle of beer. Then came a string of *petits sandwiches.* "I told the waitress you were starving but couldn't come."

"But she doesn't know me."

"Short, Jewish nose, always lugging books—she knew exactly who you were. With her compliments."

"And the books—?" I began, fearing the worst.

Suddenly, my heart sank. He had totally forgotten about the books!

"Right, the books—" he started. "I couldn't find some of the ones you wanted . . . so I took out these instead."

There he was being Harpo again. Out of numberless pockets in his faded army camouflage jacket, he produced six books.

"Not bad," I said, as I looked at their titles. They were good books. When I looked in the inside cover, my heart sank again.

"But you forgot to check them out!"

"Well, yes, see, that was a bit hard. There were long lines, and they were all asking too many questions, and frankly 'appy bower was about to end, and I didn't want to miss it. So I put the books in my pockets and decided to leave. I can assure you nobody saw."

I was horrified. I was pleased.

"Now, I must let you work. Any books to lend me? I still can't sleep at night."

I let him borrow Sade, Maupassant, Balzac, and Stendhal. *"Bonne soirée."*

And he was gone.

I'D BEEN THINKING of the next morning's meeting with Lloyd-Greville for so long that it had begun to seem unreal, as though lodged forever in the future. I decided to type up my notes, thinking that jotting down my ideas about Chaucer might help firm them up in my mind. But I was not prepared to see that I hardly nursed one interesting idea about Chaucer. He'd want to discuss *Troilus and Criseyde* or "The Knight's Tale" whereas I'd much rather go on about "The Tale of Sir Thopas," where Chaucer makes fun of himself as a totally feckless raconteur who is ultimately interrupted by the inn-keeper and told to stop, because none of the pilgrims could stand his silly prattle. Chaucer the anti-narrator: there was gold in this idea. By 11:00 p.m. I realized that I had circled the wagons too many times to know what I had to say about Chaucer. I could already hear Lloyd-Greville: *What, in fine, are your thoughts about "The Book of the Duchess," sir?* Lloyd-Greville had probably picked up the Gallic *in fine* from Henry James, about whom he was also an expert. *My point was . . . well, you see, gentlemen*—and suddenly I saw myself for who I was. I was, like the narrator of *Notes from the Underground,* an arrogant, jittery, posturing, paranoid, dysfunctional, capricious fop. Like him, I was all double-talk, even when I was alone and nobody was listening, even when I whispered things to myself that were truer than true—imponderable double-talk just the same.

I had no idea what my thoughts on "The Book of the Duchess" were going to be, but the more I wrote, the more I jotted down ideas, the more I seemed to depend on the page itself to tell me what I was trying to say. Trying to say? I didn't know what I was trying to say until I'd said something that looked good enough for the Lloyd-Grevilles and Cherbakoffs of this world. If they thought it passed, then it passed for me. My ideas, however, were as transient and provisional on paper as I was at Harvard, in Cambridge, on this planet. I was, and my ideas were, like Kalaj himself, all talk. And the trouble was I couldn't tell the difference between an idea and its malingering double, chatter.

By one o'clock in the morning the phone started to ring again. I picked it up without thinking. "I'm not asking you to come over. But can I come over?" It was Niloufar, she needed to speak to me.

"I am not alone," I lied.

"Already found someone else? Bravo," she said, and right away hung up on me. A few minutes later she called again. "I just want you to know you're the worst person I've ever met. And I've known some very bad ones."

"Thank you very much." My turn to hang up.

She called again. "What I said was not true. You are the best person I've ever loved. Please come back. Or I'll take a taxi and be at your door, begging."

"I can't talk."

"Oh, I see, of course. Are you ready for tomorrow morning?"

"No, not yet," I said, thinking she was changing the subject if only to maintain a semblance of composure but also, perhaps, to thwart whatever pleasure I was enjoying at the moment. I was wrong.

"Listen to me, Monsieur Chaucer screwing *La Princesse de Clèves.* I hope he tears you to pieces and exposes you for the shallow, bungling *petit con* you've always been, even, and especially, in bed. I curse you and your children if they're unlucky enough to have you as a father. A curse on you—did you hear me?—a curse!" And out came a string of words in Farsi, tears, yelps, followed by an endless series of French words sobbed out of her lungs, as though she were talking not to me, not to her lover, but to her mother, pleading first, then cursing again, then apologizing for cursing, and cursing all over again. "I curse you." As in some of her most passionate moments, she had turned to Old World-speak, and if my heart was racing as she kept heaping curses upon me and on the children of my children, it was because I too, like her, came from a world where curses, like blessings, like pledges, like all protestations of enduring love are, even when you don't mean a word you're saying, binding legal tender, the currency of the soul, because once spoken, they cannot be taken back, dispelled, or parleyed with; they will hunt you down, find you, and carry out their sentence.

I didn't sleep that night. I couldn't sleep. The meeting with

Lloyd-Greville and the curses were enough to keep anyone up. I had crossed the line, stepped into the lepers' colony of the damned; there was no redemption, no pardon. From here on, I'd live out the term of her curse. As for my comprehensives, they were cursed long before I'd met her, before Kalaj, before I'd even applied to Harvard—for this had started as a fantasy and, before I'd known it, the fantasy had crossed the line and wriggled its way into real life and was now outliving its time.

I went into the kitchen and decided to make the strongest coffee I had in the house. It would take ten minutes to brew a big cup of espresso—but I needed a break. I had five hours before me; the job could be finished by then. The stovetop espresso pot was dirty from the last time I'd brewed coffee in it, probably as far back as the month of May. My friend Frank had come over one evening to grumble about his girlfriend who wouldn't stop complaining that he wasn't doing something to avoid losing his hair. Claude, who was also present that evening, and who never liked to listen to Frank's amorous bellyaches, interrupted, as he always did when Frank started about Nora, saying we needed to add Cointreau to spike the coffee. We brewed three cups, then brewed three more. Eventually, we turned to wine until Frank offered to cook something in my kitchen for the three of us. All I had were eggs and tomato sauce. Any cheese? he asked. Grated Kraft Parmesan. "I'll make dinner," he said, having located an unopened box of pasta.

I hated being alone in my apartment, though I also welcomed being alone again. But suddenly, and, once again, because of the coffee, I remembered the day when I'd returned from Widener Library the previous winter with several books and on walking into my apartment had found it all lit up with Frank and Nora setting my kitchen table for the three of us. "You forgot to lock the door, so we let ourselves in and brought dinner. Don't you ever lock your door?" Nora had asked. "Not always. What would anyone want to steal?" I'd said. "True," they'd agreed. The sofa, the bed, indeed, all my furniture, as everyone knew, had been lifted off the streets of Cambridge. Even my plates and my coffee mugs and director's chairs were the legacy of friends of friends who had left Cambridge. Nothing belonged to me. I paid month-to-month rent, without a lease. The only key I used was the mailbox key. Frank had brought cooked lasagna that night and was busy reheating it. I loved them both that evening. This had never happened before, which is why stepping into my apartment and finding that people had lit up my place and made themselves at home had turned that evening into one of my happiest and most memorable days at Harvard. Lights, friendship, wine, lasagna, coffee.

The coffeepot that morning was stuck shut. So I banged it against the kitchen counter. Then, to empty the hardened coffee grinds, I opened the service door, lifted the top of the trash container on my landing, and gently banged the metal funnel filter against it, once, twice. My neighbor opened her service door right away. "Did you knock?" she asked. "No," I said, apologizing for the noise. "I was just emptying the coffee grinds," I said showing her the funnel as proof I wasn't lying. "The last time I made coffee using this thing was months ago."

"Oh," she said. Then because I stood there, hesitating to shut my kitchen door before she had shut hers, she asked why I was up so early.

"Work," I said. "What about you?"

Work too, she smiled.

"Funny, though," she said, "I happened to see your light late last night and wondered about you."

Was this the equivalent of telling a man she's dreamed of him?

"What did you think?"

"Nothing."

"Good or bad?"

"Nothing special, really."

I still did not shut the door though I could tell from her body language that she was about to shut hers.

"Tell me the next time we meet then."

But I still didn't signal I was shutting the door. I just stood there with parts of the dirty coffeepot in both hands. "It's a promise then."

She smiled but did not answer, and because she did not answer I knew at that moment that she knew about Linda and me and that she'd make sure to open her kitchen door in three days at the latest, unless she was like the Princesse de Clèves and would never open it again when she was alone in her kitchen precisely because she was dying to throw it wide open. Then, if indeed she was like the Princess, she'd tell her boyfriend, not what she had done one afternoon when he was away at work and I'd knocked and asked to borrow, say, a bottle opener, but that she had intentionally resisted opening the kitchen door because she knew who was knocking and didn't trust herself.

I WENT TO meet Lloyd-Greville that morning at 10:00 feeling buoyed and uplifted not by my readiness to discuss Chaucer but by what had happened at 5:00 that very morning. And perhaps it was because I was in such high spirits that I must have persuaded Lloyd-Greville I was more than prepared to take my comprehensives that coming January. As I was stepping out of his office, he handed my file to Mary-Lou, saying "Our friend here could, if he wished, write a dissertation on Chaucer." Lloyd-Greville was always stingy when it came to praise; he preferred compliments by proxy, by speaking to you via someone else, by not even looking at you. I went home, unplugged my phone, and threw myself on my sunbathed bed totally naked.

4

THE INDIAN SUMMER WASN'T LETTING GO, EVEN AS
September dragged on into early October. Mornings were
chilly, but by midmorning the weather would grow warm, then
unbearably hot, and then quite cool again. Ersatz weather,
Kalaj called it. Why should this surprise anyone? Everything
about this place was sham, bogus, fake, phony, counterfeit.
Contrefaçon, he'd say, meaning that everything was counterfeit in America. Still, I liked the extended illusion of spring
weather with its heady presage of summer oddly trailing on
the last, first days of fall. It took me back to spring break,
when summer was still weeks away. I remembered the end of
the academic year. Back then I had drawn up lists of books to
read or reread and had just discovered the use of the terrace
upstairs. My friends Frank and Claude were still in town and
Nora hadn't even left for Europe yet. Nora, when she wasn't

with Frank, would come by sometimes and cook a Cornish hen for the two of us, though we both knew that she was coming simply to vent about how hard Frank was to live with and how she couldn't wait to be without him for a while, which is why the two had decided to spend their summer away. The whole thing with the Cornish hen and the half-liter bottle of wine always ended up in tears. One evening we'd gone to see *Annie Hall* in Boston. She kept laughing; I couldn't begin to understand why, and finally decided that perhaps Frank was right, there was something wrong with her. It never occurred to me that I had not yet grasped Woody Allen's humor. Kalaj, when I thought back on those spring days, was still months away, as if unborn yet. To think there was a time when Kalaj hadn't stomped into my life and altered its rhythm. I tried but didn't really wish to restore that sheltered rhythm, though I knew that continuing on this path of bar after café after bar after café seemed equally unthinkable a way to spend my time as a scholar. But Cambridge without Kalaj seemed unthinkable now. And yet after spending an hour with Lloyd-Greville, I was starting to recover my confidence and, with my confidence, my old love for scholarship and for Cambridge and for the life it presaged.

I went back to Lowell House more frequently as soon as I received Lloyd-Greville's temporary thumbs-up. I liked going there almost every day. I liked having a study where I could meet students and discuss their work. I liked my new students. All History and Literature majors were unusually bright and well read, and most spoke at least one foreign language. Students were in the habit of waiting for me outside my study after lunch. We discussed the books they wished to read, drew up lists, chatted, talked about life, which invariably meant sex, or the absence of sex. With yet another student, I discussed the topic of her senior thesis, things we had more or less already agreed upon before she'd left for Europe in early May. Now, five months later, she wore a tan, had perfected her French, couldn't wait to be back in Paris for Christmas. I hadn't seen Christmas in Paris in at least a decade. Sometimes I held tutorials in my office, or I'd invite someone over for coffee after lunch, and liked nothing more than to feel back on track with everyone else in Cambridge, liked the view into the main courtyard where students and younger tutors alike seemed to lounge about for hours on beach towels in the early afternoon, reading and studying, without another care in the world, graced by the towering, watchful presence of the blue-domed belfry and the protective manor-house gaze of this spot of paradise called Lowell House. For a few years in everyone's life here, Harvard cordoned off the world, was the world.

Kalaj didn't have a place in this world, and yet I knew that he'd barge himself in one way or another.

A few days after my meeting with Lloyd-Greville I ran into Kalaj at the café. He still couldn't sleep, he said. He was, once again, as he so often was these days, in a foul mood, worse even than the last time. Could I do him a favor? Of course.

He needed me to go with him to visit a lawyer. Tomorrow morning? Yes, I could do it, I said. Did he have an appointment? What for?

"You can't walk right in to see your lawyer, you need to make an appointment."

"So? Call now and make an appointment," he said.

But it was past six o'clock; the lawyer had probably left already.

"Call anyway," he said, producing the phone number from his tiny notebook after removing the rubber band. We called, or rather I called.

The lawyer picked up the phone himself.

I hadn't had a chance to ask for an appointment when Kalaj interrupted me in French to ask if the lawyer could see him now.

"Can we come over now?"

"Now as in right *now*?" he asked, raising the pitch of his voice, as if the idea seemed totally outlandish.

"*Maintenant?*" I asked Kalaj, hoping he'd change his mind.

"*Oui, maintenant,*" he answered.

"Now."

The voice at the other end of the line hesitated. "Frankly, I was getting ready to head home."

I whispered the message to Kalaj. He immediately put an index finger to his lips, meaning *say nothing*. It was the equivalent of a *fermata* in music, the strategic prolongation of a sound, except that the sound here was silence, the deliberate silence of someone who has just plopped down a penny on the table and is waiting for you to do the same before raising you with yet another. This was the very essence of lingering. Once you've asked your question do not say a thing more; when you've put your one chip on the table don't add a second simply because the other person is hesitating or because the silence between the two of you has become unbearable.

"How long will it take you to get here?" the lawyer asked.

Once again I whispered in French: how long did he think it would take?

"Ten minutes."

I was baffled. It usually took almost three times as much to get there from Cambridge.

"Quick," said the lawyer.

Standing up, Kalaj gulped down the remainder of his coffee, left some change on the table, picked up his things, and off we went. We hopped into his car and right away, after a few awkward turns through narrow alleys to the river, his huge Checker cab—the tank, the Titanic, the armored vehicle and intrepid war machine—was zipping its way at breakneck speed on Memorial Drive with the wonky grace of an aging dowager on wheels.

In my life I had never traveled so fast. We were begging for an accident. Why had I ever befriended such a nut?

"Where did you learn to drive?" I said, my way of asking him to slow down.

"In a driving school owned by a Tunisian Jew in Marseilles.

That's why we make the best pilots in the Israeli air force, didn't you know?" he jested.

It was the lawyer himself who opened the doors to his firm on the twenty-sixth floor. "This way, gentlemen." The collar of his striped white and blue shirt was unbuttoned and his sleeves rolled up above his elbows. This, Kalaj signaled, was not someone getting ready to head home.

We entered an office overlooking the harbor. Boston looked magical from such a height. Both of us must have gasped, the way hired waiters do when they're first shown the way from the kitchen to the main dining room in a posh mansion.

We had rehearsed our spiel in the car. What Kalaj wanted was not just for me to translate, but to read between the lines, to extract, to interpret, to intercept, from what the lawyer was saying the core of what he wasn't saying. In this as in everything else, he wanted *complicité*. The lawyer put both feet on his desk, took out a fresh yellow legal pad, removed the cap of his pen with his teeth, and placed the lined pad on his thigh, meaning: *OK. I'm listening.*

"Kalaj's wife is suing for divorce," I explained.

Nod, nod, meaning: *And this is surprising?* He lit a giant meerschaum pipe.

"They haven't been living together for over two months. He's living in a tiny rented room in Cambridge. The question is: Will this hurt his chances for getting a green card?"

Nod, nod from the lawyer, meaning: *Did you honestly believe that it wouldn't?*

"If both agree to go for an interview before divorce procedures are set in motion, might this help things?"

Nod, nod. *It might.*

"Is there anything that can be done to hasten the process before the issue of his divorce comes up?"

"We can try to ask them to hold an interview sooner—but it's not good to push the people at Immigration. They get very suspicious. And let me warn you, they do deport people they suspect of operating in bad faith." Silence. "Why is she suing for divorce?" he asked, as though more out of personal curiosity.

"Pourquoi veut-elle divorcer?" He understood the question, but I had to go through the motions of asking him. He whispered a few words in French.

"She alleges he cheats on her."

Nod, nod. *No shit.*

"Well, gentlemen, all I can promise is to request that they move up the date of the interview."

Kalaj did not ask me to translate.

"His father is sick in Tunisia. He needs to leave the country for ten days."

"Not advisable."

"Il se fout de notre gueule, ou quoi? Is he fucking with us or what?" whispered Kalaj. Then, to the lawyer he said, "Well, thank you. And by the way," he added, turning to a series of framed photo portraits on the wall, "they're all wrong."

The lawyer cast a disbelieving look at his framed photographs of heavyweight champions. "Not Carnera, Baer, Braddock, Schmeling, Louis, Charles, Marciano," said Kalaj. "It was"—and he proceeded to list them by heart the way every French schoolboy knows his La Fontaine's *Fables*—"Willard, Dempsey, Tunney, Schmeling, Sharkey, Carnera, Baer, Braddock, Louis, Charles, Walcott, Marciano, Patterson, Johansson, Liston, Ali."

"Wow. I'll have to look into it. Does he know Köchel numbers too?" asked the lawyer with irony in his voice as he turned to me.

"No, he's not a Mozart fan, but if you ask him, he'll explain exactly why asparagine emits that unmistakable smell each time you eat asparagus and go for a piss."

I didn't have the heart to tell Kalaj that the lawyer's cold, disaffected replies spoke volumes and couldn't possibly bode well. But Kalaj didn't need me to tell him that. "I paid him three thousand dollars and all he does is smoke his huge Sherlock Holmes pipe and nod." He made his usual imitation of Yankee nasal sounds as they're mimicked the world over. *Not advisable. Not advisable. Not advisable.*

Kalaj knew of a lovely small Italian place in the North End where we could stop for dinner. He liked to show he could speak some Italian, which he had picked up in Milan. We had veal stewed in thick buttery wine sauce. I had not eaten so well in months. We usually split the bill right down the middle. This time Kalaj insisted on paying. I refused to accept. "I make five times in one day what you make in a whole month," he said.

He was right.

He ordered a second bottle of wine. On the small television placed above what looked like a makeshift bar, the news bulletin showed Egyptian President Sadat landing in Israel, with the Israeli army band playing the Egyptian national anthem. I recognized the anthem from my old school days in Egypt. I liked the anthem now. What a glorious moment.

Did he believe there was going to be peace now?

He lifted his left wrist, looked at his watch, and said "Yes." *For the next five minutes.*

"The Arab and Jew go to dinner. It should be the title of a movie."

"When every Jew and every Arab will have killed each other, there'll still be one Arab and one Jew left and they'll continue drinking *cinquante-quatres*. I just hope there are more like us," he said. "Do you think there are?" Then, not waiting for an answer, he added, "Some friendship. The Arab and the Jew."

I said I didn't know. He said he didn't know either. We laughed. In Cambridge, there weren't.

The waiter and the cook were muttering something in dialect. We were, Kalaj said, no longer in Boston but in Syracuse. Not too far from Pantelleria.

"Did you like Syracuse?" I asked.

"I hated it."

"So did I."

We started to laugh.

"Let's have a *cinquante-quatre Chez Nous*."

On the way back to Cambridge he told me that he'd loved Maupassant. Stendhal was good, yes, but Balzac was a genius. "But this fellow Sade disgusts me. Please take it back and let's forget you ever lent me such a book."

I had never believed that a man with so much life experience could be easily shocked. But he was genuinely upset. He was, his lifestyle aside, an unmitigated prude.

When we parked the car outside Café Algiers, I hinted that the interview with his lawyer had left me feeling very worried.

"I know. But I don't want to think about it now." He had a date with his *Pléonasme* in half an hour and had no room for more bad thoughts in addition to those she'd probably stir in him tonight. "Trust me," he added. I assumed things were in a rocky phase.

"Did you have to go through one-tenth of what I'm going through for a green card?" he asked once we ordered coffee.

"No. I had a green card more or less waiting for me when I arrived, courtesy of my uncle in the Bronx."

"What did your uncle in the Bronx have to do?"

"My uncle was a Freemason. He asked a Freemason to write a letter to a congressman who was also a Freemason, and from one Freemason to the other, someone finally allowed me to become a legal resident."

"Just like that."

"Masons are very powerful people."

"Like Jews?"

"Like Jews."

In less than ten days, Kalaj had not only managed to get himself invited to join a Masonic lodge, but had placed glossy stickers bearing the Masonic square and compass all over his cab—on the hood, on the dashboard, on the front and back fenders. He had even snuck two discreetly beneath the armrests right under the ashtrays.

Someone he had recently taken to the airport happened to be a Freemason who happened to have a Freemason friend who—

"You're a genius," he said to me.

ONE NIGHT, AFTER a heavy meal at High Table at Lowell House, I was awakened by a sharp pain on my right side. I waited for it to pass. It didn't. The Persian curse, I immediately thought. I took some Alka-Seltzer and went back to sleep. But sleep didn't come. The pain intensified and kept growing worse. By five in the morning I decided to call Kalaj. But he wasn't answering. I put on some clothes, and unable to find a taxi on Concord Avenue, I had no choice but to walk all the way to the student infirmary. If I got sick I'd have a good excuse for putting off work on my comprehensives. Then the thought occurred to me: if I died, I wouldn't have to take my exams at all. Clearly, the shot in the arm after my meeting with Lloyd-Greville had worn off.

By the time I was seen by the doctor at the infirmary, the pain had subsided. Probably trapped gas, the doctor said.

What had I eaten for dinner? Harvard's Dining Services, I explained. Figures, he replied.

This reminded me of the time a few weeks earlier in September when a wasp had stung me in my sleep and the pain was so excruciating that I put on my clothes and rushed myself to the infirmary convinced I was poisoned. They applied a few drops of ammonia where the wasp had stung me, and the pain was instantly gone. I had never seen Harvard Square at four in the morning before. It felt like an abandoned lunar station. Empty but sealed.

In both cases, as I walked out of the infirmary and felt a fresh morning gust course along the totally deserted Square, I suddenly could see how, bare of people and its usual bustle, this town couldn't have been more foreign to me than it was at dawn, and that I was living a totally foreign, mistaken life here: this wasn't my home, these weren't my streets, my buildings, my people; and the hollow bland-speak spoken by the head nurse and reiterated by the attending night doctor to lift my spirits came in a language that my mother wouldn't begin to fathom. Curses I understood. But *Try to feel better, OK?* and other honeyed *mièvreries*, as Kalaj called them, seemed to isolate me even further. I was already isolated as it was. Get sick and you realize you are a scuttled boat in a maelstrom.

To think that a few days earlier in the North End of Boston I'd been making fun of Sicily when I'd give anything to be there right now, strolling along the dank, ugly, bracken docks of Syracuse. Harvard wasn't me, even Café Algiers wasn't me. Nothing was me here.

I thought of Kalaj as well: he was more alone than I was: he didn't have the illusion of an institution behind him—he barely even spoke English. All he had was his camouflage jacket, his sputtering bravado, his *zeb*, and his rickety man-of-war mottled all over with ridiculous Freemason stickers.

After the infirmary, I didn't go back to sleep. I went straight to Cambridge's only twenty-four-hour deli and ordered a full breakfast, sausages included. I took the day's newspaper from the counter and read it. Then after Cambridge's notorious bottomless coffee, instead of going home, I headed to my office at Lowell House. I wanted to see people. But the courtyard was entirely deserted. I was the only one alive at Lowell House. If a student happened to cross me on my way to my study, he'd probably suspect I'd spent the night with someone and was making a discreet exit before daybreak. I liked stepping on the dewy grass. I could live here, I thought. I couldn't wait to see everyone up. How I liked the beginning of the school year, with its busy ferment of people rushing up and down Mass Ave when the town was abuzz with students winding up for a busy day. I loved Harvard Square in the fall.

There, I'd said it.

I did love it.

The feeling would go away. I knew it. It would peter out the moment I asked myself if it was possible to have a home somewhere and never belong to it.

I was the first in the dining hall for breakfast that morning. I neared the half-open window to the kitchen area where the cooks were still setting up the food and managed to send a heartfelt greeting to Abdul Majib, the kitchen attendant who wore a white uniform and always recited a beautiful, long-extended morning or evening greeting each time he saw me. It put me in a good mood. Then some students began to arrive. I sat down with two of them. Others were just waking up and stumbling in like sleepwalkers in a rush, their hair still dripping from showers taken minutes earlier. There was talk of heading out by car to see the leaves that weekend, miles and miles of leaves blazing through the landscape like wildfire over New England. Would I like to come? I didn't care about the leaves. A wealthy producer had arranged for a private screening of *Saturday Night Fever* in Boston—did I care to join? I didn't care for disco either, I'd said. It took me a few moments to realize that I was sounding exactly like Kalaj. Had I always been this way or was I learning to ape his hostility about everything whenever I felt uneasy with others. "He hates everything," someone said about me. "No," said a girl, who seemed to be coming to my defense, "he just doesn't like to say he likes things." I paid her no heed, didn't even know her name. But I knew she'd read me through and through.

I excused myself and went back to my study, where I burrowed for hours. Could an American really see through other human beings with such uncanny insight? I had never bothered to ask myself such a question in the past. Obviously, I must have never thought that Americans understood human nature, much less had a human nature—otherwise, why would I be asking the question? Still, I admired her insight and the forthright aplomb with which she had spoken.

By noon I felt I needed to escape to Café Algiers, my base away from my base at Lowell House. Kalaj was there. I would have been perfectly happy to be by myself: corner table, smoke, read, lift my head up occasionally, order another cup, watch the people come and go. But his presence changed this. I seldom went there at lunchtime and was startled by how different the place looked, especially on a sunny weekday. Even Kalaj's behavior seemed different at that hour, more relaxed, as though he had dismantled his Kalashnikov and was leisurely oiling and cleaning part after part. He was happy to see me too. Things must have worked out well with Léonie. Yes, they had. He asked me what I was doing that day. I was planning to head back to my office at Lowell House. Then at five I had to go to the Master's Tea at Lowell House, followed by a cocktail reception at Lowell House. "*Je me fou de ton Lowell House*, I don't give a fuck about your Lowell House," he finally blurted. Lowell House had become *my* Lowell House. "You and your Lowell House." He disparaged it and seemed to wince each time I mentioned the word. I learned to avoid speaking of it.

In fact, Kalaj never asked, and I never explained what Master's Tea was, but it was a weekly reception that I happened to like because there were always people I enjoyed meeting and chatting with. It was, it occurred to me, the exact opposite of Café Algiers, a touch ceremonial, quite Anglo, yet never stuffy.

He said he had a few minutes to kill before picking up his girlfriend and the boy; they were going for a picnic at Walden Pond with a Romanian au pair and the boy she babysat. Did I want to join? I thought about it for a while, wondering all along if it wasn't going to be a bit cold for swimming. But then, it was an intensely sunny day and I had already removed my jacket and was indeed sweating. Kalaj was wearing a T-shirt only. He too had removed his jacket.

"I'll come," I said, "but I have to be back at Lowell House in time for dinner."

When I explained that as a tutor I was given free meals at Lowell House he almost fell from his seat. "Free food, for an entire year!" he said, amazed at the munificence of American institutions. "What's the catch?" There was no catch, I said, just sit and talk with students. I told him that I was hoping to be appointed a resident tutor the coming February, which could mean that the same institution would throw in not just food but two free rooms for what amounted to mere talking. "If they're willing to give you room and board just for yaking with strangers—and, let's face it, you and casual chitchat aren't good together—what would they give me, then? Harvard Square? Boston? The world?"

We stopped the cab to pick up Léonie and her boy, and a few blocks farther down stopped by a private house on Highland Avenue where Ekaterina, the Romanian au pair, and her five-year-old ward were waiting for us. The women had brought wine, cheeses, lots of food—French country style. The two boys wanted to sit on the old jump seats, but Kalaj said the seats were unsteady and dangerous. On our way, I asked him to stop at one of the supermarkets and, five minutes later, returned with a huge watermelon that made everyone crack up laughing. "And how do you plan to cut this giant gourd? With karate chops?" he asked. I'd thought of every-thing, I said, and produced a super-cheap Japanese steak knife that I'd seen advertised time and again on television. Every-one was overjoyed.

Kalaj decided to take the scenic route to Walden Pond. On the way, we couldn't agree which song to sing together because no one knew the songs the other wanted to sing. The only songs we all knew, including Ekaterina who had learned them from her parents in Romania, were French songs from our parents' generation. So we started with these, and in the Checker cab headed to Walden Pond, here we all were, like two couples with their children headed for a Sunday picnic in July somewhere in the French countryside, singing Aznavour, Brel, and Bécaud songs, which the younger ones mimicked, just as all four of us had mimicked them in our childhood. Everything seemed right with us. It was a Monday, not a Sun-day, and it was October, not July, and this was Massachusetts, not Provence. Details!

No one knew what Walden Pond was famous for. I didn't want to break the spell by playing Mister Learned Professor.

But I couldn't resist telling everyone there used to be a time when investors would harvest the iced water of Walden Pond and ship it to India.

"You mean to the Indians of Arizona."

"No, to Indians of the Ganges."

Kalaj was totally nonplussed. "But that would be like selling sand to the Arabs," he added, "or ice to Eskimos, or cloth to your people." We all burst out laughing.

When we arrived, we parked the cab in a sodden, narrow alleyway in between a row of trees. We got out, took off our shoes, rolled up our pants. Not a soul in sight. The pond was entirely ours. "So what does one do here?" Kalaj finally asked, already feeling awkward.

"You swim. You picnic. You relax."

Kalaj refused to swim. Too cold, he said. Plus he didn't want to change. Then he looked around and said, "Tall cypresses and bathing water. They don't mix for me." He began describing Sidi Bou Saïd, just south of Pantelleria. Now there was a heavenly spot! "One day, we'll all have to go there, you, me, the children. And all our friends."

On second thought, it was peaceful here. The air felt clean, he said, and there were no people, and he liked walking along the shore on bare feet. And yet, as though catching himself, *Tout ça ne me dit absolument rien*, all this means absolutely nothing to me, he added once he spotted row upon row of thick, drooping tuft fringing the water, every clump of trees already looking glum, autumnal, and bereaved. This was no beach.

He played with the children. Then he said he'd take care of cutting the watermelon. It took him back to his catering days. "Is the water cold?" he asked.

"No, you can swim in your undies if you want," said his girlfriend.

"And what do I wear afterward?"

"You'll find something. You'll wear your trousers only. Or swim naked."

"He's really a prude, didn't you know," said Léonie.

The babysitter Ekaterina took out a large tablecloth and laid it out on the grass and asked Léonie to watch her boy. She had, it took me a moment to realize, the awkward, boyish walk of dancers, a sort of flaunted waddle that was not unattractive to look at. Then she leaned down with her back completely straight, spread her thighs on bended knees, and began to undress. To my surprise, underneath her shirt, her bra, and blue jeans she wore no bathing suit at all. She was getting naked. "I'm going for a swim. Coming?" I said yes before realizing that what she meant was completely naked. I liked the way she waddled into the water, noticing for the first time that with her dancer's walk came the perfect legs of a dancer. I took off everything and jumped in after her, not realizing that the water was freezing. "This is the most wonderful place in the world," she said as we treaded water away from the others, "even if it's totally American."

"You're starting to sound like him," I said.

"Jumbo-ersatz, jumbo-ersatz," she began to mimic, pointing her wet index finger at me in an imitation machine gun, *rat-tat-tat, rat-tat-tat.* We laughed out loud: "The water is ersatz, the plants are ersatz, even the fish are ersatz—there are no fish. I hate fish." We both took turns imitating his rants when he harangued the human race and damned every man, woman, species, child, fish, tree, vegetable, mineral, *rat-tat-tat.* To imitate her final round of bullets she splashed me in the face, once, twice, three times.

We swam farther out where the water felt yet more chilly. Then we swam underwater, came up to breathe, then back under again. I hadn't swum naked in years. Eventually, we saw people on one of the shores and decided to swim back. "Turn around, everyone," she said as we came rushing out of the water. "You too, *iepurașul meu,* my bunny," she said to the five-year-old who couldn't help staring, as I couldn't help staring at her legs, wondering all along whether God had made her thighs or whether they were the product of some strict Eastern European ballet school regimen. "And don't stare," she said. Even her cagey bantering felt familiar, warm, intimate, as though something of hers had touched my hand and then held it and didn't mean to let go. I wondered if this was because we were all speaking in French or just simply because Kalaj, as usual and without knowing it, had been stoking everyone's libido and we were all playing by his rules, where contact among humans was easy, natural, untrammeled, and necessary. Or maybe, in the end, we were all four of us truly happy to be together and no longer felt like stranded members of a disbanded company who'd given up on themselves in a Lotusland called Cambridge. The pond wasn't exactly ours to claim, but it let us play there, the way an empty tennis court can be yours for a day when the owners are out of town. Mild-mannered poachers trying to catch a few hours in the sun, not rogues or squatters. We were borrowing America, not settling in. The diffidence and haste with which we kept throwing the watermelon rinds in plastic bags so as not to attract bees or litter the grounds told everyone we were determined to keep a low profile. I said nothing, but I realized I was the only one among them who had a green card. Léonie plopped herself right next to Kalaj, and they embraced.

Later, during the picnic, when Ekaterina produced some Cheerios for the children, Kalaj, who had never seen the likes of Cheerios in his life, asked to taste one. Before he had put it in his mouth, she silently mouthed the words *jumbo-ersatz*, *jumbo-ersatz*, meaning: *You watch, he'll start*. The square container was immense, the food was totally artificial, nature never spawned these flavors—Kalaj was starting to load his Kalashnikov. When Ekaterina took out a Ziploc bag with five large, juicy nectarines, he exploded. "You should never buy nectarines. Nectarines are totally ersatz . . ."

"Like mules," she said.

"Yes, exactly," he said, missing the joke at his expense. "*Sesame Street* is all ersatz too. It teaches people to be ersatz. Just listen to the voices of each character. Not one has a human voice."

"But children like it, and children like nectarines, and I like nectarines. Do you want one?" she asked.

"Yes, I do," he conceded.

Her two little packs of Twinkies produced the same outraged response. Abject scorn followed by stoic acquiescence. "So, let's see what this Twinkie thing is," he finally said.

Then he got up and took a short stroll along the shore, dipping his toes in the water again, staring at the tops of the trees in the distance. He was enjoying Walden Pond, even America.

And right then and there I finally understood Kalaj. Behind his wholesale indictment of America, he was desperately struggling not to give in in case America decided not to yield to him first. The lawyer had mentioned the word deportation, and both of us had winced. Kalaj preferred to turn his back first, in the hope that America might ask him to look more favorably on her and give her a second chance. He was, without knowing it, doing what he'd always done: flirting . . . but this time with a superpower. America, as far as he was concerned, had not really put a penny on the table, and he was getting tired of staying in the game. America was busy stacking up its chips, while he—anyone could tell—was obviously bluffing.

Perhaps, also, by degrading America and nicknaming *amerloque* everything that was wrong with the world, he was forging for himself an imaginary Mediterranean identity, a Mediterranean paradise lost, something that may never have existed but that he needed to believe was out there in some imaginary other shore because otherwise he'd have nothing and nowhere to turn to in case America turned its back on him.

When it was time to fold everything back into the car and throw the garbage out in the appropriate bins, we looked at each other and realized that we had all taken more sun than we had hoped. It gave us a sort of heady good cheer, as if we'd finally caught up with a summer that had slipped us by.

Before entering the car, Kalaj asked everyone to clear their feet of any sand or mud, especially *you there in the back*, meaning me. Then he said he needed to piss. "So, pee," said Léonie, who was already sitting in the seat next to his. He looked about him uneasily, slightly at a loss, then headed back to the shore, and, with his back to us, as he stared into the quiet expanse of water, started to pee. He took his time, but the idea of someone pissing so irreverently into Thoreau's hallowed pond seemed too comical not to be put into its historical context. So when he returned to the car I explained to them the importance of Walden Pond in American literature. They all listened, attentively. "And I who simply needed to go," he finally said after mulling the matter a while and bursting out in loud guffaws, as we all joined in, the children included, all of us breaking into song as we rode back to Cambridge, swearing we should do this again in a few days.

I was the first they dropped by car, just in time to take a very quick shower and head to Lowell House on foot. All through cocktails, though, I had one thought in mind: I wanted the day to start all over again. Just as I wanted it never to end. If I did not know in whose camp I belonged—with Lowell House or with Kalaj—what I did not mind was oscillating between the two, with one foot in each, because I belonged to both, and therefore to neither—like having a home without belonging to it. Like staring out the window of my twenty-four-hour deli early in the morning after spending the night at the infirmary and feeling a rush of love, loathing, and bile.

After the cocktail reception, I ducked dinner and found my way to Café Algiers, then to Casablanca, then to the Harvest. But Kalaj was nowhere. When I asked the waiters and bartenders, they said they hadn't seen him. Suddenly I felt something fierce. Why did it take so long to admit why I'd come looking for him? I wanted to find all three of them, him, Léonie, and Ekaterina. And if I didn't find the three of them, I wanted Léonie to tell me where to find Ekaterina. And if Léonie was nowhere, I wanted to find Ekaterina sitting alone. If only I had skipped the Master's Tea and the cocktails immediately following. Perhaps it was the three sherries on an empty stomach speaking, perhaps it was too much sun, or perhaps it was just that we hadn't had a real moment together except while swimming, and tonight it seemed there wasn't going to be a similar moment again. And yet I was sure that something had happened when we were in the water together, from the way she'd been looking at me while drying herself, knowing I couldn't keep my eyes off. I wasn't making it up, and maybe this is why I couldn't let go of that fleeting something between us, because I couldn't quite put my finger on it or know when precisely it had happened. And then it hit me: the sheer obvious simplicity of it. I should have seized my moment then. Or asked for her phone number when we were in the car together. So what if Kalaj might guess why. This was the first thing Kalaj assumed about every man and woman on the planet. And if Léonie knew, what of it? I was there when she met Kalaj, and he had asked for her number in front of me—it was the kind of thing you asked without thinking. Had I not asked because I didn't want to seem interested, or didn't want to ask in my usually flustered way and look more flustered yet if she hesitated?

I tried one more place. But no one was there either. I headed home by way of Berkeley Street, passing by all those patrician houses, thinking now of the nectarine Kalaj had bit into and said he liked.

I could just imagine Kalaj speaking to her about me. "Of course you should call him. Better yet, go to his house," he would have said. "When?" "When? What a question. Tonight. Now. His door is literally always open." I could just hear him speaking to her while driving her home and shouting at his windshield. *Maintenant, aujourd'hui, ce soir!* Would I have gone and waited outside of her employer's house on Highland Avenue?

"My instincts are intact," he had once said, meaning that mine were totally warped, tarnished, compromised. "Intact," he had said on the night he took me to see his car and, on impulse, had made me knock on the hood of the car parked right next to his. The Western man's instincts were like pockets with holes in them. Sooner or later, everything slips through. "But I am like those beggars who line the inside of their tattered pockets with steel. Their clothes are all frayed, but the inside is a vault."

I decided to knock at Apartment 42.

Linda opened the door and right away walked back to where she'd been sitting and watching TV on her sofa. I shut the door.

She had passed her exams. I congratulated her. Mine were almost slightly over three months away.

She tucked both legs under her light blue terrycloth bathrobe. All I had to do was pull the belt and the knot was undone.

WHEN I AWOKE the next morning, it was almost eleven. The first thing that raced through my mind was that a whole day had passed and I had not read a single page. All that sun, and the swimming, and all those sherries, and then the agitated night in Apartment 42.

In the middle of the night I had decided to leave her apartment. I had opened her door, uttered a loud *good night, leman mine* in Chaucerese, then let her door bang itself shut, also loudly, and right away opened mine as fast and as noisily as I could and slammed it shut as well. I wanted my other neighbor to hear and to put two and two together. I decided to call her the Princesse de Clèves, because part of me already knew she'd heard the two doors bang and was already not pleased by what the noises implied. Tomorrow at dawn I'd play the same trick with the coffee grinds and see where that took us. I'd say something about work, I work all the time. No you don't, she'd reply. What do you mean? You know exactly what I mean.

Then I'd do what I did best: allow myself to blush. You're blushing, she'd say. I am blushing, but not because of what you think. Why are you blushing? I'd look down and say: Seeing you makes me blush. And I'd wait for her to say something, anything, even if it was as gauche and gimp-legged as what I'd just said. Provided she said something, I'd always have a comeback.

But I was so tired that night that I slept through five o'clock, six o'clock, seven o'clock, eight, nine, and ten. By now she'd be walking their collie through the Cambridge Common. Too late.

5

SOMETHING VERY NEW WAS HAPPENING TO ME. I FELT
as though every sinew, every bone, muscle, and cell in my
body was thrilled to belong to me, to be alive in me, through
me, for me. I knew that Ekaterina had longed to be with me
last night and that, if I'd found a way to call her, she'd have
met me anywhere, taken a taxi, rushed upstairs. The truth is
that on that strange morning I didn't give a damn about my
exams, because it was clear to me that anyone I'd cast a glance
at from here on would simply crave to touch me, to sleep with
me. Whence had this strange, unusual feeling sprung? Why
wasn't I always like this? What must I do to keep this thrill,
this buzz alive in me? And where had it been hiding for so
very long? Was this what living Kalaj meant?

Would the feeling die as soon as I returned to my usual
life—my old self, my old, tired, humdrum home that had no

lock, no food, no life, my books, my rooftop, my students, my little corner where I whiled away the hours thinking I was indeed headed somewhere, my Lloyd-Grevilles, my tea parties, my cocktails—were they all going to come back when I least wanted them?

More importantly: how did one feed this fever? Did one walk around brandishing a Kalashnikov? How did one keep this fervor of might, abundance, and pride forever alive? It reminded me of how primitive people were said to have carried live embers wherever they went simply because they hadn't learned yet how to light a fire. I had embers in every one of my pockets, and my pockets were lined with steel, and I loved the feeling.

The first thing I did that day to make sure I didn't lose this feeling was not to shower. I wanted to reek of sex, touch every part of me and know where it had been, what it had done, what had been done to it last night.

When I arrived at the department, Mary-Lou was just coming out of the supply room adjacent to her office and immediately reminded me that I had yet to give her the names of my other two examiners. I'd do so as soon as I met with them, I said. She swung around her desk and photocopied a list of instructions for the exam, because, she said, Harvard had very fussy guidelines when it came to comprehensives and I wasn't always mindful of them. As I was sitting and reading over the instructions, she said I looked better without a beard. I told her that this was the first time anyone had complimented me on my face. Don't people compliment you often? she asked. I said nothing, thought of Kalaj, and could almost hear her loose change being stacked on her side of her huge desk. All I had to do was raise her by one tiny penny and, who knows, we'd be doing it in the windowless supply room where she kept the extra jars of freeze dried coffee, the paper clips, the blue books, and reams of stationery bearing the department's letterhead. The question facing me now was: would she hold it against me if I omitted to raise her by that penny? The sight of her beefy face and Botero legs that tapered into tiny feet shod in satin blue pumps made me hesitate.

I decided to say something about the summer's terrible weather and manage to throw in a casual reference to my girlfriend and her parents' summer home in the Vineyard where they'd had air-conditioning recently installed in the television room and where we ended up spending so many hours, the whole family together. That, I figured, would take care of things.

Outside the tiny office reserved for teaching fellows to which I had a key, and where I kept some books, a student was standing and was waiting to meet her tutor. She was wearing sandals and an orange dress that flattered her dark tan and her thick, light brown hair. While I stood there with her, I asked about her courses, she about those I was teaching. We spoke about her senior thesis. As we were speaking, I couldn't keep my eyes off hers. She, I discovered, couldn't keep hers off mine. I loved the way her eyes kept searching mine, and mine hers, and how each caressed and lingered on the other's gaze. We were making love, and yet, without denying it, neither was calling attention to it.

We both discovered we loved Proust. She was writing her senior thesis on Proust. Could we talk sometime? I normally met students in my other office at Lowell House. But, not being my student, she was welcome to drop by at Concord Avenue if she wanted. In typical bland-speak that meant everything and nothing at all, the girl in the orange dress simply said, "I'd like that very much." I could just imagine how Kalaj would have mimicked the phrase. Her first name was Allison. The last name was dauntingly familiar. I told her it was nice meeting her. She said we'd already met once before. I must have given her a quizzical look, for she immediately said, "When you said you didn't care to see the leaves or to watch *Saturday Night Fever*."

This was the girl who had disabused me about America. Why hadn't I noticed how beautiful she was that time over breakfast?

What on earth was happening? I loved this new me. Here we were discussing Marcel Proust and building all manner of bridges, while part of me hadn't quite left and indeed still smelled of Apartment 42. If only Emerson, Thoreau, and Justice Holmes, to say nothing of Henry James, father and son, knew what slop was being visited on their beloved and pristine Massachusetts!

I was crossing Harvard Square when I heard someone yell

out to me in French, "Do you always talk to yourself?" It was Kalaj. He had stopped for a red light and was leaning his head out of his cab as I was crossing the street. In the back sat a slim white-haired lady dressed in a well-pressed lilac business suit.

"More ersatz than this you cannot get," he said referring to his passenger. "Where were you headed?"

"To have a cup of coffee and read."

"Ah, the leisurely life." he said. "I'll see you later."

It was nearing noon. I loved Cambridge at noon. It was time to head to the roof terrace before the weather finally changed. All I wanted now was to read the memoirs of the seventeenth-century Cardinal de Retz, which I'd started a year earlier and promised I'd read as soon as I could. Put everything aside, and spend an entire afternoon with this man who, of all men on this planet, was more an intrepid soldier, courtier, lover, jailbird, and diplomat than a man of the cloth.

I walked by Berkeley Street. Nothing pleased me more than to pass by these old New England houses and be greeted by the beaming palaver of Anglo-Saxon housewives busily plant-ing next spring's bulbs.

Stuck in between my mailbox and my neighbor's box was an index card. *"Dropped by but you were gone. I'll try later. Ekaterina."* She had left no phone number. I wondered if this was the handiwork of Kalaj. On the rooftop, we could have replayed yesterday's excursion to Walden Pond. The sun was no more intense up there than it had been on the shore, and I still had some of the watermelon left and an uncorked bottle of Portuguese rosé. It would have been wonderful sweating it out under the sun until we couldn't stand it any longer and headed downstairs to my apartment.

I removed the card and wrote a few words and then teased it back into the narrow slot between the two mailboxes, hoping that my next-door neighbor would see it when leaving the building a second time to walk her dog. *"I'm waiting upstairs."* But on my way upstairs, I ran into Linda. What was she doing now? Nothing. Did I want to come for a visit? A short one, I said. When I walked in, I suddenly realized what I hadn't noticed the night before. Unlike mine, her apartment was decorated and looked as though someone had put the whole place together with a humble, loving hand; the place had domestic longevity written all over it, while mine was roughly furnished with a scattering of odds and ends picked up anywhere for nothing or almost nothing and thrown together in an ill-assorted, slapdash medley that bore no trace of any hand, loving or otherwise. I had a feeling that Kalaj, Ekaterina, and Léonie's bedrooms were thrown together in as rudimentary and hasty a manner as mine—i.e., savage with niceties, impatient, hostile, and transient. Furniture didn't stay long with us.

I soon told her I was expecting someone, and headed back to my apartment. In fact, I heard the buzzer ten minutes later. "A woman with a dog opened the downstairs door for me," Ekaterina said as she pushed open my door. The news thrilled me to no end and made me happier than I already was to see her.

"Did you tell her you were coming to see me?"

"Yes, I did."

She walked in with fresh muscatel grapes, whose scent suddenly suffused my living room. "I brought you these, I knew you'd like them."

I took the grapes into the kitchen. I was looking for an excuse to open the service door, and decided that getting rid of the paper bag in which Ekaterina had brought the fruit was as good an excuse as any. I put the grapes in a bowl, crumpled the bag, and threw it in the larger trash can on the landing outside my door.

"I am so glad you came," I said, still leaving my kitchen door open.

"Me too." And because I felt no hesitation whatsoever, I came up to her and kissed her on the mouth. I loved her breath.

"We can eat them in the living room or upstairs on the terrace, which do you prefer?"

"I could also mix drinks," I added. No, she couldn't drink. She had to pick up her boy from kindergarten at 2:00.

"So let's eat them in the other room," I said. I took the grapes back into the bedroom, and we sat on the bed, her legs beautifully crossed on my sheets. "I want to eat these grapes naked," I said, and before she had time to even say yes, I began removing everything I was wearing. I loved being like this. I loved watching her dancer's thighs on my sheets.

I promised to read two whole books the moment she left.

ONE FRIDAY, TO celebrate our newfound friendship, we decided to have a dinner for all four of us and a few friends. Kalaj invited one friend, I invited Frank who had come back from a summer in Assisi and who, as my ex-roommate, had helped me through thick and thin, especially in the loan department. We had spoken by telephone but hadn't managed to meet since his return. He was going to bring along his new Armenian girlfriend who promised to dazzle us with sensational pastries from an Armenian bakery in Watertown. There were also others: Claude, who had also recently returned from France, and a friend of his named Piero, a count in his last year at Harvard Law. I would have invited Linda had I not invited Ekaterina first. Bring both, said Kalaj. I could invite Niloufar too, he suggested. "She'd cook wonderful rice and spiced meats," said Kalaj, bursting out laughing, because I'd told him all about the powerful effect of her spiced meats.

"No, it would hurt her, and what I've done to her I'll never live down."

"You are right," he said.

Kalaj and I met at Café Algiers as soon as I was done teaching that Friday. It was before noon, and he was seated next to the young American whom I'd not seen since that first time in early August. Young Hemingway and Kalaj were arguing politics again. Kalaj finally called him an anarchist in diapers. The American suggested that Kalaj was a Malcolm X manqué and "might do well to revisit" his political views. Kalaj stared at this strange locution as if it were a stray dog that had come up to his table for a bite of his sandwich. He licked the end of his cigarette paper, then, staring the American in the face, finally interjected: "You have no balls."

Startled, Young Hemingway sputtered and replied, "I have no balls?"

"Yes, they're in your throat, here," and with the bare tips of both thumbs to suggest tiny gonads he placed each thumb against either side of his Adam's apple and began to emit a reedy little squeal, with which he echoed, *might do well to revisit, might do well to revisit.* "If you wanted to tell me I was an idiot, you should have told me, *Kalaj, tu es un idiot.* Can't even speak and expects to argue . . . Just go back to your scrap metal shop of a university where they mass-produce you like rinky-dink umbrellas good for one rainfall."

"I thought we were friends, Kalaj."

"We are nothing. We just drink coffee together." He turned to me and said, "Let's go!"

We hopped in his cab and headed straight to Haymarket Square to buy vegetables. He had already purchased the beef for a song from the head cook at Césarion's the day before and it was being marinated in my kitchen in a sauce of his own invention. "What's in the sauce?" I kept asking.

"You'll see."

"Yes, but what kind of sauce is it?"

"A *you'll see* sauce."

He was also going to prepare a mousse the likes of which we had never tasted. He had not used a kitchen in more than six months, so this was something of a celebration. We asked everyone to bring wines. The vegetables were going to be easy—but he needed fresh chestnuts, and these were almost impossible to find. So we purchased dried chestnuts instead. They were clearing up the stalls that Friday afternoon, so the potatoes, onions, green peppers, mushrooms, and celery we managed to get for free. I was under the impression that I was going to be responsible for the cheeses. Bread and cheeses he had already taken care of, he said. "You know nothing about cheeses. The first thing you'll do is think you're buying French cheese when all you'll serve is a curdled brew made with liquids that had never been inside a cow's udder." Kalaj did not believe in small spice jars; he bought large bags of everything from cumin and thyme to paprika.

More people said they would come, including Zeinab and Sheila. Even the woman with bathroom problems had uttered a vague maybe. Kalaj never broke up with anyone. People simply drifted in and out and back into his life, the way sand castles go up and down and are rebuilt time and again on the same spot of beach.

Kalaj wanted to find a man who was *bien* (right) for Zeinab, so I thought of Claude. But just in case things didn't work out between them, I invited a young Hungarian who had studied in Turkey. And then there was the Count. "I can just see them," said Kalaj, "Zeinab and the Count discussing Balzac on a park bench in the sixteenth arrondissement, he with an umbrella and a tennis racket between his knees, and she with a broomstick and a mop. Lovely couple!"

The evening started on the wrong foot. Earlier, while Kalaj was busily cooking the meat with all manner of diced vegetables, and Ekaterina was helping with the salads and the vegetables, we heard the voice of Maria Callas on the radio singing one aria after the other. This was quite unusual until the announcer said what I was beginning to dread. Maria Callas had died that day in Paris. It put a damper on everything. My ex-roommate's girlfriend and I were both fans. Count, as Kalaj suddenly dubbed him, thinking it was his first name even though he'd introduced himself as Piero, was beside himself, since his father had been a lifelong friend of hers and had her signed portrait in his office. The talk turned to Callas, and because I owned a few recordings, I decided to play two to three arias, trying as best as I could to explain why she was *prima donna assoluta*. A comparison of a few arias sung by other sopranos was meant to drive the point home.

Kalaj, who had nothing to say on the subject, was unusually quiet for a man used to brandishing his loud weaponry wherever he went. Asked by Léonie why he wasn't speaking, he simply put on an affected simper that was meant to call attention to its contrived character. "Me, I'm listening," he replied. "I like to listen." But I could tell that he was seething inside and, without instant recourse to his Kalashnikov, had lost his ability to say anything. This was probably not the scene he had imagined, and he must have felt like an outsider at his own dinner party. Ekaterina began to talk to him, trying to draw him out, but he'd lapse into silence as soon as he uttered a few words. Something was clearly bothering him. Zeinab finally put her arm around him: "*Tu boudes*, are you sulking?"

"I am not sulking," he said, shrugging his shoulders to free them of her arm. "Just leave me alone, will you?" We left him alone.

We changed topics and someone spoke of a movie he had just seen called *The Lacemaker* about a humble, self-effacing apprentice who works in a beauty salon and who becomes the mistress of an intellectual who soon tires of her and ends up dropping her. This was more to Kalaj's liking, and right away, he had loaded and cocked his gun, ready to aim and fire, and was soon inveighing both against all women for wanting to rise in the world by exploiting men and against all young men for exploiting the women who exploited them. There were no prisoners, everyone was being mowed down.

Kalaj and Léonie, however, disagreed. Claude, clearly happy to have brought along a count and still eager to shine in his eyes, said this was a circular argument and was headed nowhere. But Count was willing to be more indulgent and said that history was filled with similar instances and that it was no longer possible to take sides, but if sides had to be taken, he'd side with the woman. "Why with the woman and not the man?" *Rat-tat-tat-tat.* Because in the end men are frequently given second chances, women seldom are. "Are you so sure that men get second chances—are you so sure?" *Rat-tat-tat-tat-tat.*

"I think everyone in this room will agree with me."

"And what about the men who always give women a second chance but are never given a second chance, what about them?" *Rat-tat-tat-tat-tat-tat-tat-tat.*

"I am not competent to comment on this, sorry."

"Not competent, not competent, I'll tell you why you're not competent. Because you've never really had to help anyone, man or woman. What do you know about poor girls from the country or from another country who land in strange, big cities and whose last recourse is always the same—*le trottoir*, the sidewalk—what could you possibly know except as a consumer, and even then, what does a consumer know about the exploitation of women after he's said *au revoir et merci*, or of the exploitation of men, because, yes sir, there are men who exploit men in that very same way among the dockers in Marseilles."

"How do *you* know?" asked Count.

"I know, and how!"

The skirmish between the two men would have devolved into something ugly if the large pot with the meat didn't require Kalaj's attention. Moments later, the food was ready and everyone was urged to sit down around a table that could handle no more than four persons. People sat on the sofa, on the floor. We improvised a chair by using a tiny stepladder I'd found on the street; Zeinab could use it as a stool. I had an impulse to go downstairs and invite the twins from Apartment 21, but then thought better of it. As for the neighbors across the service entrance, I had no doubt that they knew a party was going on. Had they wanted to, they could have invited themselves. We drank lots of wine, and thank goodness Frank had prepared enough baked lasagna for a regiment, because we would have moved from the beef and the chestnuts and vegetables to the breads and cheeses without much of anything else in between. Kalaj was ecstatic and kissed Frank on his shimmering bald pate. "One doesn't sit around a table for the food only. Food is there to feed friendship," he said. I don't think any of us understood the wisdom of the saying, but it sounded good, and perhaps we were all in the mood to believe just about anything that spoke well of friends and good fellowship. Count had brought many goodies from some hilly area in Umbria, and no one doubted that this had turned into a feast far, far superior to the tiny supper originally planned.

At some point, a song I had long ago taped on a tiny cassette came on, and Kalaj immediately pricked up his ears and asked us to be quiet for a moment because he wanted to hear the words. He hadn't heard the song in a very long time, he said. "A very long time," he repeated. Then, having caught the right words and synced his lips to the singer's as he sometimes would with Om Kalsoum at Café Algiers, he began to whine the words ever so softly, as though he was ashamed of being seen singing, because for all he knew, he was just singing to himself because he needed to hear the words from his own mouth for him to feel them. The song was about a man thinking of a woman he hasn't seen in a very long time but whom he knows he'll meet again when their paths cross. The path to each is crooked and filled with detours—she's met other men, and he's met women too—but he knows that eventually they will meet and make love and speak of the incidental lovers each had loved along the way.

"This is not necessarily about a man and a woman," said Frank, "It could be about a man who's lost his way and decides to give his homeland a woman's name. The woman is just a metaphor for home." Kalaj listened attentively. Had Count said such a thing he would have strafed him with a machine gun filled with ire and contradiction, but coming from Frank, the comment seemed to placate something very deep in Kalaj. *The woman is a metaphor for home,*" he said, echoing Frank's impromptu remark, *"the woman is a metaphor for home,*" he repeated. Then he asked me to play the song again. But before the second stanza started, he suddenly rushed out and headed straight into the kitchen.

When he came back and Zeinab had started serving the Armenian desserts and the mousse, Léonie could still be heard carrying on about the woman who had sacrificed her life for a man who'd outgrown her too soon.

Léonie and Count agreed that the issue wasn't as simple as all that. Kalaj disagreed. Why they had resurrected the topic wasn't clear at all, especially after the song we'd heard had put him in so contemplative a mood. But as soon as it became obvious that Count had joined forces with Léonie, Kalaj left the table, went into the bedroom, and slammed the door behind him. Maybe he was making a phone call, maybe the food wasn't agreeing with him. Zeinab seemed perplexed but didn't say anything, and the Armenian girl and Frank kept exchanging mystified looks, all the while determined to sample their desserts and stay out of the Tunisian's bad temper. Something was definitely wrong. A few moments later, I opened the door slowly and stepped into my bedroom. He had not only shut the door but had turned off the lights and was lying on my bed in total darkness, smoking.

We all have our phantoms, and I was seeing Kalaj's for the first time, perhaps because, for the first time, he wasn't able to shoo them away by shouting.

Something very serious was troubling him. Was he missing someone, was this reminding him of something somewhere else, were his problems catching up with him—the green card, money, solitude, divorce, deportation? "No, nothing, *nothing*," he replied. I made a motion to leave the bedroom to let him be by himself, since it was clear he didn't want to speak. When I was about to open the door, he simply asked me to stay.

"What is it?" I asked. "Tell me."

He caught his breath. "I cooked this whole dinner for everyone and everyone is having a great time, but, you see, what about me?" He hesitated a moment, "*Et moi?*" he said. "*Et moi?*" "I don't understand," I said, "everyone is happy because of you. Everyone is grateful. And no one is ignoring you or has even done or said anything to slight you."

"That's because you see the surface, but you don't look underneath. *But what about me?*"

I still had no idea what he was getting at or what was eating him.

"In exactly a year's time I will not be here. Each and every one of you will be here, but I won't be among you. I will miss all this so terribly, that I don't even want to think beyond this minute. You see now? Has anyone thought about me?"

I was dumbfounded. Silence was my only way of agreeing with him and of saying what I would never had had the courage or the cruelty to say to his face: *You are right, my friend, we completely failed to think of you, we do not see your hell, you are all alone in this, and, yes, you may be right about this too: you may not be among us next year, may not even be in our thoughts next year.*

"Now you see?" he asked.

"Now I see," I said, meaning: *There is nothing, nothing I can say to buoy your spirits.* I was helpless. I felt like the captain of a cruise ship who shouts "Man overboard . . . but, ladies and gentlemen, there is nothing we can do, it's time for lunch, and the food is waiting." To say anything so as to say something would have forced me to utter fatuous palliatives, and I had drunk too much already to lie persuasively.

But I suddenly realized one thing very clearly in this dark bedroom. By looking at him I was almost looking at myself. He was the measure of how close I might come to falling apart and losing everything here. He was just my destiny three steps ahead of me. I could fail my exams, be sent packing to New York, and in a year from now, no one would recall this dinner party, much less remember to think of me.

"See? I'm like someone who prepares a whole feast knowing he is dying, and everyone is happily eating and drinking away and forgets that the cook will be carried away by the end of the meal. I don't want to be the dying cook of the party. I don't want to leave and be elsewhere. I need help and there is no one, no one."

I heard the catch in his voice.

"So, what about me?" he asked, as though coming back to a nagging question that hadn't just cropped up because of this evening but that he'd been brewing perhaps since childhood, since forever, and the answer was always going to be the same; there is no answer. "*Et moi?*" he repeated, feeling desperately sorry for himself, while I still stood there, unable to say or do anything for him.

And, for the first time that evening, I saw that this short mantra of his also had another meaning, which had simply eluded me all the time I'd been standing there in the dark listening to him. It didn't just mean *And what about me?* but spoke an injured, hopeless *What happens to me now?*

He wasn't asking me for an answer, or invoking my help, or

even pleading with the god of fairness and forgiveness overseeing his affairs in North America; he was just groping in the dark and repeating words of incantation that would eventually lead him out of his cave in the only way he knew: with tears. With tears came solace and surrender, pardon and courage.

That night as I watched him cry, you could almost touch his despair and its ephemeral balm, hope. When, seconds later, he actually started to sob as he'd done on the day he heard of his father's sickness in Tunis, I knew that here was the loneliest man I'd ever known in my life, and that anger, sorrow, fear, and even the shame of being caught crying were nothing compared to this monsoon of loneliness and despair that was buffeting him every minute of his days.

A part of me didn't want him to know that I could see he was crying, so I made to go back to the living room and attend to the guests.

"Don't go yet. Sit down. Please."

It's what one said to a nurse when one didn't want to be alone once they'd turned off the light in your room and dimmed those in the corridor. But all the chairs were in the living room and there was nowhere to sit except on the bed, so I sat on the edge, next to him. He wasn't speaking and he was no longer crying, just breathing and smoking.

When, a minute or two later, after thinking his crisis had subsided, I made a motion to leave again, he said, "Don't go."

I wanted to reach out to him with my hand and touch him to comfort him, maybe even to show compassion and solidarity, but we'd never touched other than fleetingly, and it felt awkward doing so now. So, instead, I reached for his palm but found the top of his hand and held it, gently at first, then more firmly. This was not easy for me, and I suppose it was not easy for him either, because he did not respond or return my grasp. For two men who claimed to be so inveterately Mediterranean we couldn't have been less expressive or more inhibited. Perhaps we were both holding back, perhaps he was thinking the exact same thing, which is why, in an unexpected gesture, instead of standing up again, I lay down right next to him, facing him, and put one arm across his chest. Only then did he reach out to hold my hand, and then, turning to me, put a leg around me and began to cradle and hug me, both of us entirely silent except for his muted sobbing. We said nothing more.

Shortly after, I got up and told him, "Pull yourself together and let's step outside." I did not shut the door behind me.

WHEN I RETURNED to the living room, I noticed it right away though I thought nothing of it at first, and perhaps didn't want to register it. Léonie was sitting on the sofa and Count was sitting on the floor, his neck resting against her knees while the back of his head lay flat against her thigh. Frank had put on more music by Callas. The others were busy cutting the two desserts Zeinab had brought.

Catching my glance in his direction, Count stood up and said he was going to buy cigarettes around the corner. Claude immediately offered him his. But Count smoked Dunhills only. "I should have known," said Claude, "you always pick the very best, Piero." A matter of minutes, said Count, trying to justify his brief exit. Léonie looked up and said she'd walk him downstairs and, seeing Kalaj entering the room, asked to let her have the keys to the car to get her sweater.

He gave her the keys.

"You should learn to roll your own," said Kalaj to Count.

"I don't need to," replied Count as he let Léonie out the front door, then discreetly shut the door behind him.

"*Nique ta mère*," muttered Kalaj under his breath.

We carved the cakes in long wedges and served dessert on paper napkins, and because there weren't enough clean forks, we ate with our hands. Pecan pie is the best thing since the invention of the telephone. No, cheesecake, said someone else. Cheesecake too, said Kalaj. We opened more wine, there was even talk of finally finishing the gallon of vodka I had appropriated along with the Beefeater gin from the departmental party last April. We passed the freezing cold vodka around, everyone agreed it was stupendous, so that a second round was *de rigueur*, and I was just on my way to the kitchen to start the coffee when I saw Kalaj bolt out of the living room, tear open the front door, and rush down the stairs.

The rest of us looked bewildered and exchanged panicked glances. "What got into him tonight?" asked Ekaterina.

Zeinab, who knew him better than any of us, simply said, "He's always a pill when everyone else is having a good time."

Ten minutes later he was back upstairs. Not a word. He headed directly into the dark bedroom again and slammed the door shut once more. Everyone looked at one another very puzzled. Zeinab said she'd seen him upset before, but never like this.

The rest of the evening seemed to last forever. We wanted to put a happy face on things, but everyone's thoughts were turned to the man who'd locked himself in my bedroom. No one, not even I had the courage to go inside to look in on him. To kill time, we cleaned up, put things away, washed dishes, wrapped everything, and everyone was asked to take something home. I'd take care of the garbage, my mind already thinking of the trash container on the service door landing. It seemed to me that Linda and Ekaterina, for all their newly sprung friendship, were perhaps vying to see who of the two would outstay the other. Part of me wanted them to sort it out among themselves; the other part began to hope they'd both come up with a better plan.

Kalaj came out only after most of the guests had left. Someone had dropped a strawberry from one of the cakes on the carpet and then stepped on it. It was impossible to remove the stain. Ekaterina said it was Count. A friend had lent me this antique Persian Tabriz because my living room was larger than his. One day, though, he'd want it back exactly as he had lent it to me.

Kalaj said he'd clean the rug. He knew how to remove stains. But by then I had scraped the strawberry with a sharp knife and then poured stain remover on the rug.

"I wish I had thrown gasoline on her face. And on his."

"What happened?" we asked.

"What happened? What happened? Couldn't you hear?"

None of us had heard a thing.

"I beat them up. That's what's happened. Now you know."

"What do you mean you beat them up?" I asked, unable to believe the obvious.

"They were in my cab. Together. *Neeking*."

Ekaterina exclaimed *What!*

"Well, she's a woman, so I slapped her a bit. But he's a man. So I punched him in the face."

Kalaj didn't have a scratch on him.

"Where are they now?"

"They ran away, both of them."

I looked at him.

"Let me call her and make sure she's all right," said Ekaterina.

"Don't you dare."

Ekaterina quickly picked up the receiver and called her friend.

There was no answer.

"I know what she's doing."

"What?" I asked.

"I already told you. They're *neeking*."

"You should never hit anyone."

"Pummel her, that's what I should have done."

He picked up his fatigue jacket and turned to Ekaterina and said he was driving her home.

"I'm staying," she said, "or I'll walk. I don't know, I'll see. You go home."

With that he uttered his usual *"Bonne soirée"* and was abruptly gone.

All three of us sat on the same sofa dazed and immobilized. As I awoke to the reality of the night's events, I made my mind up never to have anything to do with Kalaj again. Enough was enough. "That's the end of that friendship," I said. "And I'm never speaking to him again," Ekaterina said.

But none of us budged from our spot on the sofa. Perhaps we needed to seem more dazed than we really were. Perhaps we wished to stay dazed, for all three of us had a good inkling of where things were headed tonight, though neither would do anything to bring them about or interfere if they happened. I turned off all the lights and in the dark brought out the big bottle of vodka and poured a generous amount for each in three plastic glasses. This, whatever spell we were under, needed booze. I knew I'd start with Linda's shoulder. I wanted Ekaterina to kiss her other shoulder.

IN THE MORNING, my buzzer rang.

It was Léonie. When she appeared on the landing of my floor, I couldn't believe my eyes. She had a big bruise on her cheekbone and red blotches all over her face. "And that's nothing," she said, once she realized how shocked I was. "Feel my head." She grabbed my hand and let me feel under her hair. Her scalp was full of lumps and bumps.

"And he pulled out my hair. And tore my clothes too."

She had no one to turn to except me, she said. Her employer, Austin's mother, wanted to report the incident to the police. But Léonie said she needed to see me first. Why? I asked. Because it was complicated, she said.

She sat down in my kitchenette area while I started to boil some water for tea.

First of all, was she in pain? I asked. And Count, how was he?

"He too wants to report it to the police. Kalaj broke two of his teeth, and to top everything Count is furious with me. He says I should have told him I was with Kalaj. I told him we were over quite a while ago."

"I didn't know. You seemed so lovey-dovey at Walden Pond."

"By then it was long over. We were just friends."

I was surprised.

"So what are you going to do now?" I asked, like a lawyer opening a file with a new client. All I needed was to take out a yellow legal pad, intersperse my questions with a few nods, and light a giant meerschaum pipe.

"If you report him and file a complaint," I finally said, "they'll deport him. Even a restraining order will get him deported."

I didn't know a thing about the legalities of what I was saying, but what I said seemed to make sense.

"I know," she said, "but what do you want me to do? He's

crazy. He'll kill me. I don't want him near me. I was so scared last night that I ended up calling my mother in France. I was almost ready to go back, but I love Austin and Austin loves me, and I love the family also."

"Perhaps too much," I threw in.

"So he's told you about that too—of course!"

"Yes. It upset him a lot."

"Everything upsets him a lot."

"So what do you want to do?" I asked, nodding, meaning: *Let's get down to brass tacks.*

"If Austin's mother reports him to the police, Kalaj will let her know that I've slept with her husband. I know he'll tell her, I know him. If I file a report, he'll still tell the wife. If Count goes to the police, he'll right away tell Austin's mother. If they could deport him this afternoon without giving him a chance to call anyone, I would do it. He is the worst mistake of my life, and I've made huge ones before, which is why I came to the States. Better yet, if he could disappear somewhere in the Midwest I'd be perfectly happy, because then I won't even have it on my conscience that he was deported because of me."

I had every sympathy for Léonie. But, without knowing why, I wanted to prevent Kalaj's deportation.

The best thing I could do was, first, to persuade her not to file a complaint and, second, to make sure they made up, or at least had a talk—in my presence if they wished. I'd seen it done in movies. People airing their differences, their grievances. "Very ersatz," I finally said.

She laughed. Then, seeing herself laugh, she began to cry. It was the first time she was crying about this, she said. She'd held up well enough until now. No one had ever beaten her before, not even raised their hand against her. And now this fellow, this convict wanted to lord it over her? Who did he think he was?

The big question was how to prevent Count from going to the police. "He's vindictive. You saw how he argued with Kalaj last night. Plus he probably feels mortified for getting beaten up without putting up a fight, not even to protect me. He doesn't want to see me again."

The first thing I did after she was gone was to call Claude. Claude was aware of what happened to his friend, whom he refused to call Count, as we all did to make fun of him. "Piero knows some very powerful people in Italy. They could cause Kalaj serious problems. He could also make things difficult for you for hosting the brawl and for me as well for bringing him to it."

"Plus Count has two broken teeth," I said.

"Plus Piero has two broken teeth," he corrected.

We had to come up with a plan.

I told Claude not to do anything. I would rush over to his house and together we'd work out some sort of plan to discourage Count from filing with the police.

When I arrived at Claude's house, nearby, he'd already had a conversation with Count.

"But I thought you were going to wait for me?"

"Well, I had an idea and I called him right away."

"Were you afraid I might insist on talking to him first—is that what it is? Now you've just made things ten times worse," I told Claude.

"How could I have made things worse if Piero says he won't file anything with the police."

"Count won't?" I asked, dumbfounded.

"No, Piero considers Kalaj a wretched *marocchino* who'll soon enough get himself deported one way or another. Besides, this is his last year in Law School and he wants to put last night completely behind him. He's already made an appointment with a famous dentist in New York and is flying there this afternoon to be seen on Sunday. Then he comes back and wants nothing to do with your friends, or my friends, which means you, of course, and that poor woman."

"Count gets new teeth and she goes back to babysitting. Count was right about women seldom getting a second chance," I said, trying to underscore the irony of the situation.

"Your problem is you lost someone who could have been an important friend to you."

Claude, a social climber? I'd never seen that side of him before.

I WAS SO happy to hear that Count was not going to go to the police that I immediately called Léonie and told her the news. She was not happy to hear that Count had buckled, but she was relieved. Things would get back to what they'd been before Kalaj. This, I felt, was perhaps the story of his life. No matter how long you knew him, and how he disrupted the world of those around him, eventually he'd be out of your life and things would go back to being what they'd been before him. Despite his dogged efforts to recast the world in his own image, he made no impact, changed nothing, left no mark. In fact, he'd already walked out of history and the family of man long before he or any of us knew it. He reminded me of a mythological beast that the earth sprouts forth on some demented whim and that wreaks great harm on earthlings, ravages the countryside, and then, without explanation, is suddenly swallowed back up by earth. The dead are forgotten, the wounds heal, people move on.

Eventually I did arrange for Kalaj and Léonie to meet. Perhaps they should not have met, for both managed to unearth a demon neither probably suspected they had in them. When they met in public a few days later, things seemed to go very well. Kalaj took Austin under his wing again and was kinder than any father could be to the boy. But one evening, he showed up at Café Algiers with scratch marks streaked all over his neck. When he rolled up his sleeves, I saw that his right forearm was full of bruises. "What on earth is going on?" I asked.

He smiled it off.

"Do you guys beat each other up now?" I asked, trying to make light of it. Had I suspected the truth, I would never have asked.

He didn't answer. Then, a few seconds later, as if out of nowhere, he said, "Sometimes."

"Sometimes?"

"We like it."

"You *what*?"

"Some people need drugs. Others alcohol. She likes to slap me."

"Do you really like it when she slaps you?"

I couldn't believe my ears.

He thought about it as though the question had never occurred to him before. Who in his right mind would dare ask such a question of a Berber?

"I don't mind," he said.

"You're both sick."

"We are."

Had he pushed his self-destructiveness so far?

It couldn't last. Léonie broke up with him one evening at Café Algiers. She dashed in through the back door, walked up to our table, told him *"Écoute, c'est fini,"* gave him a plastic bag in which some of his things were folded, and walked out.

"Everyone does this to me," he said. "Either they shut their door to me or they bring me remnants. As if I needed remnants and underwear." And with all his might and all his rage, he hurled the plastic bag into the kitchen area. The owner of the café came out of the kitchen, walked to our table, and said, "If you go on like this, you won't be able to come here."

"What did I tell you?" Kalaj turned to me without even looking at the owner. "Everyone shuts their door in the end."

The whole scene put me in a terrible mood, because it did not just make me think of the numberless times I too had promised to shut my door at him and have no more to do with him, but of how close I myself had come to seeing Harvard's door shut in my own face.

6

I BEGAN TO AVOID KALAJ. PERHAPS MY TEACHING
obligations, now that the semester was in full swing, took me
away from him. Perhaps I felt I belonged to Harvard more than
I had allowed myself to believe. At a meeting of the Committee
on Degrees in History and Literature, I had made a proposal
pertaining to the quality of senior theses. Someone objected
to my proposal, I began to explain its merits, there was a vote,
and my proposal was approved. I felt validated and vindicated.
All it took was a near-unanimous show of raised hands, and
suddenly I loved Harvard, loved rubbing shoulders with the
brotherhood of Americans.

There was also the possibility of a new woman in my life,
Allison, though I still wasn't sure which way things were
headed. I didn't want Kalaj to see us together, nor did I want
him to see who I became, or how I behaved or even spoke when

I was in her company. He would undoubtedly have dubbed me affected, precious, no less a social climber than Claude was in my eyes—and perhaps I was. But the irony is that I was probably no less affected as a Mediterranean among the habitués of Café Algiers than I was among WASPs at Lowell House.

But then something else was troubling me, and Allison's presence made me see it more clearly. It's not just that I did not want Kalaj to see me with her; I didn't want her to see me with him. She was candid, bold, straightforward, and freethinking in so many unforeseen ways, willing to try many things that were not part of the immediate world she'd been brought up in. Nor was she a snob, though some might have thought so, if only because she moved in circles where everything was rarefied and where you never had to think of cost, even when you felt you needed to pretend to. She knew the things she liked and was used to and was seldom aware of their far inferior and cheaper version everyone else in the world purchased. Her family always traveled first-class; it would never have occurred to her that one could also travel coach. She had never in her life seen the back of an airplane or thought it possible to sit in the cramped spaces everyone else flew in. But she was discreet in everything. She never ordered more than two drinks because she didn't like being sloshed; I never ordered more than two drinks because I'd have no money left for dinner. It would never have occurred to her that buying four drinks each, three days in a row, could mean my financial ruin. But she had perfect judgment, and once she was told about the rest

of mankind and its strapped budgets, she made all the necessary adjustments with the surefire ease with which a rich person knows how to dress down when visiting poor relatives in
the suburbs. Above all she was a very canny reader of people
and could instantly have distinguished an uncommitted tru-
ant like me from a confirmed vagrant like Kalaj.

Allison had come to my apartment on Concord Avenue
early on the afternoon of Yom Kippur. Not intentionally of
course, and not that it bothered me in any way, since I had
never observed Kippur in my life. But it was emblematic of
how far apart our worlds were. When she buzzed me early that
afternoon, I told her to come right upstairs; I'd recognized it
was a woman's voice but couldn't make out whose. When she
walked in wearing her orange dress I was totally surprised. I
was wearing a pair of shorts and a T-shirt and had just come
back from a jog. I was also sweating. I must have looked a mess.
I told her to please sit on the sofa, to pick something up to
read, and that I'd take no time to shower and get dressed.

She was unfazed by this. Perhaps, in her mind, she was
not visiting me at home; she was just visiting a Lowell House
tutor in his off-campus digs, hence the relaxed drop-by-and-
show-up-whenever-you-please informality of her visit and the
ease with which she adjusted to everything.

"Tell you what, do you know how to make espresso?" I
asked in my distracted and flustered state.

She loved espresso but didn't know how to make one.

"Five minutes," I said. I'd make us two terrific lattes.

I was trying not to allow myself to get aroused by the situation.

She must have taken a good look at my bookcase and, before I'd even started the water running, shouted that she was amazed I had the complete first edition of Proust's *A la recherche du temps perdu*. Had she read the whole thing yet? I shouted back behind my closed door, feeling that if she didn't feel uncomfortable shouting back and forth with someone she scarcely knew while he was in the bathroom, who was I to quibble.

"Yes," she replied.

Then came total silence. Was she going to undress and step into the shower with me? The thought gave me a sudden thrill that was difficult to restrain but that part of me did not wish to temper. Would I come out of the shower and expose myself? Or would she have already snuggled in my bed, naked under my sheets, her clothes dropped on the floor along the way to my bedroom as a preamble to what lay in store for us? I didn't want to say or shout anything for fear she'd make out the arousal in my voice. All I knew was that in Kalaj's book of rules, if I was as aroused as this, so was she.

When I came out of the shower in my bathrobe, she was lying flat on her stomach on my living room floor leafing through my diary.

"What on earth are you doing?"

"Reading," she said, as though it was the most natural thing in the world.

"Where did you find it?"

"In your bedroom, on your desk."

I was speechless. So she'd gone into my bedroom, seen my totally unmade bed, rifled through my things, found the diary, what else?

"Do you really, *really* mind?"

I thought about it.

"No, I don't mind really, really mind," I said. "Actually, it thrills me."

"Thrills you? How, *actually*?" she said, echoing my own word.

I had no idea where this was going—was she a total ingénue or did she know exactly what she was doing, which could be exactly why she showed up in the first place.

They always know. I could just hear Kalaj's voice.

"I'm going to get dressed and make coffee."

"Why don't you do that."

I'd never in my life uttered a sentence like "Why don't you do that" to mean yes. Who knows what these words implied or meant in her world.

Naturally, I banged the espresso filter against the garbage container as loud as I could, left the door wide open for the time it took to boil the milk, then closed the door again.

Allison had come to talk to me about her senior thesis on Proust after I had encouraged her to look me up. She was working with another tutor at Adams House, she said, but was intrigued by our brief conversation outside my office. Someone else had mentioned my name to her. She wished she had known earlier, but it was too late to change tutors, she said. Now, as we both stood in the kitchen waiting for the coffee to brew, she gave no sense of being interested in discussing Proust. She had brought my diary into the kitchen and continued poring over it as we stood silently by the gas range. For someone reading someone else's diary without asking permission to do so, she didn't seem in the slightest bit ill at ease. What did *ersatz* mean? she asked. I told her. Who was K. then? I explained, without giving away the seamy underside. What about Walden Pond? Skip that part, I said. "So tell me about N. You wrote about her less than three weeks ago," she said.

This was not placing penny bets. She was putting weightier, Monte Carlo chips on the table.

"You really want to know about N.?"

"I asked, didn't I?"

"Why do you want to know?"

She hesitated.

"Maybe I'm trying to figure you out."

I admired her. I've always like such disarming candor in a woman. Or was this something you said to someone you'd just met, no hidden agenda, nothing implied—not a penny chip at all?

"Yes, but why?" I asked.

Maybe I was ducking, or maybe it was my turn to place a bigger bet than I was used to. Maybe I wanted to make certain that heavier bets were not untimely.

"You know why," she said, "you know exactly why." And,

changing the subject right away, she added, "I want you to read me this paragraph here so that I can hear it in your voice."

"My voice?"

"Just read."

It was a description of how Niloufar and I had kept staring at each other at Café Algiers one afternoon and, without saying anything, without warning, she'd started to shed tears as I reached out and held her hand, and with one thing leading to the other, had found myself in tears as well.

I caught my breath. I was too aroused. I knew I couldn't continue this, but I certainly did not want to fold. I read it for her, with sincere feeling, all the while sensing that I was using the arousal with one woman to arouse the other.

"OK, now read me the poem."

"What poem?" I asked, unable to recall having written a poem in my diary. My mind was beginning to draw one huge blank over everything around me right now. I could think of one thing only, and I had to struggle not to touch her.

"This poem, here," she pointed to something I'd transcribed two months before.

I saw what she meant. To please her without disabusing her, I began reading with expression:

Dresser.
Turntable.
Television.

Striped ironing board.
A standing lamp to the left.
A night table to the right.
A tiny reading light clasped to the headboard.
She sleeps naked at night.

But then, sensing my voice wavering and feeling unequal to the task of the cad, I broke down and said:

"I can't concentrate on any of this right now."

She waited a second.

"To be honest, I can't either," she said.

And because she was much younger and because I still wasn't sure whether any of this was appropriate, I drew close to her and asked if I could kiss her.

MY BIGGEST WORRY that afternoon and every other afternoon after that day was that Kalaj might decide to drop by unannounced, which he'd done in the past. Allison was open-minded, but watching a swarthy Che Guevara wearing a mock-guerrilla outfit open the front door and lumber into my apartment while we were making love on the Tabriz would have freaked her out. There was something very wrong in their meeting. She understood "illegal immigrant" and she understood "poor" and "very, very poor." But what she might not understand and, outside of her very distant brushes with Harvard's drug scene, had never rubbed shoulders with was sleaze. Everything about him was wrong, and knowing he was my friend might lead her to assume that he and I shared more in common than she was aware of.

Allison liked to drop by after her classes. We'd have lattes together and sometimes we'd cook dinner. Sometimes we read or studied in separate corners of my living room. Sometimes we listened to music together. And there were times when I would surprise myself at the voluminous number of pages I was capable of reading in her presence. By ten o'clock, which was very early for me, but not for her, we'd go to bed. At school, we made a point of not showing signs that we knew each other other than casually. This was more my decision than hers. She had nothing to hide; I, on the other hand, did not want department chairmen to start talking about my friendship with a student whose senior thesis was more than likely going to end up on my desk and whose name represented more wealth and therefore more "pull" than twenty Heathers put together. She was not invasive, but she brought some items of clothing over, and left them discreetly folded in a closet. She brought an extra bathrobe, and because mine looked ratty, decided to buy me the "His" version of the same bathrobe. The striped made-in-Germany terrycloth bathrobe, I discovered, cost more than my monthly rent. I called Kalaj and told him not to show up these days.

"Why," he asked, "is *la quarante-deux* moving in?"

"No," I said, "someone else."

"But I thought you, Ekaterina, and *la quarante-deux* had

become friends?" I told him not to mention that night to me. "Why not?"

"Because the two women ended up being more interested in each other than in me." I wanted to tell him about Allison and about what was so different about her, but the only word I could come up with was the one I needed to avoid because he'd have resented it the most: she was *respectable*. Everything about her was respectable.

This finally came to a head one early afternoon later that fall when she took me to meet her parents at the Ritz-Carlton for tea, and all I could think of, as we parked her car and walked toward the hotel, was, *Please, God, don't let Kalaj's cab pass by now, don't let him pull over and speak to us, don't let him be anywhere close, because it'd be just like him to turn up as I'm trying to look dapper at the Ritz-Carlton.* I was ashamed of him. Ashamed of myself for being ashamed of him. Ashamed of being a snob. Ashamed of letting others see that what we had in common went far deeper than this surface thing called lousy cash flow. Ashamed that I wasn't allowing myself to own up to how deeply I cared for him and had found it easier to think of us as transient, dirt-poor louts with a penchant for low-life café fellowship.

Tea at the Ritz-Carlton went swimmingly. The father tried to impress me with his knowledge of *The Odyssey*; I told him I had studied with Fitzgerald; he spoke of his years in the Middle East, I dropped all the right names. He listed the spots he loved in Paris; I told him of mine. It was a draw, but it brought us closer.

That evening we had dinner at Maison Robert, a stately French restaurant that suddenly resurrected a world I hadn't stepped into in over a decade. Waiters, wines, luster, affluence. What did one do these days with a Ph.D., he asked? Well, one could always write or teach, I said. Then, sensing he wasn't convinced, I reminded him that my father had become a wealthy businessman in Egypt even though all he'd ever wanted was to write books. Was I amenable to other professions as well—another career, perhaps? he asked, as he looked down, toying with the edge of his knife on the tablecloth. Absolutely, I replied, trying to sound at once earnest and casual and determined to keep an open mind.

Was he going to ask me about his daughter too? The man was too tactful for that. I never brought her up either, and the shrewd lover of *The Odyssey* must have read the message clearly enough. But he wasn't going to let me off so lightly either. So he made subtle prods: about my plans, my future, my hobbies, trying best to steer clear of the stubborn if muzzled word *intentions* bouncing under the table like a leashed dog looking for his bone. I did not come to his rescue. Then came the heavy bream fish in some sort of buttery white sauce, served with Montrachet wine, then the chateaubriands with their sauce and the sautéed potatoes and haricots verts, accompanied by a delicious Pomerol, and at the very, very end, the tarte Tatin with a dollop of crème fraîche for each. Our dinner ended with Calvados.

Kalaj's thundering advice, repeated every time I'd spoken to him about her these last few days, was never far. Marry her.

Become rich. Buy me a fleet of taxis. I'll make you a millionaire. Then, if you have no children and she bores you, dump her.

During dinner, while waiters tiptoed around us, I imagined that one of them was Kalaj, winking at me, whispering, *Do it, just do it. The fleet of taxis. We'll do the math later.* How I longed to see him now and catch his complicit leer as he'd eye the jumbo-sized tarte Tatin they'd brought for us, immediately followed by Calvados. *They like you, otherwise the interview would have stopped over tea at the Ritz-Carlton.*

Father, mother, and daughter saw me to the cab that was to take me back to Cambridge. "When I was your age, my father wouldn't give me a penny for the bus, let alone a taxi," he said, passing me a twenty-dollar bill when his hand shook mine.

I was caught by surprise but genuinely refused the father's money. He insisted. Finally, I relented. I remembered how a rich student had right away accepted a similar offer from me when caught without money at the ticket office of the Harvard Square Theater. Poor people refused because their dignity was already in tatters, the way an underling might refuse a tip, because it screams his poverty. Rich people accepted the money because it was not perceived as a gratuity, or charity, or a reflection on their station in life, but simply as a favor that comes with friendship. A poor person would make a point of returning the money right away. The rich man simply forgot.

I accepted, hoping he would mistake me for the second.

But because I was not, I stopped the taxi two minutes later, got out, and took the underground back to Cambridge.

At Café Algiers that night, I didn't tell Kalaj what I'd done. "In your place I would have taken the money, gotten off the cab, and headed back by train."

I looked at him and smirked.

"That's what you did, isn't it—that's exactly what you did— and you weren't going to tell me!"

I don't think I ever bought a round of XO Cognac at *Maxim's* with more gusto in my life than I did that evening with Kalaj.

The image of Kalaj as a leering waiter and me as a plutocrat had come and gone. Poverty had changed me. I was ashamed of the twenty-dollar bill. I tried to cloak what I'd done with all kinds of excuses and wished to shrug the whole thing off with affected insouciance, but there was no hiding the truth. I'd hustled the man who'd bought me dinner and whose daughter I was sleeping with.

THAT NIGHT I paid dearly for our dinner and our drinks. The pain I'd felt weeks earlier returned, an ache in the kidney area extending all the way to the right of my rib cage. One of the doctors had warned me to stay off fatty foods for a while in case it turned out to be what he feared. Well, last night's meal was anything but lean. They had already run a test a week earlier, but I had never bothered to check the results, since I had never had a relapse. I tossed and turned, thinking of the girl who was probably wondering why I hadn't asked her to drive me back to Cambridge, especially when it was clear that her parents liked me and knew we were sleeping together. I, on the other hand, couldn't wait to run away from the three of them—like a Cinderella whose livery would turn into cabbage and turnips if she didn't rush back to her little hovel.

An hour into the ache I figured I might as well return to the infirmary. As irony would have it, I had no money left to take a cab and was too much in pain this time to walk myself to the Square. I called Kalaj, but once again there was no answer. Linda had no car—so there was no point in waking her. Allison, I didn't dare call. Sexual intimacy was one thing, pain-and-money intimacy, quite another. Frank and Claude, out of the question. I couldn't have felt lonelier or more helpless in my life. So with complete despair, I decided to knock at the kitchen door of Apartment 43. It took them a while, but eventually the boyfriend opened the door, wearing nothing but pale blue boxers. Obviously I had woken him up. "So sorry, I know it's very, very late, but I'm in great pain. Can one of you drive me to the infirmary in the Square?" I was begging for help. I had never in my life felt so denuded of dignity. On second thought, perhaps I should have called an ambulance. But it was now too late for this. "It'll take me a second," he said. I heard him whispering to his girlfriend, explaining, using my name. So they knew me by name. Even doubled over in pain I wondered if she'd ever liked my name or whispered it to herself when she was alone.

The car smelled of their dog. "I hope it's nothing," said the boyfriend, who insisted on dropping me at the door of the

emergency entrance and then helping me out of the car, holding me with one hand under my armpit as I limped to the door.

I was admitted by the same head nurse and the same doctor
as before. As soon as I was stretched out on the gurney, the pain
began to subside. Could it all be psychosomatic? Most people
feel better the moment they step in here, said the genial head
nurse in her British accent. As she sat down and spoke with
me—there were no other in-patients that night—she began
to ask me where I came from . . . I figured it was small talk to
get me to relax. I normally answered the where-from question
by saying France. Then when asked more specific questions I
might add Paris. If the person happened to know French well
and was in a position to detect my accent, I'd instantly switch
and say that I was really from Italy, which would sufficiently
throw them off the scent and prevent them from inquiring
further into my origins. But this time I wanted to open up to
someone without too many detours and went directly to the
source: Egypt, I said.

"Well, you don't say!" she said. She had been trained as a
nurse in Egypt, during World War II.

I asked where.

"In Alexandria."

"That's where I was born!" More coincidentally yet, it was
in an English hospital that my mother was trained as a volun-
teer nurse during the same war.

I missed my mother, I said. Suddenly I wanted to cry. What
was happening to me? Was I going to be very sick? What was

this pain? And as I lay there I remembered Kalaj's own words, *What happens to me now?* What happens to me now? I started to feel the tears roll down both sides of my face.

Without a word, the nurse reached for a tissue and wiped one side of my face, and then the other.

There was something so irreducibly earnest and guileless between us that I was perfectly happy to spend the rest of the night in that area with the head nurse sitting next to me in the dimmed lights of the emergency room. "Maybe I should let you rest a while," she said. But she didn't move. Perhaps all she meant was there was no need to talk.

Toward dawn, they decided to admit me to an upper floor. By then they'd had a chance to look over last week's test results. The head surgeon was going to speak to me. He was an early morning type, so I shouldn't get too comfortable, said my new nurse.

The doctor knocked at my door around seven in the morning, carrying a manila envelope with the X-rays sticking out. He slipped them under the glass panel with the gliding, effortless grace of a man who does this thirty times a day, lit the panel with a cavalier flick of the switch, and after musing a while at what looked like an off-gray paisley design called my inner organs, said that I had gallstones. The Jewish organ par excellence, I jibed. The tall WASP gentleman stared at me with a quizzical look, more amused perhaps by my attempt to be funny than by the joke itself. "I thought Jews were obsessed with another part of the male anatomy."

The man had a sense of humor.

He sat on my bed, crossed his legs, dangling his top leg up and down, while his penny loafer hung from the tip of his toes, exposing his entire sock.

"Anyone else in the family with gallstones?"

"All of them."

"On both sides?"

"All four of my grandparents."

What had I had for dinner last night?

I said, Maison Robert, as though that offered explanation enough.

A long silence elapsed between us.

"Is this going where I think it is?" I finally asked.

He bit his lower lip, looked at me, and said, "What do you mean?"

"Knife?" I asked.

He liked my joke.

"Well, we don't like to say 'knife.' The dictionary is full of friendlier terms—but the long and short of it is probably *yes*."

The operation was not urgent. But I had to watch my diet. No fats, no alcohol, no coffee. Meanwhile, they wanted to run a few more tests, so I should stay in bed and eat the bland food they fed me on the house.

"May I ask a question?" I finally said.

"It won't hurt," he answered. Apparently everyone asked that same question.

"No, that was not my question."

"Yes?"

"How long after the operation can I have sex?"

He smiled.

"You will be very tired afterward." And to send the message home, he let his head slump down to his chest.

I called no one. I wanted to be alone. I was ashamed of being stricken with an old man's ailment. Might as well have the ague or the gout. By around two that afternoon, I heard a timid knock at the door. It was Allison. How on earth had she found me here? My phone wasn't answering. She'd been ringing all morning. Rather than suppose I never wanted to see her, or had spent the night with someone else, she'd assumed the worst and checked with the hospital. What amazing confidence in herself, in people, in the power of truth and candor. In her place, the first thing I would have imagined was that I had disappeared—or, better yet, absconded with her father's twenty-dollar bill. If only all humans were like her and thought her way, there wouldn't be an oblique ripple left on earth.

She sat next to my bed and we spoke. She held my hand. By the way, she had some bad news. What? Chlamydia.

"Not—" I started.

"No, from me," she said.

"Does that mean I have it too, now?"

"Yes." The good news is that her parents loved me. They thought I was funny. They loved the way I'd complained there were no fish knives at Maison Robert. It was typical of them to have noticed this.

Later that afternoon, one or two students straggled into my room, then a few teaching fellows, colleagues. Professor Lloyd-Greville dropped in to say hello. He too, apparently, had heard. Then my entire sophomore tutorial. There were about sixteen of us in the room, the hospital staff came and complained there was too much noise and that no one was allowed to smoke.

"But I smoke," I protested.

"Well, you can, but no one else can. And, by the way, you shouldn't either."

Mrs. Lloyd-Greville showed up with a tiny pot of verbena from her garden and a box of chocolates. "They're not for you, of course, but for your guests." It was a double-decker box with a transparent parchment sheet placed above the chocolates indicating the intricate ingredients of the equally intricate assortment. The box was being passed around the crowded room when the unthinkable finally occurred. Kalaj walked into the room, bearing three porno magazines. I wanted to disappear under my bed covers. By eight-thirty, long after official visiting hours were over, I heard the loud voice of a woman. It was Zeinab, who had heard the news through the grapevine on Harvard Square. Then, minutes later, Abdul Majib, the old Iraqi kitchen attendant from the Lowell House kitchen, decided to make an appearance as well.

So here I was in bed, trapped and helpless, in a universe where all my clever partitions had totally collapsed.

Kalaj and Allison, my students, the department head, Cherbakoff, who came by on cat's paws, then Zeinab the waitress, my colleagues, everyone, careerists and lowlifes, were thrown together as in a Fellini movie or a clambake on Cape Cod.

I knew that, with the exception of those in the room who'd had to recobble their lives and reinvent themselves to live in the States, very few would understand that no human being is one thing and one thing only, that each one of us has as many facets as there are people we know. Would it upset Allison to discover that the person I was with Zeinab couldn't ever be who I was with her, and that this was my unspoken reason for keeping Kalaj away from her—because I showed him far more facets than the one or two I felt laid-back enough to share with her?

I could tell Allison seemed ill at ease. She sat on a chair in a corner, silent and remote, waiting for everyone to leave, not sure whether she should be my student or my girlfriend. Kalaj, who must have originally assumed I'd be alone, leaned against one of the walls with his camouflage jacket, his beret, his gunner's scowl, and the three porno magazines rolled into the shape of a rain stick picked up on some guerrilla expedition in the Amazonian hinterland. If you didn't know, you'd think he was a foreigner on some Third World scholarship who'd spent all-nighters working in a soup kitchen.

He had already put one of my students in his place by saying that the Marquis de Sade disgusted him. With another he
insisted that all American writers were no better than rock
'n' roll con artists, including those he hadn't read and wasn't
likely to start now, ending his after-hours, sotto voce shoot-
out-with-silencer by reminding everyone in the room, including the nurse who came to remove my tray, that hospitals,
like courthouses—including doctors and lawyers—were put
on this planet to beat down your soul till it was flattened into
toilet paper—and of souls, ladies and gentlemen, we were each
given one only, and it had to be returned, when we were well
and done with it, intact and as good as new for the next person. As Nostradamus says— And he began quoting quatrains.

In the space of five minutes, after an initial period during
which he had intrigued and charmed all those in the room, he
eventually managed to scare everyone away. "Who was that
crackpot?" someone asked weeks later.

EVERYTHING I FEARED since school had started was beginning to happen. From a traveling companion picked up in an
oasis during my lonely summer days in Cambridge, Kalaj had
become a deadweight that was impossible to shake off. After
my release from hospital, there was nowhere to go in Cambridge without running into him. I could not sit with anyone in public without being joined by him or, as was more
often the case, without being invited to join him at his table,
or, worse yet, constantly having to dream up new excuses

to explain why I couldn't talk to him just yet. In the end, I grew tired of dreading to bump into him or of running out of excuses. I was crammed with emergency excuses and white lies the way people with runny noses stuff their pockets with too many handkerchiefs. I hated myself both for being too weak to fend him off and for worrying about it all the time.

I tried to avoid the bars and coffeehouses where I was likely to bump into him. Once, at the Harvest, I was sitting with two colleagues, and there was Kalaj at the bar, drinking his usual *un dollar vingt-deux*. I'll never forget his eyes. He had seen me of course, as I had seen him, but he was allowing a glazed look to settle over his eyes, as though distracted by troubling, faraway thoughts—the Free Masonry, his cab, his long-term projects in the U.S., his father, the green card, his wife. Five minutes later, I heard his explosive, detonating, hysterical laugh in response to one of the bartender's jokes. He was sending me a message. It was impossible to miss. *I don't need you. See, I can do better.* There was something overly histrionic about his laughter that reminded me of the first time we'd met. *You're trying to be like these friends of yours*, he seemed to say, *but I know you'll stiff the tip when no one's looking.*

I'll never forget that vacant look on his face. He wasn't pretending he hadn't seen me. He was pretending he hadn't seen me pretending not to see him. He was letting me off the hook.

A few days later he was waiting for me outside Boylston Hall. He needed two favors. "I'll walk with you," he explained.

His landlady was remodeling the house, and God only

knew when she'd be able to let him have his room back. She was therefore *giving him fair notice.*

It didn't sound very convincing. Had he done something wrong, tried to bring women into his bedroom? I asked. "Me, soil my sheets, when I could dirty a woman's instead? Never."

He wanted me to go with him to help find another bed-and-breakfast. But as we knocked at door after door and were already approaching Porter Square, the old, prim ladies on Everett, Mellen, Wendell, Sacramento, and Garfield Streets took one good look at him and had no vacancies. "Can you put me up for a few days?" he finally asked me. The question had never occurred to me and I was totally unprepared for it. I was surprised by my own answer. Of course I could, I said. All he needed, he said, was a sofa to sleep on, a quick shower in the morning, and he'd be out of my way till nighttime. Maybe he'd arrange to sleep at his current girlfriend's, though he didn't want to push things with her right now. "I promise I won't be in your hair."

I was a good soul, helping a friend in need, opening my place up to someone who'd be on the street otherwise. But as I was telling him that he should make himself at home except in the afternoon and early evenings (Allison), we passed by Sears, Roebuck, which immediately made me think that perhaps it was time to start planning to install a lock on my door in a few weeks.

Midway back from Porter Square, he bought me a warm tuna fish grinder at a Greek sandwich shop. While we were eating, he told me the next news item: because of a minor infraction, they'd revoked his driver's license for a month. With all my contacts, he began—this was his typical phrase— couldn't I help him find a job.

I thought for a while. The only jobs I knew anything about were in education.

"I've taught before."

"I mean university education."

"Teaching is teaching."

I'd see what I could do. Instead of going to my office, I decided to pay my chairman a brief visit.

"But has he ever taught in an American institution?" Lloyd-Greville asked, when I finally brought up Kalaj's predicament.

"He barely speaks English—which is exactly what you've always said we needed in a French teacher."

Professor Lloyd-Greville concurred and asked me to speak about the matter to Professor Cherbakoff.

"And he speaks real, live French, the kind students are likely to speak when they land in France next summer," I explained.

Cherbakoff also concurred.

As it happened, he said, there was a slot open for a part-time French-language instructor. One of the teaching fellows had had to resign owing to a complicated pregnancy that required extended bedrest.

Ten minutes later, I was back at Café Algiers telling Kalaj to go and see Cherbakoff right away.

I could tell he was nervous.

"Kalashnikov meets Cherbakoff," taunted the Algerian, who'd overheard the conversation. Everyone laughed. Cherbakoff, *Cutitoff,* Cherbakoff, *hadenough,* Cherbakoff, *Jerkhimoff.* Parodies came breezing in from the kitchen area as almost everyone in Café Algiers clapped.

An hour or two later, Kalaj walked into the café bearing a large teacher's edition of *Parlons!* with accompanying teacher's manual, exercise book, reader, and lab book.

"Tomorrow at eight o'clock, Lamont 310."

He looked at me more puzzled than ever. What was Lamont? The name of a building, I explained. He had never heard of it. Corner of Quincy Street and Mass Ave. He knew exactly what I meant. I explained to him that there was a periodical room in Lamont. After teaching, he could read all the French newspapers and periodicals he pleased without having to pay a cent. He liked the idea of reading newspapers and periodicals after teaching.

Where was he going to hold his office hours?

He thought about it.

"Here," he said. "This way they'll get a taste of French cafés."

He said that Cherbakoff had mentioned something about an ID card, but Kalaj figured it would take too much time. He'd simply borrow mine when he needed it. It was useless arguing how this would have complicated matters for the two of us. I let him borrow mine. He said he had to prepare for his class tomorrow morning.

Had they suggested how they wanted him to teach French?

"I told them I already knew," he replied.

This was not boding well at all. Suddenly I imagined a small village school outside Tunis where a local teacher, brandishing a long stick, walked around a classroom filled with cowering frock-clad boys. When one of them hesitated with the answer, *whack!*

"You can't yell," I said. "And you can't hit anyone."

He thought for a while.

"How am I going to teach them anything then?"

"You can't yell, you can't strike, you can't even make them feel bad about themselves."

"So, if someone is an absolute idiot, what do I tell him—that he's a prodigy?"

Zeinab, who had overheard the conversation, started laughing at Kalaj when she realized that his teaching at Harvard was not a joke. "How can he teach them anything when he doesn't understand the agreement of the past participle with the direct object?"

"I understand it well enough."

"Prove it."

"It would take too long and I don't have the time."

"Prove it."

"I don't want to."

"Because you don't know."

"What I know is that you'd do anything to go to bed with me—but it won't work."

Near us a couple was just about to leave. They hadn't touched the huge wedge of Brie they had ordered.

The young man stood up and went to pay. The girl was already waiting for him outside the doorway.

Kalaj grabbed the piece of cheese and spread it richly on a slice of baguette, which he then cut neatly in two, one half for me, the other for himself. Zeinab cast an angry look at him.

"They throw away everything in this country. I, I, I, Kalaj, am not ersatz. And I'm not a thief. Food is food, and this one has already been paid for."

"If you wanted food, Kalaj, all you had to do was ask me," said Zeinab, who would have cut off her right hand and given it to him had he just stared at it long enough.

"You won't even tell me how the past participle agrees with the direct object, and now you want to feed me?"

"I told you: I'll do everything for you."

"Back to that again! Just leave me alone. I need to study what I have to teach these ersatz minds."

"Just mind your past participle. I'll explain it if you could only learn to listen," said Zeinab.

"Explain. But be brief."

I left them, went home, and changed into better clothes. I had to be on Chestnut Hill for cocktails at Allison's parents. I had originally thought of asking Kalaj to drive me there, but then remembered he'd had his license revoked. Besides, arriving by cab all the way from Cambridge would send the wrong message. Now, without his license, the question was moot.

I was going to take the train. "Try to find me a job with all those rich contacts of yours," he had said. "I'll be their driver, cook, bodyguard, pimp. Anything."

All I kept thinking for the remainder of the evening was: Now he has complete access to my apartment, has my ID card, and even teaches where I teach. I'd never felt so invaded or taken over before. I hated the feeling. It was as if my double were squeezing me out. Why had I been so weak? And why was I thinking like a tightfisted, skinflint Jew? The Jew who likes his little things in their little place, who wants what people borrow instantly returned, who doesn't open his doors too wide for fear strangers might storm in and never leave, the Jew who doesn't want others to open their heart, fearing he might have to open his, who won't venture in though God knows he's been invited in so many tacit ways. Or had I become an American now: my space, your space, and lots of spaces in between?

I hated myself both for not wanting to let him into my apartment and for surrendering without a struggle—for not refusing to go to the cocktail party at Allison's parents, and for taking the long train ride to get there, for saying I wasn't sure I would go and for begrudging having to go, for not wanting to marry Allison and for letting her think I wanted nothing more, for not wanting to be a student of literature, for not wanting to be in Cambridge, or in the United States, all the while continuing in a rut that felt, and indeed was from the very start, the best that life had to offer.

As I watched my own reflection on the glass panels of the

Green Line car heading out to Newton that evening, I kept asking myself: Was this really me, and were these really my features standing out on this totally alien Boston scenery? Who was I? How many masks could I be wearing at the same time? Who was I when I wasn't looking? Was I simply a being without shape, ready to be molded into what everyone wanted me to be? Or by acquiescing so easily was I simply making up in advance for the treachery I invariably brought to those who trusted the face?

I looked at my face against this strange Boston background and saw a lawyer who overtips the waiter at lunch because he knows he'll be vicious in court that afternoon. I saw a husband who buys his wife expensive jewelry—not after cheating on her, but before finding the person who'll help destroy his marriage. I saw a priest who absolves everyone because he has lost his faith and no longer trusts in his vocation.

That evening, Allison wanted to drive me back home. I let her, though I would have preferred the train. There was a moment at the party when I wished to undo my tie if only to let fresh air into my system, but also to show I had less in common with the guests than with the waiters, who were all wearing open-collar, buttoned-down white dress shirts. Suddenly, I wanted to be alone and watch Kalaj roll a cigarette as he made fun of this entire party with its jumbo gravity hanging from its jumbo chandeliers, the jumbo levity of the frou-froued guests who kissy-kissed and huggy-hugged with their jumbo show of plenitude and ease. *Amerloques*, I could hear him say.

"Take this one," he'd point to a woman in the crowd. "Skin like burlap. Three generations ago she was scrounging turnips out of the dead land. And as for these two," he'd snicker, "they may have come on board a sailboat, but look under, and you'll find the coarseness of a sea dog and the larceny of stevedores."

I wanted to sit by myself in the empty train car and let the hypnotic rhythm of the wheels dull the fire within me. All these wealthy people who simply belonged. Their large cars. Their large mansions. Their startled large eyes when they repeated my name. Their professed love for the Mediterranean which they couldn't, if you gave them ten lifetimes, begin to understand, because what they always liked instead was the cold Atlantic and the limitless Pacific, because Kalaj was right, this was another world, and this was another tongue, and these people were a different order of beings, just as their women were women plus something, or maybe minus something that made them different from the women we'd known and been raised by and been taught to worship, because, among so many things, they were everything that a man was not and could never be. Kalaj would understand. And yet now, strangely enough, I didn't want to have anything to do with him either, because I was ashamed of him, because I was tired of him, because however much I was closer to him than to any of these people at this party, the distance between him and me was big enough to remind me, even when I missed him, that estrangement was carved into me with acid and barbed wire. I was no closer to him than I was to them.

Allison and I sat in the car outside my building. "Tell me what's wrong?" she finally asked.

"Nothing," I replied.

"I know something is wrong, very wrong, why won't you tell me?" I hoped she wasn't going to cry or make me feel sorry for her. I didn't want to hate myself more than I already did.

I saw my building, and I saw my own reflection on the window of her car, and I thought of the train I'd have taken from Chestnut Hill and would probably still be on before changing at Park Square. Yes, there was plenty wrong, everything was wrong, but how could I begin to tell her when I didn't know myself? What truth would I speak, when I didn't even know the truth? "Is it that you don't love me—or not enough—or not at all?" How to explain that I did love her, that of all the women I'd known, she was the one I would want to live with, and be loved by, and have children with. "I don't want to give you up," she finally said.

All I said in reply was "Sometimes I need to be alone." I didn't know I was going to say this until it had come out of my mouth.

"I thought we were happy."

"We are."

"Then what is it?"

I didn't know. Like an actor who wants to sit alone in his booth after all the lights are out and everyone's gone home, I wanted to take my time removing the makeup, the wig, the false teeth, the skin glow, the eyelashes, take time to recover myself and see the face, not the mask, not the mask again, always the mask again. I wanted to talk to myself in French, in my own French accent, speak as those who brought me into this world had taught me to speak. I was tired of English, tired of anything that didn't smack of sea salt in the summertime and of the brine of foods prepared in our kitchens on those endless summer afternoons when the cicadas rattled like mad and time slackened and the sea beckoned, listless and sleek, through the windows of our bedrooms when we didn't wish to nap but found ourselves lulled by the sound of the waves all the same. I was even tired of my make-believe Paris, tired of the screens I put up, tired of thinking I wore a mask, tired of longing for my face, tired of thinking it wasn't the mask I was quarreling with, but the face—tired of fearing there'd never even been, might not ever be a face. Tired of fearing I was incapable of loving anyone or anything.

"I'm going to drive back home now. I'll call you tomorrow. If you can't tell me the truth, then I'll know, and I swear I'll never bother you again."

She did as she promised. She called me once the next day. And then never again.

To Kalaj, when I told him what Allison had said, hers was all corporate ersatz-speak. But it was, and I knew it even then, the most honorable and most tactful behavior I'd witnessed in any woman in my life. She'd been candid and bold from start to finish. She knew what she wanted. I didn't even know how to want, let alone what I wanted. I admired her.

As we said good night that evening, I caught myself already wishing she'd never call me the next day. I didn't want to have the one-on-one postmortem I knew awaited us tomorrow. If to avoid that call I'd have to lose her to a fatal car accident on her way back to her parents' house that night, so be it. I was ashamed of myself. But shame was just a metaphor, a word, nothing. In the large exchange house of the soul, it was another bankrupt word that didn't help me get any closer to what I was feeling.

On my way to the fourth floor that night, my heart almost sank: I remembered that Kalaj would be upstairs. I caught myself making the same wish for him as well. If only they'd deport him tonight so that I wouldn't have to explain why I wanted him out of my life. And if he and Allison were to crash into each other tonight, so much the better.

Kalaj was not upstairs. I felt for him as I pictured him cramming for his first day of teaching. I felt for Allison too, weeping, or perhaps not, as she drove all the way back to Newton tonight. And for her parents, rich and self-satisfied as they were, I felt for them too; they worried over their daughter's crush on a man who kept ducking and slipping and leading people on like a fish who nips but never bites.

7

I WAS NOT READY FOR THE COLD WEATHER OF LATE fall in Cambridge. Usually I welcomed that time of year, with its early twilight and the look of bare trees against the sky and the lull that hovered over Cambridge past seven in the evening. But the late summer had been so intense that I was reluctant to see it go. Kalaj, however, fell in love with the colder weather. He put on a heavier jacket, wore a gray scarf around his neck, and would frequently walk with his hands dug deep in his coat pockets. This would be his first winter in Cambridge, and the prospect thrilled him.

In the darkening days before Thanksgiving, Kalaj would come over to consult my dictionaries and correct sheets of homework, staying up till two in the morning. It made him feel as though he too were a graduate student and that we were roommates living it out in some sort of American Bohemia. He took whatever extra jobs he could find to tide him over. Money was always scarce. But somehow we always managed, and there were days when, by one miracle or another, we could always arrange to head out to the North End and bring back food to organize a few intimate dinners with friends. When we felt we had more women than men and needed an extra male, we'd always say, by way of a joke, why not invite Count? Someone always ended up making a joke about Count Dracula and his two missing teeth.

Late that fall a group of us got together one Sunday evening to see a double feature at the Harvard Epworth Church. We paid a dollar each and saw an old film called *Desire*. It left us indifferent. Then we went to Casablanca, had a glass of wine each, then went home our separate ways. If Kalaj wasn't dating someone, he'd walk back home with me. Once home he knew I'd have to read, so he made no noise whatsoever.

We each had our students. On occasion we'd compare notes. He liked that. I helped him compose his first grammar test. I then taught him how to print and collate his exams. Then I helped him determine an A from a B– from a C+. This was an altogether new world to him, and part of him, you could tell, was starstruck and awed, like an immigrant who, on board a steamship at the break of dawn, suddenly spots the first glimmers of Manhattan's skyline. Kalaj liked the new rhythm his life had taken.

A week or so before Thanksgiving, one of the greatest shocks in his life occurred. A student had submitted Kalaj's name to the administration. The letter arrived in care of my address. He was being invited to a teacher-student dinner at one of the river houses. What was that? Had a student lodged a complaint against him? No, it was an honor, I explained. A student invites a teacher and has a formal dinner with him, one-on-one. He thought about it for a long time. "Can I go dressed like this?" he asked. "No, you need a jacket and a tie." He listened, all the while rolling a cigarette, staring at the tobacco without saying a word. "*Oké, oké.*" I felt for him. "I'll lend you any tie you want, but my jackets won't fit you."

On the evening of the dinner, he knocked at my door wearing a double-breasted gray flannel suit with a light blue shirt and a dark blue tie. I recognized the Charvet tie. He saw me admiring it. "Courtesy Goodwill," he said. But the suit was French. As was the shirt. Either he already owned the suit, the shirt, the black shoes, or he'd gone out and bought them in Boston for the occasion. Che Guevara wearing a bespoke suit. Kalaj had shaved off his mustache, combed his hair with a touch of brilliantine and looked at least seven years younger. He made me think of someone who was going to the opera for the first time. "I'll call you when it's all over. Maybe you'll meet me for a drink at *Maxim's*. We'll find new women."

I watched him leave.

The munificent dinner sold him on the wonders of America. He never ate pork, but the sight of the juicy roasted ham with pineapple slices and cloves, coupled with the most over-sized shrimps he'd ever seen elsewhere in his life, were sim-

ply too much for him to resist. And the best part of it was
that every time he thought it was time for dessert, something
would always remind him that this was only the beginning.
He ate things he had never seen alive and couldn't recognize
if you whispered their name to him, but they tasted of heaven,
and there was so much of it that part of him kept looking for
a paper bag in which to put extras either for me, or for his
friends at Café Algiers, or to remember the evening by. The
American paradise was an inexhaustible PX of all that was
ever jumbo and ersatz on earth. He loved it. "When we have a
party we must cook roasted ham with pineapples."

Then he mused a little while.

"I must tell you, all evening long I was thinking of one
thing and one thing only."

"What?"

"You must marry Allison."

"Why?"

"If you won't do it for you, do it for your children, do it for
those you love, and do it for me too, because this country is
ersatz-fantastic."

AS SOON AS he was hooked, he became weak. Until then,
he had flaunted his hatred of America because it dignified
his pariah status. He could survey the New World from a
quarantined balcony, but he couldn't get near, much less
touch it, so he shouted curses at it. But being invited in,
if only to take a tiny peek for an evening, made an instant

convert of him. In his heart of hearts, I am sure, he couldn't wait to say the Pledge of Allegiance. I asked him what did it—the opulence, the abundance, the sheer self-satisfaction of the rich? "Actually," he said, "it was the ham. And maybe the fact that their red wines put to shame our measly *un dollar vingt-deux.*"

He began to like his students and to have lunch at some of the houses that were willing to offer him a free meal if he sat with students and chatted in French with them. He discovered the wonders of Harvard's French Tables where students gathered for dinner in smaller dining rooms where only French was spoken and for which he was asked to purchase the wines and cheeses every week. With students, he never spoke about politics or women. Instead he spoke about computer syntax. They all listened with rapt faces that reminded me of how his lawyer had gawked at him on hearing him list all the heavyweight champions. But after the famous dinner party, after his first and only football game, after all those eager students who had never known a man like him before and who'd timidly step into Café Algiers to meet him during his office hours and sip a Turkish coffee instead of conjugate verbs, his resistance began to flag. Even when he was allowed to drive his cab again, he continued to wake up earlier than usual to teach his eight o'clock class. Sometimes he worried. "One Friday night one of my students will leave an after-hours club, hail a cab, and it will be mine. What do I tell them then?"

"You tell them the truth."

"Do *you* tell them the truth?" he asked. I was going to say that I seldom did. Instead, I suggested he dodge the subject altogether and say that there is little he loved more than listening to jazz *en sourdine* on Storrow Drive.

Harvard sucked him in during the fall semester. His crowning moment came when he was invited to two Thanksgiving dinners, one in Connecticut, the other in Boston. Same suit, same tie, same shoes, he joked. He opted for the Boston dinner. For the lady of the house he had purchased roses that cost him close to half a day's worth of fares. "No speeches, no screeds, no jumbo this, ersatz that," I told him. Zeinab, who was present during my short exhortation, added, "And no talking about asses and pussies, Back Bay is not Café Algiers." America had embraced him. He embraced it. It was a fairy tale.

Being the superstitious Middle Easterner that he was, he kept waiting for the other shoe to fall. What he wasn't prepared for was how brutal American doors can be when they suddenly shut you out. By early December, just when he was preparing to savor his first Christmas in America with some of his students who weren't going to be traveling back home, he received a letter from Professor Lloyd-Greville sent in care of my home address, *thanking him dearly for stepping in when they needed his help . . . Too many adjunct teachers at this time . . . Wishing him the best for his career.*

Kalaj was not surprised. "For the past few days every time I crossed Lloyd-Greville in the corridors, he looked away."

He knew that look. "It's the look on cab passengers who, even before opening their wallet, have already decided not to tip. The look of people who have already signed your death warrant and can't look you in the face. The look of a wife who kisses you as you head out to work at seven in the morning but has already scheduled the movers for ten."

He'd seen that look in women many times. The look of treason, not after it happens but while it's still incubating. "I don't make these things up," he said, in case I wanted to warn him against paranoia. I suspect he was also referring to that moment at the Harvest when I tried to avoid speaking to him because I was with friends. But Lloyd-Greville's letter made him more desperate. I had to write to Lloyd-Greville and explain that Kalaj was very important to his students, that the sudden departure of a teacher would demoralize the entire class, that in good conscience he, Kalaj, could never allow this to happen.

I tried to explain that such letters never work and very often backfire, turning you into more of a pariah, a pest, especially if your boss must continue to see you until next January. But he wouldn't hear of it. "It's a matter of my dignity," he finally explained.

Instead of the long letter he wished me to write, I wrote a short acknowledgment, *thanking Lloyd-Greville for his letter . . . It disappointed him no end that adjuncts were no longer needed . . . It had been a rewarding experience . . . He would treasure it for life.* Etc.

He thought I was yielding too easily—"It's because you don't want to get your hands dirty," he said.

It had nothing to do with my hands. What he wanted never worked—not here, not in France, not in Tunisia, not anywhere.

He accused me of being a coward, an apologist, *un réac*, a reactionary.

If I thought it would help to write the three pages that I know no one will read, I would write the letter. But it will do nothing. Protests are pointless, reasoning is pointless, guerrilla tactics serve no purpose, especially when you've lost.

"So what do we do then? Surrender?"

"You're starting to sound like the Che Guevara from Porter Square. There is nothing you can do."

He did not take it well.

"I must resign effective immediately."

"You will do no such thing. You will teach till the end of your term, and when you look back on it, you'll have nothing to reproach yourself with."

He listened. "I won't be able to hold myself back."

I wanted to tell him that Harvard was no Italian Count. No threats, no broken teeth, not even as a joke!

And then it hit me: he couldn't face his employer, he couldn't face his students, he wouldn't even know how to face the people at Café Algiers who had been watching him sit next to one or two students and go over the agreement of the past conditional with the pluperfect in counterfactual clauses, and never once raise his voice, always positive and upbeat, and in the end always throwing in a *cinquante-quatre* to make them feel better about themselves.

He wanted to hide. He didn't even have it in him to mention the matter to Léonie, who, even after they were finished, still came around to Café Algiers to have a *cinquante-quatre* with him. "Do you still pummel each other?" I asked, trying to change the subject.

"No, we stopped that nonsense long ago." Then after thinking: "Can I stay at your place for one more night?"

Of course he could.

When it got very cold and I had no more blankets, I explained to him that there were people in America who slept under electric blankets.

"What do you mean?"

I explained. He'd never heard of such a thing. He was horrified. "No wonder it's a nation of vibrators and electric chairs."

The next morning I made coffee and eggs for the two of us. I wanted to make sure he was on a full stomach. Then he went to teach.

It was only later in the day that I learned what had happened. He'd gone to class, distributed the homework he had meticulously corrected the night before, told everyone in class what the department had done to him, and right then and there walked out of the classroom, not before dropping his copy of *Parlons!* and his other textbooks along with the teacher's manual into the garbage bin. He knew he'd be for-

feiting his monthly paycheck but it gave him no end of satis-
faction. "I have three things: my cab, my *zeb*, and my dignity.
Without one, the other two are worthless." On his way out of
the building, he happened to cross none other than Professor Lloyd-Greville, who was walking with visiting scholars,
and, miming the gesture with his hand, told Lloyd-Greville
to beat off. Kalaj had socked it to him, and in front of everyone. Lloyd-Greville retaliated by saying he would report him
to the dean of the faculty. "The who?"

We laughed about it. He wanted to cook dinner for the two
of us. Then, as if it came as an afterthought, "I think I'll sleep
here tonight also," he said.

I could see this was going to become a pattern. Without
knowing it, I caught myself wondering how long it had taken
poor Lloyd-Greville to write his letter to Kalaj. When was I
going to break the news to Kalaj and prove to him yet again in
his life that the world was made of two-faced people? I thought
of his wife and of Léonie, and of his first wife in France, and
of the U.S. government—everyone had had to battle with the
same thing, how to tell poor Kalaj that he wasn't loved, wasn't
wanted.

The matter reached a point when Lloyd-Greville, who
had always been a friendly mentor to me, particularly after
our Chaucer interlude, began to shun me in the corridors.
It was not Kalaj who had overstepped the line now; it was I.
He greeted me hastily, obviously feeling very angry but also

somewhat guilty of the bad thoughts he'd been nursing about me. Eventually, I figured I had to repair the damage before I too was cast out as a pariah.

"I had no idea what Kalaj was capable of," I told Lloyd-Greville when I stepped into his office. I'd thought him an overeducated man from the colonies who had run adrift and needed to be gently nudged back into the world of the academy. But I had very recently discovered from his wife that he had a very, very serious problem.

"What problem is that?" asked Lloyd-Greville, clearly impatient with my visit and not looking me in the eye as he shuffled a few papers in an effort to seem busy tidying up his desk. I looked at him and lowered my voice.

"Drugs."

A rooster should have crowed at this very instant.

Lloyd-Greville said he would report him to the police.

"No, he's already in a program now." I said. "But these things take a very long time. And his wife says he's doing much better than when he first started."

"I never knew he was married."

"Yes, they have a lovely little boy too."

The cock would have crowed a second time, a third, and a fourth. It helped buttress the impression that I too, like everyone else, including his wife, had been taken in, but that deep down he was a good family man with good values and well on his way to recovery, slow and treacherous as such recoveries always were—unfortunately.

"Poor fellow."

"Poor fellow indeed."

Then upon reflection.

"He made fun of me to the students."

And well he should have, I wanted to say.

Lloyd-Greville added: "Even though he is married I have a suspicion he was crossing certain lines, if you know what I mean."

You don't say!

I tried to drop my jaw and put on a startled, disbelieving face.

To mend fences, I offered to teach Kalaj's course until the department could find a replacement before the beginning of spring semester. And if a replacement wasn't available, I'd be happy to teach his course the coming spring. "I've heard rumors his grammar wasn't what I thought it was," I said, hoping to seem a judicious and impartial observer who was not about to let friendship stand in the way of my loyalty to my department.

Fifth and final crow of the rooster.

"You'd be helping us tremendously," said Lloyd-Greville.

"Still, a sad story."

"Yes, very sad."

He asked how I was coming along with my preparation for my forthcoming comprehensives. "Well." I told him I'd finished reading a seventeenth-century author called Daniel Dyke.

Lloyd-Greville winced, then confided he wasn't sure he'd ever heard of a Daniel Dyke.

"A minor influence on La Rochefoucauld," I said, as though it were the most obvious truth in the world. That kept him quiet.

To Kalaj I lied no less than I'd lied to Lloyd-Greville. I told him I had tried my very best to explain to the administration how eager he was to continue and how much his students liked him, but there was a quota of graduate students who had to teach, and the preference always went to those who were studying at Harvard—nothing personal.

"But who will teach my course?" he asked.

I had hoped he'd never ask.

"Everyone refused to teach so early in the morning, so I was obliged to say that I would—" This was my evasive spin on the fact that, without intending to, I'd just given my cash flow a thirty-three percent boost.

A FEW EVENINGS later I invited him to an all-you-can-eat place around Porter Square. Ever since he received the letter from the department, I made a point of not being seen with him around Harvard Square. We ate a huge meal and then walked back to my home. To my dismay, I saw him come up the stairs with me. Things with his last girlfriend were obviously not going well at all. That too had cast down his spirits. I pretended that things with Allison had resumed and that we needed the apartment. "I promise I won't make any noise, I'll come very late, take a shower at dawn, and be out." I didn't have the heart to refuse him. But I asked him not to keep his things in my home. Allison didn't like this, Allison gets nervous when, Allison would much rather—I kept blaming Allison for everything. "And who does she think she is, your Allison, anyway? Your fiancée or the woman you *neek* every day?"

What saved me were rumors of two robberies on our street, rumors I built up to justify finally putting a lock on my door—exactly what I'd planned to do on the very day I told him he was welcome to stay in my apartment. We'd passed by Sears, Roebuck and I was already pricing locks. Kalaj had enough tact not to push the matter, though I am sure it didn't go down well with him. He never told me where he slept when he didn't sleep on my couch. I never asked. I stopped going to Café Algiers or to any of the bars around Harvard Square.

We saw each other a few weeks later. It was his idea. Same all-you-can-eat place off Porter Square. Allison was busy visiting her parents, I said. We stayed out late. Then he dropped me at my door, and I watched him drive his Checker cab toward the river and disappear. Another night with his music *en sourdine*, I thought. I felt like a shit.

Weeks went by without more than a couple of phone calls. Things were cooling off between us, and perhaps it was better this way, I thought. I was working very hard, knowing that I had slightly more than a month before the dreaded date. There were a few parties to go to. At their early winter get-together,

Mrs. Lloyd-Greville took me to "our intimate little corner" at their house where we bandied mock-flirtatious quips. Mrs. Cherbakoff continued to ask about my parents' health, both to find out if they were still alive and if I planned to pass my exams so that they could continue breathing a while longer. And there were the usual pre-Christmas student parties, to which normal protocol required you bring either a bottle of red or a wedge of Brie.

After the third pre-holiday party, I woke up at night with another attack of gallstones. There had been no warning whatsoever, but this was far worse than the previous two. I could hardly stand up, felt nauseous, and when I finally touched my forehead, knew I had a fever. I dialed Kalaj's most recent phone number, but the woman who picked up the phone hadn't seen him in quite a while and said she hoped he'd drop dead.

"I am his friend," I said.

"And so was I, whoop-dee-doo! Drop dead too."

"I need to be taken to the emergency room," I said.

She came to pick me up fifteen minutes later and drove me to the same infirmary. Brunette, curly hair, made and sold her own jewelry, parents lived on the Upper East Side, and, yes, twice a week, when I asked if she was seeing a shrink. I never saw her again.

After walking into the emergency room, I found the familiar gurney, the placid English nurse, the same young doctor who'd been called in for me and who still showed signs of wetness from his 4:00 a.m. shower. Two days later I was operated on and had my gallbladder removed. At the infirmary, as had become routine by then, my room was continuously mobbed. Students and professors dropped in, including Lloyd-Greville, husband and wife, and Cherbakoff, husband and wife. Frank and Nora came together and left together, as did Niloufar, who came, as one does at a funeral, with one flower ready to be tossed at the tombstone of the deceased. Unannounced, even Young Hemingway stopped by. Six months later, in fact, we became good friends. But Kalaj never came, though he must have known, since Zeinab came to see me every day, sometimes twice. I kept fearing he might show up, all the while another part of me wished that he would and that he'd be the last to leave so that we might crack jokes at the expense of all those who had come with kindness in their nectaro-syrupy hearts. I would have loved nothing more than to see him tell Lloyd-Greville's wife, as I'd heard him tell a woman who complained he never helped her achieve orgasm, that she should treasure the memory of her last orgasm, since it probably predated the French Revolution. But having him stand elbow to elbow with my examiner would have been madness, and the last thing Kalaj may have wanted was to run into his old students. Actually, I didn't want him to run into anyone I knew. I wanted my partitions back up.

Allison had heard about my operation but did not come. Instead she sent me a lavish bouquet of flowers. "I don't need to say it—my feelings haven't changed. Please get well. A."

I wanted to call her on the spot and ask her to come see me

right now, even if it was past visiting hours. I wanted her to stay up with me all night and hold my hand over the blanket until, with morphine, the pain subsided and I fell asleep. She'd do anything for me, as I knew I would for her. But I didn't trust myself, didn't trust my love, didn't trust my own promises, much less those who trusted them. Just the memory of how she'd barged into my life and lain down on my carpet and read through my diary without paying me any heed could stir up something like love for her. But it was not love, just lovelike. Something in me had withered; soon it would wither in her too. Right now I remained a mystery to her; but this mystery was precisely what stood between us. She was drawn to the foreign inflection in everything I did, thought, and said. Soon she'd spot the bruise behind the inflection. I blamed her for not seeing the bruise so I wouldn't be blamed for hiding it from her.

THE FIRST PLACE I went when they let me out ten days later was Café Algiers. No one had seen Kalaj in days, I was told. Nor was he anywhere to be seen at the Harvest, or at Casablanca, or downstairs at Césarion's. When I asked if they had his number, the only number they gave me was my own. I decided to go home. But home, when I got there, was too stultifying; it reminded me of the loneliness I had managed to put behind me ever since meeting Kalaj and that I was convinced was a thing of the past now. There was no one to call. I missed Allison. I missed Ekaterina. Missed Niloufar. Even

Linda would have been welcome. Everything felt soulless. By nighttime I began to miss the hasty patter of footsteps of the night nurses. I went back to Café Algiers, a ten-minute walk. Kalaj saw me before I so much as started to look for him. Actually, he was yelling at me. "Are you out of your mind, are you crazy?" He seemed in a panic. "You should be in bed." Zeinab, who was nursing a drink between Kalaj and a young Moroccan cabdriver I'd seen only once before, took one look at me and said I should sit down right away. "You're all white. You're going to faint." They brought me a glass of soda water which Kalaj forced me to drink, all the while sprinkling my face with drops from a piece of melting ice. For a moment I felt like a wounded Victor Laszlo stumbling into Rick's Café Américain in *Casablanca* and being bandaged by staunch and loyal partisans.

I had not seen Kalaj in weeks. He seemed changed.

"Are you all right?" he asked.

"I am all right. And you?"

"Could be better."

Typical strains of veiled sorrow fringing self-pity.

"They took my license away and will never renew it. The FBI. I had to sell the car."

"We're going to have to see your lawyer."

"You know as well as I do that he is a crook. He'll end up costing more than the car."

"But you can't just let them take your car away without trying to do something about it."

Léonie's boss had a lawyer friend who might be asked to help. Except that Léonie felt that her ex-lover hadn't forgiven Kalaj, and might be happier having him totally out of the way.

"And the Freemasons?" I asked.

"The Freemasons, well, we'll see about the Freemasons."

Silence.

"And if these don't work, well, all of you in this bar right now—and that includes you too, Zeinab—will say that the last Checker cab in Boston was driven by a pure Berber who was proud of his skin and proud of his friends."

Kalaj was in top form.

"If I had a car I'd drive you home right this instant."

"I'll take him if he wants," said the young Moroccan cabdriver.

"How many times do I have to teach you," said Kalaj, reprimanding the cabdriver who was more my age than Kalaj's. "Never say 'if he wants' with this kind of honeyed, ersatz tone in your voice. Instead, say, 'I'm taking you home. Let's go.' "

"Well," said the shy Moroccan, "should we go?"

Everyone laughed.

"They said I could drink if I wanted," I insisted.

"They said you should go home," said Kalaj, as patronizing as ever.

I knew that he cared for me. But I could also tell that he was holding a grudge and had finally seen through all of my wiles. A chill seemed lodged between us, and although I'd long wished for it, I hated seeing how easily it had settled, as though reclaiming what had all along been its rightful place.

It was Zeinab who spoke about it as soon as Kalaj said he needed to go to the bathroom.

He was going to be deported, she said. Even the Freemasons, to say nothing of the Legal Aid Society, were unable to stop it. His impending divorce hurt his chances a lot. Actually, it wasn't a divorce. The marriage had been annulled.

"We're still going to have to find a way," I said, feeling that simply resolving to do something was already a way of doing something.

"I don't think there's anything he can do at this point."

"What if he decides to stay as an illegal and disappears, say, in Oregon or Wyoming?"

"I don't think it will work. He doesn't want to be illegal."

"What will he do then?"

"Probably go back. He can't go back to France. So, you see, for him it's back to Tunisia."

But that's like saying that the past seventeen years of his life—half his life—never happened, I thought. To go back to his parents' home, to go back to the old bedroom where he'd slept and might still have to sleep with his brothers as he'd done as a child, to go back to a place where he dreamed of a France he had not yet seen only to realize that he'd not only already seen France, but that he'd lived and gotten married there and might never be allowed to set foot again there—"It would drive him crazy," I said, suddenly thinking of myself hurled back to Alexandria after forswearing it forever. "It would be like being born again into a life one couldn't wait to escape."

"Not a second birth," said the Moroccan. "More like a second death."

Kalaj had lived with "second deaths" all his life both before and after France. He was not the type to say that experience is all to the good, that nothing is wasted in life, that everyone we meet and everywhere we go, down to the most squalid, insignificant job we hold, plays a tiny role in making us who we become. This was ersatz palaver, and Kalaj was too brutal with himself to think this way. There were no second chances in his book of life; you simply dipped into yourself and pawned the little that was left from earlier deaths. For him there were bad turns, and there were cruel tricks, and terrible mistakes, and from these there was no coming back, no expiation, no recovery, no turning over a new leaf. To live with yourself you had to cut off the hand that offended, cut, slice, peel, scrape, and tear away at yourself till all you were left with were your stripped-down bones. Your bones gave you away; you could not hide your bones, nor could you avoid staring at them. All you wanted was for others to be stripped down like you—lean, intemperate, and skeletal—you didn't need to confide, and they wouldn't need to confide, because both of you would know, just know, as a parent knows, as a sibling knows, as a lover, a real lover, knows that you were down to your last straw. Meanwhile, his unforgiving private God no longer manned a tablet or a staff. His weapon of choice was rage and a Kalashnikov.

He thought I was a fellow legionnaire of the bone who'd dropped by at the same watering hole with the same empty gourd and the same thirst for more than just plain water. I had disappointed him. He thought that, like him, I might be all human, raw passion. It took someone like him to remind me that, for all my impatience with life in New England and all my yearning for the Mediterranean, I had already moved to the other side.

I thought of him wearing a suit on the evening when his student had invited him to dinner. He'd been tempted by the Satan of ersatz that night, and Kalaj would have yielded. As I had yielded. As everyone does.

When Kalaj returned, he said he would join us in the car. It would give us a few extra minutes together.

It was the first time I'd been in his car with him when he wasn't driving. Without knowing it, I was making mental notes: the cigarette-rolling trick while driving, the yelling at old Boston as he cut his way through its narrow alleys with bristling rage and scorn in his voice because the streets here were simply stupid and ersatz, the occasional whistle when someone deserved a compliment and he didn't know enough English other than to just whistle. In the car he reminded me of my father after everything he owned including his car was nationalized by the Egyptian government and he was forced to ride in other people's cars, looking awkward and uneasy when he didn't have a steering wheel before him. Kalaj sprawled himself in the back of his own cab, giving directions and shortcuts on our way to Concord Avenue.

When we reached my building, the Moroccan double-parked the old car while Kalaj sprang to help me out of the car. Did I need help going up the stairs?

No. I could manage. But in typical Arab fashion, he did not step back into the car until I disappeared up the stairs to the landing on the first floor. Then I heard the car leave.

TWO DAYS AFTER I'd nearly fainted at Café Algiers, I met the woman from Apartment 43 on the stairwell. She was carrying groceries, I was carrying a light plastic bag from the Coop, so I offered to carry one of her packages upstairs. "Not throwing any more dinner parties?" she asked, that glint of irony always in her eyes.

"No, not recently." Then I realized I'd never invited her and her boyfriend to our dinner parties when Kalaj used to cook. But I didn't want to pretend I was planning a dinner party anytime soon. I was moving to Lowell House, I said. She looked crushed.

"Why?"

"Free lodging, closer to the Square and the libraries, better deal all around."

"But no privacy," she said.

"No, no privacy, that is true."

Were we speaking in double entendres? When she opened

her door, she let me in, and I walked into her apartment, and then into her kitchen, where I deposited one of her bags on the counter. Like Linda's, her apartment also was mine in reverse. The idea intrigued me, everything about her intrigued me. We talked about apartments; she'd always wondered about my place. Did she want to take a look? I had just bought a recording of Brahms' Clarinet Quintet. A gift from me to me, I explained. Birthday? No, just came home from an operation two days ago. Gallbladder, I said.

"Ouch!" She had completely forgotten about the night when her boyfriend had driven me to the infirmary. "Are you going to be OK?"

"I think so," I said. She needed to put some of her food away first, then said she'd drop by.

"Would you care for a latte? I was going to make one for myself on a Neapolitan coffeemaker."

She had never heard of Neapolitan coffeemakers.

"You'll see," I said.

"But are you allowed to drink coffee?" she asked.

"I can have booze, ergo coffee is good."

"OK," she said.

I did not leave through the front door but found something thrilling in using the service entrance and then opening my door and walking right into my kitchen, as though we had discovered an undisclosed conduit between us that had always been in place though we'd both chosen to overlook it. I liked the idea of a back door to a back door, of secret passages and hidden trapdoors for quick exits and easy access while her boyfriend was, say, in the shower or about to come in through the front door. I liked coming home to myself through someone else's home.

"I always leave my door unlocked," I said.

She walked in when the coffee was already brewing, loved the scent, she said, as she closed first her door, then mine. "I always like it when you make coffee."

"I always like it when you cook bacon in the morning."

Perhaps it was our way of saying we had been keeping secret tabs on each other and that we hoped neither suspected we did until that time when we'd both feel a special thrill in finally admitting it to each other. "We never invited you," she finally said, something like apology and regret underscoring her words.

"And I never invited you," meaning we were even, no harm done, no offense taken. "It's just that you guys keep to yourselves a lot, and I didn't want to be the pushy-neighbor type."

She thought about it. "You're really wrong about us," she said.

When the water boiled, I showed her how to turn the coffeemaker upside down. I dragged out the whole process a bit, if only to show her something she'd never seen before. "The coffee comes out milder though still quite strong," I said.

Then we listened to the Brahms. We drank lattes. "Brahms is so autumnal."

"Yes," she said, "Brahms is so autumnal."

It was the sound of the clarinet, almost keening with melancholy while trying to seem serene, that made the music so suitable for the two of us on this late, late fall afternoon.

And all along I was thinking: Would it be crossing a line to kiss her now?

And something told me that it would be.

And I didn't have it in me to argue.

My dynamo had run cold. Kalaj would have called her *la quarante-trois.*

I so envied the life in Apartment 43.

I SAW KALAJ at the Harvest a few nights later. I was with another woman. She was one of my students at the Harvard Extension School. She was older than I was and was an actuary taking my Italian class in preparation for her trip to Italy the following summer. She herself was a third-generation Italian, dark hair, swarthy skin, and beautiful lips over which she tended to use too much lipstick. One evening after class she had waited until everyone had left the classroom to ask me if I would consider having dinner with her. "Why not," I said, trying to conceal my surprise.

"When would be good?" she asked.

"I am free tonight," I had said, to make her feel at ease, seeing she seemed slightly uncomfortable.

This was our second date.

What happened to Allison? he asked merely by arching an eyebrow. I shook my head to suggest: *Let's not talk about it. It didn't work out.* He shrugged his shoulder as discreetly as he could, meaning: *You're just hopeless. That was a serious mistake.* I tilted my head in a resigned: *Well, what can we do? C'est la vie.* While we were exchanging gestured messages, he was charming my new friend. "No, not Saudi Arabia—with my skin? No, not Algeria either, not Morocco, but a little place called Sidi Bou Saïd, the most beautiful whitewashed town on the Mediterranean south of Pantelleria . . ."

She was won over. For a second I saw us having dinners together, rides to Walden Pond next spring, Sunday evenings *Chez Nous* listening to Sabatini's free guitar recitals followed by the one-dollar films at the Harvard Epworth Church.

"I am glad I had a chance to meet you," he said, "because I may never see you again."

Blank stare. *Why?*

"I'm leaving."

"For how long?" she asked.

"For good," he replied.

A quizzical gesture from my eyes meant: *When?*

"In one week."

And then, as he'd always done whenever taking his leave, he abruptly wished us *bonne soirée* and walked away. He figured I needed to be alone with her.

I watched him walk around the horseshoe bar on his way out of the Harvest, then, once he'd stepped outside, stop, cup his hands around his mouth, and light a cigarette. Having lit it, he ambled out toward Brattle Street, pacing his way ever so slowly, pensive and hesitant, as though unsure whether to go to Casablanca or just linger a while longer and take in this spot for what could very well be his last time.

"Strange character," she said.

"Very strange."

"Friend?" she asked.

"Sort of." I caught sight of him once again, as he turned around the patio on his way to Casablanca, and from there most likely heading back to Café Algiers. Something told me to take a mental picture of him threading his way through the back courtyard toward Casablanca. Then I forgot about the mental picture. I was thinking of other things when it occurred to me that perhaps I'd been spared tearful goodbyes, the hugs, the flimsy jokes to undo the knot in our throats. It felt like giving a dying friend massive doses of morphine to avoid a mournful and conscious farewell.

Why had I said *sort of* when it should have been clear to me that he was the dearest soul I'd met in all my years at Harvard?

HE CALLED ME three days later. I was in my office with a student discussing her paper. He knew the drill. "I'll ask you questions, and you answer yes or no."

"Yes," I said.

"Can you see me soon?"

"No."

"Can you see me in one hour?"

"No. Teaching."

"Can I come and pick you up in two hours?" This I certainly wanted to discourage. "No."

"I'll call you later tonight then."

When he called me that evening, he told me that earlier in the day he had needed an interpreter for an interview with Immigration Services. Why hadn't he told me so? "You couldn't talk, remember?" At any rate, it didn't matter, since Zeinab had gone downtown with him and served as his interpreter. Except he would have preferred a man from Harvard. Going with a woman who also happened to be an Arab might have sent the wrong message, what with his annulment and all that. It turned out to be a perfunctory meeting. They were closing his case.

"Do you have time for a quick drink with a few friends tonight?" he asked.

It sounded like a farewell gathering.

"Tonight I can't." I made it seem I wasn't alone. I pretended to miss the passing allusion to farewells.

"Then it's possible I may not see you. I may have to leave tomorrow. But it's not certain."

"Did they give you a plane ticket?"

"Immigration is not a travel agency." He laughed at his own joke.

"But why won't those bastards tell you when you're leaving?" I was making it seem that my suppressed anger was directed at the immigration folks, and that I needed to confront their outrageously incomprehensible behavior before dealing with the lesser matter of bidding a friend farewell forever. All I was doing was making noise to prevent him from asking me once again to join him for drinks with his friends.

He knew. He was far better at this than I.

It took me a few moments to face the terrifying fact that what I wanted to avoid at all costs was tearful goodbyes. I did not want him crying. I did not want to cry myself. No hugs. No effusive promises. No languid words that spoke more sorrow than either knew he nursed. No messy feelings. Just a clean break. I was totally and irredeemably ersatz.

"I'll call you tomorrow and let you know where things stand. *Bonne soirée.*"

I spent almost all of the next day at Widener Library, away from every phone. It was high time I started making notes of the things I needed to spill back during my comprehensives.

Later that afternoon when I got home, a piece of torn paper was stuck into my mailbox. I thought it was from Ekaterina. *"We tried to reach you. Kalaj said you must have gone to the library. He didn't want to disturb you there. He asked me to say goodbye for him. Zeinab."*

All I remember feeling at that moment was a pang of something I could never name, because it hovered between unbearable shame and unbearable sorrow. *I* had done this. No one else. Never had I sunk so low in my life. I felt like someone who has been putting off dropping in on a dying friend. Each time the dying person calls him and asks him to come by for a few minutes, the friend, on the pretext of trying to lift up the sick man's spirits, makes light of his worries. I'll try to come tomorrow. "There may not be a tomorrow," the dying man says. "There you go again. You watch, you'll outlive us all."

And yet, no sooner had I felt this burst of shame than it was immediately relieved by an exhilarating sense of lightness I hadn't felt since walking out on Niloufar that night— freedom, joy, *space*, as though an oppressive worry, which had been haunting and weighing and gnawing at me for months, had suddenly been lifted. I was soaring, as light as a kite racing through the clouds.

On impulse I wanted to seek him out and tell him about this strange, uplifting feeling—as though it were a startling revelation about a person we both knew, or a truth about human nature that I couldn't wait to share, because he, of all people, understood all about these hidden mainsprings in the twisted gadgetry of the soul.

Yet now, I could head back to Harvard Square and not think twice about running into him. I could walk through Café Algiers and never worry he'd be there, go to Casablanca and no longer prepare to listen to yet another tirade, or expect to be unavoidably interrupted, or rehearse a new litany of excuses. Instead, I could sit at a table without talking to anyone, just as I'd done that Sunday in midsummer while reading Montaigne. Simply sit, mind my own business, be alone, and keep that door shut, which I'd accidentally flung open one hot Sunday when I'd walked up to a complete stranger and found someone who, but for incidentals, could have been me, but a me without hope, without recourse, without future.

I began to feel as certain countries do when their tyrant dies. At first there's a hush in the city, and everyone mourns, partly out of disbelief, partly because life, trade, friendship, love, eating, drinking seem unthinkable without a tyrant to keep them in tow. Something in us always dies when the world as we've known it changes, and the sorrow is always genuine. But by the evening of a tyrant's death, cars begin to honk, people suddenly shout hurrahs, and soon enough, the whole city, which only this morning was bathed in stupor and trembling, feels like a carnival town. Someone steps on top of a bus waving a forbidden pennant and everyone clamors back, dying to embrace him. The squares are filled with people. Everyone is partying.

I felt terrible for him, and I ached for him, thinking how he must have turned around at the airport and taken a last, long, languorous look at Boston, defeat and betrayal and the things he feared and hated most in life souring the ever-renewed sting of exile in his life. How many times must he have driven passengers to the airport and thought: *One day, one day it will be me.*

But I was forcing myself to feel sorry for him. I knew, as I prepared to head out to Café Algiers that night, already feeling something like a blithe sprint in my gait, that even as I might go searching for his shadow and pay homage to it the way people do penance at the shrine of a saint they may have helped to murder, I was also going to see whether I really missed him as much as I hoped I would. I knew the answer. But I wanted to make sure. Plus, I wanted to see with my own eyes that he had indeed left town and was never coming back. I wanted to preview life without Kalaj. Part of me wanted to celebrate but wasn't going to until I was sure.

Just as I was growing to accept his departure, I caught myself thinking that he could easily be back, telling us it was all a mistake, that they'd taken him to the airport, but at the last minute, a reprieve had come down from the governor's office. "I'm back, Kalaj is back," he'd shout, big bear hugs to everyone in the coffeehouse.

I knew what I was doing. I'd allowed myself to fantasize his dreaded return not only to pay lip service to my nobler instincts, but also to relish the jolt of waking up from this short-lived fantasy to realize that no, he *wasn't* coming back, that he was once and for all gone for good. Cambridge felt freer, quieter, and, on this late December evening, there was even a hint of something tolerably chilly that agreed with me. Yes, I felt free, the way the world must have felt infinitely freer when the last Titans were soundly beaten and sent packing.

When I arrived, his seat was indeed empty. None of the regulars who had known Kalaj wanted to sit there. It was their silent tribute. This is where the king sat, this is where he had said goodbye to everyone. "I've got a knot right here," said Sabatini, pointing to his throat. Zeinab's mascara had bled all over her eyes. "I am glad you came," she said, as she hugged me in the kitchen where I'd gone to look for her. "You were the one he trusted." I said nothing. "Unlike any of us, you were the one who never needed a thing from him."

I didn't know how to take this but decided to let it pass. I also knew that by not saying anything I was giving every indication of agreeing. On the wall she had Scotch-taped the sketch of his face done by the woman with bathroom problems. It still bore the marks from when he kept it folded in one of the many pockets of his camouflage jacket. Even the round coffee stain left by his damp saucer was still visible, bringing me back to that summer morning when he was filled with rage against a woman who had taken him in and been kind to him.

After Café Algiers, I went to Casablanca. Even the barman and some of the waiters knew he'd left. As did the barmen at the Harvest. I ordered a glass of wine and stood at the horseshoe bar of the Harvest, pretending I was waiting for him and that at any moment now he'd show up. But all I could remember was the evening when I'd watched him leave the bar area and then suddenly stop outside to light the cigarette he'd been rolling while talking to us. I'd watched him hesitate a while and finally walk into Casablanca's back door, and through the back door presumably wander into the bar itself and then onto the back entrance of Café Algiers. I remember the elusive quiver of a waggish smile on his lips when he caught my silent signals and how our entire conversation was cut short with his habitually abrupt *bonne soirée*, which was always tinged with good fellowship, best wishes, and a flash of naughty sport. His fingerprints were all over Cambridge.

I ordered a second glass of wine before finishing the first. I wanted the barman to think I was lining them up; but I did it to nurse the illusion that Kalaj was drinking beside me. Perhaps I still wanted to see if I missed him. I ended up drinking four glasses of wine. Then I began to miss him in earnest, knowing all along, though, that it was probably the wine, not me.

When I was just about to leave the Harvest, I turned around and, for the sake of testing the words in my own mouth, or of hearing the effect they might have on me once I'd spoken them, I uttered *Bonne soirée* to the maître d', who was French, and then, like Kalaj, abruptly walked out. I repeated the words up Brattle Street and into Berkeley Street, until I realized that what I was really doing was bidding farewell to Café Algiers, to all the people I'd befriended there, to Zeinab and Sabatini and the Algerian and Moroccan cabdrivers, to everyone I'd met because of him, to the Harvest and Casablanca and the Harvard Epworth Church on Sunday evenings, to our little lingo we'd improvised from the very start and to the fellowship that had blossomed because of it. *Bonne soirée* to so many new things he'd brought into my life, to our dinners with friends, to our dinners alone together, to happy hour, to the spirit of complicity that had been missing from my life and helped us find a common ground together during those hours when his worries over his green card and mine over my career cast a pall that nothing could dispel except the women who drifted into our lives and couldn't make us happier than when we were talking about them after we'd been with them. *Bonne soirée* to our small oasis, to our imagined Mediterranean alcove, to our little corner of France immediately following last call, to the illusion of myself as a lone holdout stranded in a large, cold, solitary, darkling plain that had become my American home. I was one of *them* now, perhaps had always been, was always going to be but had never known it or was reluctant to own up to it until I'd met Kalaj and then lost Kalaj.

Christmas I spent alone in Cambridge. I read more in those three weeks than I'd done since meeting Kalaj almost five months earlier. In January, I re-took my comprehensives. I passed, and four days later I was allowed to take my orals. I passed those too. On February 1, I left Concord Avenue and moved to Lowell House.

THERE WAS A period after Kalaj's departure when I'd occasionally spot his old Checker cab around Cambridge, being driven by the Moroccan. Each time I saw it, I'd feel a sudden throb, part dread, part joy, followed by instant guilt, and then the unavoidable shrug. Sometimes I'd bump into the Moroccan, and at first we'd greet each other, and then, when it was clear that all we had to say was *Did you hear from him?* followed by a hasty *Me neither*, we began to look the other way. The Moroccan spoke French with a different accent, was timid, and couldn't ruffle anyone's feathers if he tried.

At Café Algiers, where I saw him quite frequently at first, he spoke meekly, in whispers, like a conspirator. Something told me that Moumou the Algerian had warned him of Kalaj's impending deportation and told him that all he needed was to wait things out till Kalaj was forced to sell at a very low price. It made me angry.

And yet, each time I spotted the cab, I'd remember that clear, sunlit morning when Kalaj had stuck his head out of his window as he drove around Harvard Square and volleyed a jaunty greeting that tore me out of my torpor and brought me back to the here and now. I was glad that day that there was someone like him in my life, but I was also glad he was stuck in traffic and wasn't going to join me. Those contradictory impulses never resolved their quarrel and were still tussling within me long after he was gone, for I kept wanting to seek him out all the while hoping I'd never find him. Seeing his old cab on Mass Ave or parked along Brattle Street stirred feelings and questions I didn't care to tackle any longer; no sooner had they risen to consciousness than they were whisked away, unanswered, unheeded. One day, I kept telling myself, I'll hail his cab and take a ride in it. But I never did, partly because cabs were never in my budget, and partly because I knew that after merely opening the door, I'd find what I'd come looking for: a whiff of the old cracked leather upholstery that always reminded me of a shoe store, a view of the tilted jump seats he'd cautioned the two boys against sitting in on our way to Walden Pond, the indelible scent of trapped cigarette smoke which, now that I think of it, was perennially wrapped around him. And besides, taking a cab would be all wrong: I had never ridden in the back. When we hopped into the car or when he drove me back home or took me late one night to Brookline because I craved sleeping with a girl who lived there, I always rode next to him. One day, eventually, I'd hail his cab, perhaps just weeks before leaving Cambridge. But I always forgot. Then the car disappeared. And then I did.

EPILOGUE

AFTER MY SON AND I LEFT THE OFFICE OF ADMIS-
sions, I suggested we walk to my old house on Concord Avenue before returning to the Square. It was a short distance
from the patio and was going to be the last place I'd revisit
with him. I'd saved it for last.

The front door to the building was locked as usual. But
someone was just coming out and let us in with a quick nod-
hello. The mailboxes had not changed, the smell of the lobby
had not changed, the buzzer was still the same, and there was
still no elevator. Nothing had changed.

I looked at the list of names on the buzzer: the couple in
Apartment 43 had disappeared, Linda's was gone too, and
mine—as if this should have surprised me—had disappeared
as well. Someone else was being me at Number 45. I pointed

out the names to my son as if still looking for a trace of myself here. He must have thought I was losing my mind.

I felt as awkward as an organ donor who comes back to see, just to see, whether that organ that was once his still ticks the way he remembered in someone else's body. But I could have rung the buzzer and I could have gone upstairs, and maybe later I'd explain to the police when they handcuffed me and took me to the precinct station for trespassing that I'd come back to take a look, Officers, just to take a look. But I wasn't even really up for taking a look. Whatever I'd come looking for I'd either found or didn't really care to find, or time had simply squandered the whole thing and I was just not willing to face that I'd grown numb to it.

The same had happened at Café Algiers the day before. I'd stopped first outside the Harvest and noticed without going in that it had altogether changed. The horseshoe bar where I'd had my last drink by myself thinking of him had been dismantled. The spot where he'd stood that night when I pretended not to see him, and he knew, just knew, had also disappeared. Instead, I opened the door and asked the maître d' to let me take a copy of that day's menu. *"Voilà,"* he said.

"What are you going to do with it?" asked my son, who all along had been humoring our amble down memory lane.

I didn't know what I was going to do with it. Leave it in our hotel room most likely. Or toss it somewhere. But I didn't let go of it. The menu sits framed against my wall today.

We walked back to Café Algiers and stood outside as we'd done the day before, staring at the menu's familiar green and white logo.

"Are you going to ask for their menu here as well?" he asked.

But here I caught myself hesitating just as I'd hesitated the day before. Perhaps I shouldn't go in at all. Better than recognizing things I hadn't thought of in years or remembering those I hadn't entirely forgotten, I wanted to imagine them, keep stepping back till I saw what was inside me, not what was out there. As if in order to experience this thing called the past, I needed distance, temperance, tact, an inflection of sloth and humor even—because memory, like revenge, is best served chilled.

Ersatz stuff, Kalaj would have said.

Suddenly, I wanted to imagine him still sitting there, as always happy to see me, still rolling his cigarettes, still lambasting the world for being the dirty, grimy, insipid, shallow cesspool it was. He'd have just about finished reading yesterday's paper, and he and the Algerian would have sparred a tiny bit already, just enough to get their day started. I'd be on my way to the library or to meet students and had scarcely time for a *cinquante-quatre*. Now a *cinquante-quatre* would probably cost six times as much, more perhaps. I imagined the corner table where I used to like to sit and where I'd once promised myself to finish reading the memoirs of Cardinal de Retz, which after all these years, I still hadn't finished.

They were good times. But I wouldn't want to relive them.

Nor did I want to step inside Café Algiers. I wanted to imagine that his portrait now hung framed right next to the image of a deserted beach in Tipaza. I could just imagine him scoffing at both, with a rhyme: *Kalaj à la plage*, Kalaj at the beach. What idiots, he'd have said. Then he'd pick up his things, which were always scattered on his table, and say he'd drive me to my class, *Let's go!* How much time do you have? Fifteen minutes, I'd say. Good, we'll do a tour by car and talk a bit, I need your advice on something.

That's when I wished his old cab would suddenly emerge on Brattle Street. My son and I would hail it, tell the new cabbie that we needed to be driven back to the Office of Admissions, and could he please step on it.

"And take Memorial Drive, would you?" I'd say.

"But that's ridiculous," the cabbie would object, "we're just three blocks away."

"Yes, I know."

My son and I would probably be stifling laughter at this point. And I'd be relishing the prospect of returning late to a nearly empty Office of Admissions, winking at my son and saying to the admissions officer, "Very sorry, most very sorry, we've missed the boat to Byzantium, haven't we?"

No sooner would we have gotten into the cab than I'd be reminded of that summer's oppressive heat. I'd be back to the books I read each day while drinking Tom Collins up on my roof terrace on Concord Avenue, and to those summer days so hot and so scented with suntan lotion that you'd think you were somewhere on the Mediterranean coastline, not far from Sidi Bou Saïd, south of Pantelleria, which I had still never been to, much less thought of after he'd left Cambridge. I'd be back to the French songs we sang in the car on our way to Walden Pond, or of that French song by an Alexandrian Jew about two friends ending up together after so many detours, and of the way Kalaj, who always talked so much, sat and listened to me when he came to pick me up one night because I needed to run away. I'll never forget the way his car, like a spy boat entering enemy waters to help a prisoner escape, had edged its slow, silent way from Putnam Avenue and then, with its engine still running, had turned its lights on and off twice, just as in spy movies. I'd ask the cabdriver where he'd purchased this car, who from, and when. And as I'd have him distracted, in the backseat I'd ask my son to look for a Freemason sticker somewhere. Kalaj had ended up with so many round stickers after visiting the Masonic Lodge that, not knowing what to do with the last two, he finally stuck them in the least likely spots— right below the armrests under each ashtray, in case you were a smoker and still hadn't gotten the point! Had there been such a sticker, I would have unpeeled it without the driver's noticing, and held it. That sticker would have been his time-delayed message to me—*Thank God you found me. I'm well. I have two daughters. I have good memories. I love you.*

And I love you too.

DATE			